HALFWAY TO EDEN

HALFWAY TO EDEN

A NOVEL

MICHAEL BUCCI

Published in Hoboken, NJ

Book design by Christian Storm

LCCN: 2025920105
ISBN (paperback): 979-8-9997555-0-6
ISBN (hardcover): 979-8-9997555-1-3
ISBN (ebook): 979-8-9997555-2-0

To everyone who was a part of
this journey, thank you,
with love and best wishes always.

CONTENTS

Preface xi

Chapter One: A Life Tethered 3

Chapter Two: Dating Disasters. 9

Chapter Three: Longing for a Better Tomorrow 21

Chapter Four: Tempted By Fate 28

Chapter Five: Shadows in the Post. 35

Chapter Six: The Land of Smiles 47

Chapter Seven: The Pendant's Power 56

Chapter Eight: City of Angels 62

Chapter Nine: Echoes of Arhat 71

Chapter Ten: Blinded by Trust 81

Chapter Eleven: A Faithful Friend. 88

Chapter Twelve: Fishing for Paradise 99

Chapter Thirteen: The Waterfall of Colors. 109

Chapter Fourteen: The Ultimate Sacrifice 118

Chapter Fifteen: The Temple of Arhat 124

Chapter Sixteen: The Other Side 134

Chapter Seventeen: The Village of Eternal Joy 141
Chapter Eighteen: An Outsider's Introduction 156
Chapter Nineteen: A Leap of Faith. 165
Chapter Twenty: Group Therapy 173
Chapter Twenty-One: Rising to the Challenge 183
Chapter Twenty-Two: Overcoming the Odds 194
Chapter Twenty-Three: The Strength Within 200
Chapter Twenty-Four: The Festival of Lunar Som 205
Chapter Twenty-Five: A Demon in the Garden 214
Chapter Twenty-Six: Bargaining with Bravery 221
Chapter Twenty-Seven: Point of No Return 229
Chapter Twenty-Eight: A Perfected Soul. 236
Chapter Twenty-Nine: A Dance with Destiny 243
Chapter Thirty: A Life Untethered 252
Epilogue: Sublimity 261
Acknowledgements 263
About The Author 264

"WHEN ONE KNOWS A TRUE FRIEND, THEY KNOW THEIR GREATEST GIFT."

PREFACE

HERE'S TO THE DREAMERS

Writing was always something I enjoyed, but publishing a novel wasn't a life goal until one morning, I woke up, having remembered every detail of a dream. It was so vivid that I grabbed a notebook and jotted it all down. Though most dreams fade quickly, this one stayed with me. I stored the notebook away, and it wasn't until COVID hit that I picked it back up and decided to bring the story to life. Unexpectedly, this book followed me for several years, witnessing my ups and downs, and my growth and setbacks. It became much more than just a story of adventure and travel; it evolved into a message I felt compelled to share with others.

Throughout this story, you'll come to know the village of Arhat, a name rooted in Buddhism, meaning "a perfected person or soul" or someone who has "gained insight into the true nature of existence." While absolute perfection is unattainable, the relentless effort we put toward personal growth encapsulates perfection. Often, our journey requires the insights and support of others to help us realize aspects of ourselves we might sometimes miss on our own. As we strive to overcome fears and insecurities, pursue our dreams, wrestle with self-doubt, and search for our own version of happiness, it's important to remember that even when we feel alone, there are people who genuinely care.

Each of us is on a path to enlightenment, battling life's obstacles, yet holding onto faith in our journey and hope for a better tomorrow. Despite the struggles, we keep moving forward, seeking peace, fulfillment, and a meaningful life. If you're feeling lost, that's okay. If you don't have it all figured out, that's okay. If you're afraid it won't work out after you've poured your heart into a big dream, that's okay too. Because you took action. You listened to where life was directing you, and you tried. That's a greater success than never having tried at all. So, here's to the dreamers, the doers and the believers. Stay true to your heart and happiness will follow.

HALFWAY TO EDEN

CHAPTER 1

A LIFE TETHERED

He felt the tiny particles of warm wet sand beneath his feet as he sat with his arms wrapped around his knees, peering out into the ocean. The glistening waves rolled and crashed against the beach. It was Thursday morning, around 7:00 am. Beside him sat his best friend Tyler, his wet surfboard lying on the sand next to him. Jason stayed silent, admiring the early morning joggers and their dogs playfully dodging waves. A cool breeze blew threw his hair and he felt the warmth of the sun against his face. College was over; he was ready for the next chapter.

"Can you believe it, man? Our undergraduate years are over," Tyler said, slowly shaking his head as a handful of sand slipped through his fingers.

"They flew by," Jason said, watching the rippling waves. "You gonna miss it?"

"Of course I am. Who wouldn't miss all the girls and parties?" Tyler grinned. "With all the money we're going to make, it's only going to get better. " He glanced at Jason. "Any job leads?"

"Is that all you think about?" Jason lifted his eyebrows and laughed. "No leads, just the pizza shop job and the part-time insurance role my grandfather got me."

"We all got our priorities." Tyler threw his hands up. "I'm over the pizza shop."

Jason smirked but didn't answer. Work was the only way he knew to keep himself distracted, especially now that college was over. He spent Thursdays, Fridays, and Saturdays making pies at the local pizza shop, while Monday through Wednesday dragged by in the insurance agency filing room. His grandfather had pulled strings to get him the role, and though Jason loathed alphabetizing client files all day, he didn't want to let his grandfather down.

At least he had his best friend Tyler, the life of the party, the easy-going social butterfly everyone liked. Jason, on the other hand, was the quiet one. Somehow, their personalities meshed well.

Jason stood, brushing himself off. "I'll catch you later. I got asked to come into the agency for a few hours this morning."

"Yikes, got called in on your day off, huh? Guess you're pulling a double today. Good luck, buddy!" Tyler shook his head. "Don't have too much fun without me."

Later that morning at the insurance office, Jason shuffled through stacks of folders in the cramped filing room, rolling his eyes in boredom. Every few minutes he picked up his phone, scrolling through Instagram and checking to see if he had any invites from anyone to go out after his shift at the pizza shop, but there was nothing.

Jason muttered, "Guess I'll just take it easy tonight and hang with my grandparents."

Mid-afternoon the following day, Jason lounged in his black Jeep Wrangler, parked across the street from the bustling downtown strip. He had the day off from Art's Pizza. Electronic music played softly from his car speakers and sunlight streamed through the windshield, reflecting off his sunglasses as he leaned back, finishing the last bites of his burrito.

His phone buzzed in the cup holder, and glancing down at the screen, he saw Tyler's name pop up.

"Hey, man. Gunther Beach at one for volleyball?" Tyler said, voice full of energy.

Jason checked his watch and hesitated. "I'm a little busy, but I'll try to swing by."

"Come on, bro! It's a beautiful day in lovely San Diego. Everyone's at the beach," Tyler pressed. "Anyway, hope you make it."

After hanging up, Jason placed his phone back in the cup holder, then opened his door to brush burrito crumbs from his lap. After closing his door, he let his arm dangle out the window. A soft breeze drifted in. Tyler's enthusiasm lingered in his mind.

Damn, why can't I see things the way he does? Jason thought, staring at the lively downtown street ahead. *We've grown up with palm trees, the beach, and warm weather year-round. Maybe I take it all for granted.*

He cranked up the EDM playing in the background, letting the rhythms drown out his thoughts. Music was his therapy, a safe escape from the nagging depression that sometimes crept in. He closed his eyes, falling deeper into the layered beats, nodding along. Butterflies formed in his stomach, and for a brief moment, he felt invincible.

Tyler's invite started to seem a lot better. The thought of making some new friends and having a few laughs sounded ideal.

His gaze fell on a Polaroid stuck to the dashboard. A shortness of breath overcame him. The faded photo showed a little boy with a wide smile, clinging to his parents' legs. Jason stared at it. A single tear trickled down his cheek.

He closed his eyes, leaning back into the seat. The melodic sounds washed over him like waves, blocking out painful memories. *Don't blame yourself. What happened to them wasn't your fault.*

He visualized a life far from San Diego. A place where everything was different—where *he* was different. *In my dream place, I'm fearless. I know who I am. I don't care about money, status, or looks. People respect me. I'm loved. Not by a party girl, but by someone real. Someone who sees me. I'm happy there. I have purpose.* His fingers tightened around the steering wheel. *It's up to me to find that place, to become that person.*

Jason drove to Gunther Beach and parked his car along the curb with the beach in full view. He embraced how picturesque it all was. Palm trees swayed on the hills, surrounding the cove. Surfers bobbed in the waves, longboarders cruised along the promenade, and kids sprinted across blue basketball courts while street musicians cast lively music into the air. The sturdy white volleyball nets stood tall in the sand. Jason watched Tyler and the others volley back and forth under the warm afternoon sun.

His palms grew clammy, and a knot tightened in this stomach as he thought about joining. *What if I mess up? What if they think I suck?* He lingered in the driver's seat, watching Tyler turn up the music coming from a nearby portable speaker before serving the ball.

It was an engaging game, until Tyler's attention drifted. Following his gaze, Jason spotted a girl on the sidelines smiling at him. Jason smirked. "Focus, Tyler. Focus."

When the ball flew toward Tyler, he missed it, nose-diving into the sand and losing the point. Jason laughed to himself. "Always distracted by the ladies."

The match ended, and Jason saw his opening. He could play it off like he'd just arrived late. As he opened his door, he paused, watching Tyler chat with the girl who'd distracted him. A moment later, she handed Tyler her phone, laughing as he typed something in. After she left, Jason strolled over and gave Tyler a high-five.

"What up, buddy? Winning matches and pulling numbers, I see."

Tyler lowered his sunglasses with a big grin. "Oh, you know it. She asked if she should save me in her phone as 'hot guy with slicked blonde hair.' Anyway, what happened to you?"

"Yeah, sorry, got caught up with some things." Jason tilted his head, showing his palms.

As Tyler's teammates walked by, they patted him on the back, barely acknowledging Jason standing beside him. Jason shifted his weight, dragging a foot through the sand. *How does he command so much respect and confidence?*

Tyler crouched to pack his beach bag and wiped sweat from his forehead with a towel. "Did you book that graduation trip you've been talking about?"

Jason crossed his arms, his gaze fixed on the sand as he shuffled it back and forth with his foot. "Not yet, but it's going to be somewhere abroad. Never left the country before. You'll be the first to know when I do."

"I better be. And hey, if you want company, I'm down to join." Tyler stood and held out a fist for Jason to bump. "My parents promised to spot me until I'm working full-time, so just say the word. Anyway, I gotta bounce. I gotta be at the pizza shop soon. What are you up to the rest of the day?"

Jason shrugged. "Might go surfing or stop by Stevie's surf shop. I promised my grandparents I'd help set up for their bridge party tonight."

Tyler rolled his eyes as he slung his bag over his shoulder. "Bridge party? That's your Friday night?"

Jason held his hands up. "Hey, bridge takes strategy. It's not just an old-person game."

"Sure, whatever you say." Tyler laughed. "Let's catch up on Monday. I'm taking that girl out tomorrow; maybe she's got some friends."

Jason grinned. "Nice, man. Have fun, and yes, let me know if she's got any cute friends."

Tyler slapped him on the shoulder. "Of course! Anyways, gotta run, I'll catch you later."

CHAPTER 2

DATING DISASTERS

Jason sank into his bed, still dressed in his work clothes. He had just come home from a long, tiring Saturday at the pizza shop. He felt drowsy, his mind sluggish. He fought the familiar swell of depressed thoughts. *Not tonight*, he told himself. *Don't go there.*

He hated the feeling because it wasn't always like this. Everything changed the day his parents died. He could still clearly envision himself at age ten standing at the door with his grandparents, waving goodbye as his mom and dad pulled out of the driveway. It would be the last time he saw them. He still blamed himself for letting them go on that ski trip.

College had been an escape. The parties, hookups, and late-night drinking made it easy to mask his emotional turmoil. But even then, he knew he didn't enjoy those things as much as everyone else seemed to. They were just a way to numb the pain and fit in.

A text message from Tyler distracted him. "Yo, bud, you free next Friday? Remember that girl Jessica from Gunther Beach? I'm having margaritas with her right now, and she says her friend is down for a double date. Here's a pic of her. Her name is Ali."

Jason looked at the picture. Ali was cute, he thought. Petite with bleached blonde hair and a big carefree smile. She stood between two girls who looked like her sorority sisters, throwing up peace signs. He hesitated. *She's definitely attractive, but should I go on this date? Is she just another party girl that I might get mixed up with?*

Before he could decide, he received another message from Tyler. "Any day now. I'm going to call you if you don't answer in five minutes."

Jason took another look at Ali's picture, then texted Tyler back. "She's cute, count me in. Did you send her a picture of me?"

Tyler immediately replied. "Right on! Jessica just confirmed for Friday at 7:00 pm at Putri. And of course, I sent her the one of you shirtless at the beach. She thinks you're hot."

By the grin forming on his face, Jason knew that he was kind of excited, and rather than jump to conclusions, he looked forward to meeting Ali.

He opened Google to search for Putri and saw that it was a Thai restaurant. *Looks nice and has great reviews. Damn, wish I could fast forward to Friday.*

The week dragged on, and all Jason could think about was the upcoming date. In the filing room at the agency, he imagined what Ali might be like. Maybe they'd hit it off. She could be his dream girl. Flutters of excitement rushed through him, but quickly subsided. *Wait a minute—I need to pump the brakes. I know nothing about this girl. I always do this. I always cling to things or people that I think will fill a void or fix all my problems.* Frustrated, he banged the filing cabinet with his fist, then took a deep breath to calm himself down.

When Friday finally arrived, Jason's morning started early with a quick shift at the pizza shop, and then back home in time to help his grandparents with yard work.

He cut the grass and pulled weeds from along the metal fence enclosing their quaint backyard. When he was finished, he tossed his gloves to the ground and wiped the sweat from his forehead, looking around the senior community where he'd lived since his parents passed away.

He observed the bubble he'd grown up in—all the triplex homes looked the same. *What's a twenty-three-year-old kid doing here?* It was the kind of place where everyone knew everyone else's business. It felt suffocating. At least working at the pizza shop allowed him to be in the downtown area, which was full of energy far different than here. *Thankfully, I have amazing grandparents,* he mused, a smile on his face. *But who knows if Grandma's cancer will come back?* His shoulders slumped. *That would be terrible. I'd take care of her, of course, but would she beat it again if it did? And if she didn't, how much time would I have left with her?* These questions constantly made him anxious.

His grandmother's familiar words echoed in his mind: *Your grandmother will be just fine. Go live your life, Jason.*

A warm feeling moved through him. His mind turned to the big graduation trip that he had been planning to take. *But how could I leave?* he thought, running a hand through his hair as he paced the small backyard. *What if something happens to her while I'm away?*

He walked up the three steps leading into the kitchen. His grandmother stood at the counter, making glasses of lemonade, while his grandfather sat at the head of the kitchen table, reading the newspaper.

Jason tossed his gloves into the yard box by the door. "Your backyard is spotless, and the tomatoes are almost ripe."

From the smiles on their faces, he knew his grandparents were pleased.

"Dear, why don't you pull up a seat next to your grandfather?" His grandmother walked over, placing a cold tumbler of lemonade in his hands.

Jason sat down, taking in the way his grandfather laughed at the funnies in the paper and how his grandmother hummed her favorite song as she cut up pieces of watermelon. He admired his cute little home with the fridge full of state magnets from his grandparents' bus trips, the red-and-yellow floral tablecloth, and the aloe plants that lined the windowsills.

His grandmother brought fresh watermelon slices to the table. Not for the first time, he thought she was the kindest woman on Earth. With her short dyed black hair and rosy cheeks, she still appeared youthful, and was as sharp as a tack. She'd spent most of her career as a bookkeeper.

Jason looked over at his grandfather. He'd always considered him a smart and kind man. A techie at heart with a wholesome round belly, a bristly mustache, and a full head of white hair combed to the side. He sure did enjoy a box of wine, and of course, his second love, basketball. Jason thought it was cool that his grandfather had coached in his younger days and played for the Air Force during the Korean War.

Jason stood up with his fingertips pressed on the table. "Grandma, shouldn't you be resting? Why don't you come sit down?"

"Rest! Everyone's always telling me to rest." She placed her hands on her hips. "First, the doctor said I only had eight months to live, but here I am, strong and healthy. They don't know what they're talking about." She waved her finger. With a smile, she walked over to the table to take a seat. "Anyway, enough about my health. What does a young man like you have planned for tonight? In my younger days, I danced up a storm."

Jason's grandfather took a sip of his glass of wine, then said, "Your grandmother was something else. She won competitions and everything."

"How about you, Grandma, cutting up the rug?" Jason's eyes widened. "I'm heading on a double date tonight at some Thai restaurant."

His grandmother drank a mouthful of lemonade, then rested her chin on her fist. "Jason, that's marvelous. Do you have a picture of her?"

Jason pulled out his phone to show them, and his grandfather lowered his glasses, squinting. "She's a looker."

"She's beautiful. You two have fun tonight," Jason's grandmother responded.

His grandfather crossed his arms and stroked the gray stubble on his face. "Jason, how's that insurance job going? Mr. Murphy from down the street said you're doing terrific."

"It's good, but to be honest, I don't think it's for me," Jason admitted.

His grandfather rested his elbows on the table, his hands crossed. "Insurance is a nice, secure job. You need some career direction, and this will get you started. Give it a chance, you'll be one of the managers of that agency in no time."

Jason stared back at him and nodded. On the inside, he was grateful for the part-time job, but he felt misunderstood, as if not having it all figured out wasn't okay, as if stability was far more imperative than being happy in a career and in life.

He excused himself from the table and walked down the hall to his bedroom. After a quick shower, he rummaged through his messy drawers, pulling out wrinkled t-shirts, and eventually choosing his favorite fitted black V-neck. He ironed it out and pulled it over his head. A spray of cologne and he was ready.

In the garage, he detached the doors from his black Jeep, the one he'd worked through college to afford. He selected his favorite Eric Prydz playlist, revving the engine before pulling out of the driveway. As he drove through the community gates, his grip tightened on the wheel. He took a long reviving breath, then an unexpected smile formed on his face.

"Freedom!"

The wind whipped through his hair as the Jeep hugged the bend, the vast blue ocean on his left side. As he approached the vibrant downtown, lights from all the restaurants and bars became brighter. He could hear live music playing nearby. The restaurant patios were filled with people enjoying dinner and groups strolled the sidewalks.

When Jason arrived at Putri, his stomach tightened, and his body tensed up as he spotted Tyler and the girls waiting at the door. He deliberately parked a little farther away, hoping they'd miss him so he could take a few deep breaths in the car to calm himself.

As he walked toward the entrance, Tyler was already heading his way, hands outstretched for a high-five. "Jason, my brother! Meet Jessica, and this is her friend, Ali."

Jason hesitated, timid at first and clenching his toes in his shoes. "Nice to meet you, Ali."

"You too, Jason." Ali smiled.

His hands trembled, a lump forming in his throat as Ali's smile took him off guard. She was even more beautiful in person. All he could think was how badly he wanted to make a good impression tonight.

Tyler led the way with the girls following close behind. As Jason pushed aside the red hanging beads that separated the dining area from the entryway, he felt as if he had been transported to Thailand, despite having never been there. A beautiful stone Buddha fountain sat in the center of the dining room just above a small pond enshrouded by thick green ivy. Several tiny golden Buddhas sat along the perimeter of the room. Colorful white-and-blue vases, large and small, with dragon designs were present in every corner of the restaurant. The servers looked to be dressed in formal Thai garments. They all wore red baggy pants that seemed more like pajamas and their long-sleeved golden jackets had buttons fastened up the front. The background music was soft and meditative. Jason glanced up to see golden cloths draped from the ceiling, and colorful stained-glass chandeliers.

They were seated at a large round table. Tyler rubbed his hands together as he sat down. "What should we do for drinks? I'm thinking whiskey highballs."

Jason couldn't help but smirk at Jessica's raised eyebrow, her expression telling him she probably wasn't a whiskey gal.

She tapped her chin thoughtfully. "How about lychee martinis? They sound yummy."

Tyler lifted his eyebrows, a puzzled look on his face. "What's a lychee?"

Jessica leaned forward, eager to explain. "You know, those spiky red shells with the slimy fruit inside."

"Well, at least there's vodka in it." Tyler smiled. "Make that two, please." He held up his two fingers to the server.

Ali chimed in, raising her hand. "Make that three. I tried lychee in Thailand."

Tyler glanced at Jason. "And for you? Milk?"

Jason laughed, a little embarrassed. He wasn't much of a drinker, but he didn't want to seem lame in front of Ali. "Make that four, please." He grinned awkwardly.

He sipped his water, then turned toward Ali. "So how was Thailand?"

Ali's face lit up. "I loved it. It's probably my favorite place aside from Cancun."

He leaned forward. "Did you go cliff jumping or scuba diving?"

Ali shook her head. "Na, that's a little bit too extreme for me. We mostly toured temples in Bangkok and hit up Phuket, a major party island. The rest is kind of a blur. We partied a lot."

Ali pulled a vape from her purse. "You guys don't mind, right? I've been trying to quit, but this strawberry flavor is too amazing."

Jason quietly observed her. She reminded him of some of the girls he'd dated in college, who were all about the party life. He wasn't a smoker, but he figured that since so many people his age vaped, it was something he had to compromise on in a partner.

When the drinks arrived, he raised up his glass with the others to toast, then turned his attention to the menu, scanning appetizers and entrees.

Ali glanced over at Jason and Tyler. "Were you guys in a fraternity?"

Jason leaned in, folding his hands on the table. "I wasn't. Nothing against them, I was just focused on school. I still made it to the parties, though."

By Ali's fake smile, he could tell she felt bad for him, like he was an outsider for not being in one.

"Ah, that sucks. Well, at least you went to the parties." She took a swig of her martini. "I showed up to so many afternoon classes wasted. When I first joined my sorority, I got hazed. It's honestly all about the social connections and dating. Right, Jess?"

Jessica laughed, nodding her head in agreement. "How could I forget? They made us mud-wrestle. I was cleaning mud from my hair for days. Tyler, any hazing stories?"

Tyler smirked. "Just the usual naked laps and consuming live goldfish."

Jason laughed at the girls' reaction to the goldfish comment, covering their mouths and widening their eyes in disbelief.

As the conversation flowed, Jason's attention drifted to the pad thai making its way to their table. The waiter placed the steaming dish in the center, and Jason looked over at his friends. By the look in their eyes, he could tell they were just as hungry as he was.

Before anyone could dig in, Ali threw up her hand to stop them. "Wait, I need a picture for the 'gram."

Jason leaned back and watched as she arranged the dish to get the perfect angle while everyone else eagerly waited on her. Throughout the night, Ali had spent more time checking her phone than interacting with the group. It was like she was trying to be in two places at once.

He knew it was only a matter of time until Tyler started ordering shots, and sure enough, a round of tequila was already on its way.

While they waited, Jessica asked, "So, what's everyone's plan now that college is over?" Her eyes shifted across the group. "How about you, Jason?"

"To be honest, I'm still figuring it out," he admitted. "I mean, I've got the insurance job and Art's Pizza for now, but we'll see. Maybe I'll teach English in another country."

Jessica seemed to grow curious. "I'd love to teach English abroad, but I just landed a job as a social media coordinator." She turned to Ali. "What about you?"

Ali twirled her hair. "Guys, don't judge, but I'm kind of making hella money on my OnlyFans profile. And I'm about to start club promoting. The manager there is so hot, and he hooked me up with the job. So many long nights ahead of me."

Jason stayed silent, and took a big gulp of his drink.

Tyler was the last to chime in. "I'm working for my dad's tequila business. There's serious money in spirits. I mean, I love drinking the stuff, but the dolla dolla bills are even better. Who doesn't love tequila and trips to Mexico?"

"Well, guys, sounds like we're all on our way." Jessica brought her glass to the center of the table for a toast to new beginnings.

Jason clinked his glass with the others but contemplated his lack of purpose. While everyone seemed to have a plan, or at least a direction, he felt like a jack of all trades, master of none. The toast echoed in his mind: new beginnings. He wanted one, but where to begin?

After dinner, he and Tyler split the bill. The group lingered in the parking lot, chatting. Jason noticed Tyler staring at him, then nodding his head toward Ali. He was mouthing something, but Jason couldn't make it out. Tyler finally came out with it.

"Hey, Jason, why don't you give Ali a ride home?"

Jason nodded. "Yes, of course I can."

The car ride was quiet at first, apart from the background music. Jason noticed Ali's gaze on him. "What is it? Do I have food on my face?"

Ali shook her head. "Nope, it's nothing," she slurred. "I just had a great time tonight... Josh."

He could smell the tequila on her breath and it seemed like she either just forgot his name or thought he was some other guy named Josh. Twice she leaned closer trying to kiss him, tugging at his arm and causing him to swerve.

When he pulled up to her house, he was kind of relieved. Ali was all over him, and it was hard to tell if she was into him or if it was just the booze. However, he was willing to give it another shot. He turned to her. "I had a great time tonight too. Would you like to go out again sometime?"

Ali blankly stared back, as if she was still processing the question. Before she could answer, she leaned out the doorless passenger side to puke.

Jason was speechless. "Right... let me help you inside."

Driving back, he became lost in thought. He was bummed. It had been a fun evening, but not in the way he'd hoped. He thought she was a cool girl, just not for him. She'd spent most of the night glued to her phone, barely paying attention when he spoke. And then she threw up after drinking too much. It all just made it clear that they weren't a good match.

When he finally arrived at his grandparents' house, Jason parked his Jeep in the garage and tiptoed through the living room.

His grandparents were asleep on the couch in front of the TV. They often waited up for him to come home.

In his room, he shut off the lights and crashed onto his bed, then mindlessly scrolled through his phone, switching between social media and dating apps, each one as empty as he felt.

CHAPTER 3

LONGING FOR A BETTER TOMORROW

Jason couldn't resist the mouthwatering aroma of his grandmother's famous banana French toast with peanut butter and bacon. That smell, early the next morning, quickly helped him forget about his date from the previous night. He stretched and yawned as he shuffled down the hallway.

"Now that's a smell that I'll never get tired of."

Sunlight filled the kitchen. His grandmother stood at the stove, red apron tied around her waist, spatula in hand, while his grandfather sat in his usual seat, reading his paper.

"Morning, Jason!" his grandmother said, turning to him with a radiant smile. "You're just in time. You know your great-grandmother used to make this for me. Family secret." She winked.

Jason leaned against the doorway with a smile. "I know, Grandma, you've told me a hundred times. Why don't you let me help? Go take a seat."

"Nonsense!" she remarked, with a playful wave of her spatula. "I'm perfectly fine. You sit yourself down next to your grandfather and keep him company."

Jason sat. His grandfather, who'd been hidden behind his paper, lowered it, revealing a big smile, his sparse white eyebrows lifted.

He quickly folded the paper and placed it aside. "So, how did that date go? Bet you two hit it off."

Jason hesitated. "It was okay. Nice girl. Maybe we'll see each other again."

His grandfather tapped himself on the shoulder. "See that, honey? He takes after his grandfather."

His grandmother pointed the spatula at him with a teasing look. "You mean his grandmother! But you weren't too bad in your day either, honey."

Jason smiled as they bantered. Their familiar ways of flirting, even after all these years, were special. He hoped to have the same one day.

His grandmother walked over with a bowl of fresh fruit in one hand, and a pitcher of juice in the other, placing them down in the center of the table.

She took a seat next to Jason. "Dear, we're having people over tonight for board games. You know you're always welcome to join."

"Mr. Murphy and his wife will be here," his grandfather added, adjusting his glasses. "It's a great opportunity to get in good with the boss. Enough of that pizza gig—tell Mr. Murphy tonight that you're ready to take on more hours."

Jason nodded and fiddled with his thumbs. "Yeah, sounds nice. Speaking of that pizza gig, I'm running late for work. Gotta go." He shoveled down the last bites of French toast, chugged his orange juice, and hurried out the door.

Walking up to Art's Pizza, Jason checked the shop window. The small red booths were packed with high school kids, and a line of customers stretched from the door to the counter. Jason liked working at Art's. He had fun making pizzas. Plus, it was on Washington Avenue, the heart of downtown, which was full of life.

He walked through the back kitchen and found Tyler kneading dough, forearms covered in flour.

"Look who decided to show!"

Jason grabbed a slab of the soft moist dough from one of the trays, slamming it on the counter, then dusting it with a pinch of flour. "Is Art still on vacation?"

"Yep—he can stay for all I care." Tyler tossed a handful of flour onto the counter. "We practically run this place anyway. Check it out, I've been working on my spin game." He twirled the stretched dough around his finger without dropping it.

Jason was impressed. "Not bad after four years."

"Any updates on that grad trip? What's taking you so long to decide?" Tyler spread sauce and cheese on one of the pizzas.

With a thoughtful smile, Jason said, "Don't know yet. I want to go everywhere. Maybe I'll just backpack for a year."

Tyler slapped another dough ball onto the counter. "Not a bad idea. If that happens, count me in. Once I start working for my dad, I'm done with this place. Time to make real money. I'll be driving a Porsche in no time and I'll probably have two girlfriends."

Jason laughed. "Two, huh? Sounds like you'll have your hands full."

The corners of Tyler's mouth curled up. "How about you, any interviews lined up? You're never going to get rich stuck in a filing room."

"Not really. My grandfather really wants me to stick with the insurance job."

Tyler slid a few pies into the oven. "I get it, you want to make him proud, but don't do it at the expense of your own happiness. Find something you enjoy and go where the money is. I'll talk to my dad—he might be able to hook you up."

Jason smiled slightly. "Thanks, man, I appreciate that. You gonna leave San Diego?"

Tyler flung the last pie into the oven. "Yes, sir. I'll be everywhere: Miami, Ibiza, you name it. And you?"

Jason paused chopping onions and mushrooms. "I like it here, and my grandparents still need me, especially my grandmother. There's no guarantee that the cancer won't come back."

Tyler stopped to look at him. "I know how much you care about her. She's a great woman. You're lucky to have a grandma like her. But I bet she would want you to get out there and live your life."

Jason took a deep breath. "Yeah, I know."

After a tiring afternoon shift at the pizza shop, Jason was ready to go home and crash. He felt sluggish and the smell of burned cheese and sweat clung to him. He headed straight for his room, tossing his clothes into a corner, and walked into the bathroom to shower. As the warm water ran down his back, a strange sound broke his meditation, like bamboo pipes playing somewhere nearby. He frowned, wiping soap from his eyes. Maybe his grandparents were listening to music?

The sound persisted. Curious, Jason turned off the water and listened. It faded, but then returned moments later. He peeked his head out of the shower, checking his phone to see if he'd accidentally left YouTube on.

Drying off, he wandered into the kitchen, opening the small window that looked out into the yard. His grandparents were sunbathing, but no music was playing. Then he heard it again, and followed it down the hallway to his bedroom. He searched his closet, his desk shelves, even his laundry basket, and then it vanished.

He scratched his head. "Weird!"

Exhausted, he collapsed onto his bed. His eyelids began to close, and the strange occurrence faded as he fell asleep.

A knock at the door woke Jason from his nap. Groggy, he reached for his phone and squinted at the screen. It was 6:00 pm.

"Knock, knock. How's my grandson doing?" his grandmother asked through the door.

"Come on in, Grandma. I'm doing fine." Jason rubbed his eyes as he sat up.

She walked in and sat on the edge of his bed. "Will you be joining us tonight, dear?"

He sighed. "I don't think so, Grandma. I'm kind of tired from work."

"That's okay, sweetheart. You rest up. How's that nice girl you had dinner with?"

He shook his head. "Honestly, Grandma, she's not for me."

Her smile softened. "Well, it's better to be with no one than with the wrong one."

"Always love your advice, Grandma." He hugged her. "By the way, were you playing music earlier? It sounded like bamboo flutes."

She tilted her head, thinking. "Hmm, I don't recall. Anyway, dear, your grandfather is working on his car in the garage. Why don't you go see if he needs a hand?"

"Yeah, would love to help."

After his grandmother left, Jason stayed on his bed for a moment, his thoughts swirling around his future, his grandmother's health, and the strange sound.

He turned on some music, the upbeat techno rhythms giving him a boost of energy. After a while, he jumped from his bed and headed out to the garage.

His grandfather was polishing his vintage black Lincoln Continental.

Jason leaned against the doorway. "Need a hand, Grandpa?"

"Hiya, Jason." His grandfather scanned the car, ensuring he didn't miss a spot. It was so clean, Jason could see his own reflection from the garage steps. "Just about finished. She's looking brand spanking new. I'm taking your grandmother out next week for our anniversary."

Jason smiled. "Grandma's going to fall in love with you all over again."

His grandfather laughed. "After all these years of marriage, I'm still irresistible." He got into the driver's seat, turning the key. The engine roared. "Listen to that, Jason. Music to my ears."

Jason walked over. "She sounds amazing."

"Mr. Murphy and his wife will be here soon," his grandfather said, stepping out of the car. "You should get washed up."

"I'm feeling a bit under the weather. Not sick, just worn out from work. I think I'm going to pass on tonight."

His grandfather's face grew serious. "Ah, Jason, that's a shame. Maybe later, huh?"

"Yeah, we'll see." Jason slid his hands in his pockets. "Anyway, can we take her for a spin?"

His grandfather tossed him the keys. "Damn skippy. And when you get that promotion, she's yours."

Jason caught the keys, and his eyebrows shot up at the thought of driving around in a vintage Lincoln Continental. He could already picture it: cruising around like the coolest kid in town. But was it worth it? Was a shiny new car worth getting trapped in a job he didn't like? Of course, he felt grateful for his grandfather's kind intentions, but this was just a small glimpse of what his future might look like if he got caught up in the rat race. He didn't want to end up working tirelessly, chasing that posttax bump in his paycheck while stuck in a job, not by choice but by circumstance. He had no problem with working hard, but he knew there was something more out there for him—a career full of passion and purpose, one where he worked toward fulfilling his own dreams rather than someone else's.

After a few laps around the block with his grandfather, Jason parked the Continental back in the garage. He quickly headed to his room, hoping to avoid his grandparents' friends who had arrived. As he lay in bed, he could hear them laughing and talking. Mr. Murphy's voice was deep, and Jason heard him ask where he was.

He shut off his lights to make it seem like he'd already gone to sleep, but he just lay in the dark. A deep sadness washed over him as his parents came to mind. The weight of it all felt constricting. All he could do was dream of that perfect place, one that could take all his problems away. He closed his eyes, trying to sleep, hoping that maybe his reality was just a dream that he could wake up from. He wished for a life where his grandmother was fully healthy and he had an ideal girl, more direction, confidence, and, most importantly, where he was happy.

CHAPTER 4

TEMPTED BY FATE

Tyler and Jason rolled their eyes when they saw old Art stroll into the pizza shop the next day, fresh off his vacation. Art had the kind of presence that made people notice him for all the wrong reasons. He was a short, stocky older guy, who reeked of cheap aftershave. He wore round, tinted sunglasses, a baseball cap that hid what was left of his thinning dark hair, and a gold horn necklace, which nestled in the exposed chest hair underneath his wife beater. Art's skin was a leathery brown from too many years under the sun. His thick Italian accent was hard to understand, especially when he mumbled and chewed on a cheap cigar. But his uplifting spirit gave him some kind of charm.

Jason and Tyler refused to wear the t-shirts he designed. The backs always had some cheesy pizza-related slogan, like "A slice of the action" across a steaming pie, but Art was proud of them. He wore one every day, but his shirt was different—it said, "Pizza Bum" across the chest, which was a nickname he'd given himself.

As the three of them stood in the back of the pizza shop, Art leaned against the counter with his usual grin. "So your-ah runnin' my joint now, huh? How's business been?"

"All good," Tyler said. "We're thinking about taking it off your hands."

"Don't get cute with me, Tyler," Art snapped back. "But who knows? Maybe you boys will."

Jason tried to keep things light. "How was Costa Rica, Art?"

"Jason, lemme tell ya, it was beautiful. Imma buy a big, beautiful vacation home. Maybe I'll retire there someday. And the women? They'll knock ya socks off."

Tyler burst into laughter. "Let me guess, Art—all the women flocked to you, right?"

"You better believe it, kiddo." Art winked before heading to his office.

Jason and Tyler kicked into high gear. They knew the lunch-time rush would hit soon. As Jason slid fresh pizzas into the oven, feeling the intense heat against his face, he noticed a kid about his age walk in. He looked impatient, tapping his foot at the counter.

"Let me get two pieces on the fly."

"It'll just be a minute. New pies in the oven," Jason confirmed.

"Where are we, in a senior home?" the kid scoffed. "Hey, dough boy, I'm talking to you. Get me my two slices, pronto."

Jason jerked his head back, confused. Why was this guy giving him such a hard time?

The kid impatiently tapped his fingers on the counter. "I'll come get them myself."

Tyler, overhearing the situation, whispered to Jason, "Is this guy giving you trouble?"

Jason shrugged it off. "Na, man, it's nothing. Just some dumb kid."

Tyler shook his head. "Yeah, definitely dumb, but are you going to let him talk to you like that? Tell him to leave."

Jason gave a dismissive wave. "Na. Let me just give him his slices, and he'll leave."

But the kid wasn't done. He leaned across the counter, shouting, "Hey, goofy! I'm talking to you."

Jason brought over the kid's pizza, ignoring his attitude. The kid snatched the slices out of his hand without so much as a thank you. Jason waited for him to pay, but he turned his back and it looked like he was about to leave.

"Hey, you have to pay for those!" Jason called out.

The kid took a bite, then shot a smug look over his shoulder. "This is crap!" he said, and tossed the slices back at Jason. The sauce and cheese splattered all over the counter.

Jason was getting ready to say something, but he saw Tyler run after the kid and grab him by the shirt.

"Pay up, or else I'm gonna wipe the floor with your face."

Jason stood back, watching as Tyler and the kid grappled on the floor. He jumped in to pull them apart, but it wasn't until Art came out from his office to break it up that they actually stopped fighting.

"Enough! Get out of my shop. And Tyler, you're done for today. Take a breather."

Tyler stood up, dusting himself off. "You don't have to tell me twice. Just don't let that punk come back. He tried to leave without paying."

Art muttered under his breath, "All you kids are nuts," before turning around and walking back into his office.

A few minutes later, out back behind the shop, Jason leaned against the brick wall, watching Tyler crack open a cold beer.

"You should've told that kid to get lost," Tyler said. "Are you going to the concert tonight?"

Jason sighed. He knew Tyler was right—he avoided confrontation at all costs, but he also hated the feeling of being walked all over. He wanted to be more assertive like Tyler. "I'll let you know. I'm guessing Art will expect me to work the late shift. It's okay—I could use the extra money."

Tyler rolled his eyes "You mean the extra money that Art never pays us?"

Jason smiled wryly. He agreed with Tyler that Art never paid them on time, but he was still hopeful that one day, Art would change his ways.

After Tyler had gone home, Jason stopped by Art's office, optimistic that today Art might actually have his check. He knocked and stepped inside. His boss was hunched over paperwork.

"Jason, come on in. What can I do for you?" Art said, staring at his bills.

"Hey, Art. I was just checking if the paychecks were ready? It's payday, right?"

"It's always about the money with you and Tyler. When I was a kid, we worked hard. The money came later. Look at me now—I run the most successful pizza joint in town."

Jason paused, trying to mask his frustration. "But Art, that's what you said last time."

"But nothing. Your check is coming. I'm just a little behind. Look, I need you to take the extra shift tonight. I'll include the money in your paycheck next week. Anyway, I got some paperwork to catch up on."

Jason thought, *It's been a month. Why can't he just pay us on time? Was he going to even ask if I could work tonight, or did he just assume I'd say yes?* He huffed, but said, "Sounds good, Art, and thanks for the extra shift," then walked away.

He pulled his phone from his pocket to text Tyler. "Hey, man. I'm sorry, but I'm not going to make it tonight. Art needs me to work late."

His phone vibrated in his pocket with Tyler's reply, "Come on! You were supposed to be off. Art's place is going to be dead tonight anyway. You gotta learn to say no sometimes, buddy."

Jason wrote back, "Yeah, my bad. Would have been great to join. Next time I will. I just want to stay on good terms with Art."

Jason kept himself busy in the kitchen, scrubbing counters and refilling ingredients. The occasional regulars always showed up, like the old woman who came in dressed to the nines, her make-up heavy but precise. Jason watched as she settled into her usual booth with a single slice of anchovy pizza and a cup of white wine with ice.

She'd always ask him and the staff if they had found love yet. She'd say that she had fallen in love once, long ago, on a trip, but that was where the story ended. No details. No names. Until tonight.

"Thailand," she blurted, swirling her wine and staring at him. "We met in a tiny village. We locked eyes, and suddenly, he grabbed my hand. We danced to the sound of a bamboo flute."

Jason paused; the image played vividly in his mind. Bamboo flutes, a strange coincidence. *Why of all nights is she revealing more about her love story now?* It seemed random. He didn't think much past that and carried on working.

At closing time, Jason's feet ached with every step, and after a final cleanup, he left the pizza shop at midnight. The neighborhood off the main street where Jason usually parked was dark and quiet. He searched for his car, but a strange sound stopped him in his tracks. The eerie tones of a bamboo flute drifted through the air. He froze as goosebumps formed on his arms. He nervously blew air from his nostrils and his throat tightened as he swallowed.

"Who's out there?"

He spotted a peculiar-looking food truck parked under the streetlight next to his car. It hadn't been there earlier. It was worn on the outside, but the inside glowed. Someone was hard at work. Jason was drawn toward the truck by the intoxicating scents that poured from the little window. He stepped closer. His fingers traced the pictures of classic Thai dishes posted on the front of the truck. Inside, a little old woman cooked with joy. Her wrinkled face surrounded her smile, and her thick gray ponytail bounced slightly as she moved. The bamboo flute music played in the background as she cooked.

Jason stood there, feeling a mix of curiosity and confusion. He was speechless until she asked what he'd like to order.

"Pad thai, please."

When he tried to pay, she shook her head and waved her hand. "No need for money."

Jason blinked. "Thank you."

She handed him the food, but as he turned to leave, her voice stopped him. "You will find happiness soon."

Jason turned, nodding awkwardly. He didn't know how to respond.

Walking back to his Jeep, he couldn't shake the feeling that she was still watching him. When he glanced in his rearview mirror, her smile lingered in the dim light.

On his drive home, Jason couldn't stop thinking about the interaction. He was baffled and even a bit creeped out. His mind played her cryptic words to him over and over. *You will find happiness soon.*

What did she mean by that? Was it that obvious? Does everyone see me as some kind of unhappy person?

And the food truck—what was it doing on a residential street at this hour? And why didn't she want my money? He could still hear the bamboo music in his head, which gave him shivers. *What are the chances that it was the same exact sound that I've been hearing all along?* He ran his hand through his hair. *I need to sleep.*

CHAPTER 5

SHADOWS IN THE POST

Jason loved how peaceful and quiet the beach was early in the morning. He paddled out into the ocean, catching a few waves, the cold water waking him. Afterward, he sank back into the wet sand and closed his eyes, letting the sun warm his face. The sound of the crashing waves always calmed his mind. It was a meditation he felt grateful for. He was startled by the vibration of his phone, which was resting atop his backpack. His eyes flickered open, and he glanced down, picking it up. It was a text from an unknown number. His brows lifted in curiosity. The message contained strange characters: ความสุข. He translated the meaning, which caught him off guard. It was Thai for *happiness*. He fixated on that word. *Could it have come from the Thai food truck lady? But how? She doesn't have my number.* He sent back a question mark and waited a couple minutes for a reply before giving up.

After placing his phone in his bag, it vibrated again almost instantly. He quickly reached for it, intrigued by who it might be. His eyes widened when he received the same exact message. He stared at his screen for a moment. *Is someone playing a joke on me?* He even looked around the beach as if he was trying to find the sender. He responded this time with, "STOP!" He didn't want to be bothered, assuming it was just spam or someone who had the wrong number. Though the fact that the text was in Thai and translated to happiness was a bit eerie, especially after the food truck lady had told him he'd find happiness soon. He gathered his stuff and walked over to his Jeep parked just off the beach. He strapped his surfboard to the roof and drove back home to get ready for his day at the agency.

Later that morning at the office, he worked as usual, filing portfolios, logging client details into the system, and grabbing coffees for senior management. All the while, he couldn't take his mind off the strange occurrences that recently happened.

The next two days were quietly spent at home with his grandparents, watching TV, playing gin rummy with his grandmother, and zoning out in his bedroom with travel videos on YouTube. He was still searching for that special place he'd want to go to. He hadn't mentioned anything about the Thai food truck lady or the odd message to anyone. How would anyone even understand, he thought, especially when he didn't?

When Thursday rolled around, he started his morning as usual with a surf session at the beach, then went straight to the pizza shop.

When he arrived at Art's, he walked into the kitchen and right into the middle of a heated debate.

Tyler waved a bag of cheese in the air. "Art, I'm telling you, the shredded mozzarella from Carpeta's Deli is the best."

Art crossed his arms. "Tyler, how many times do I gotta tell you? The mozzarella from Vito's is all I buy. The prices are good too."

Art turned, looking at Jason. "And look who decided to show. Let me guess—surfing again? I can smell the ocean on you from here." He tossed Jason an apron. "Here. Get to work. If you two weren't my best employees..." He stomped off to his office.

Jason slipped on the apron and turned to Tyler. "How was the casino? Any luck?"

Tyler rotated his hand side to side. "So-so. Let's just say it wasn't my best game. I've been up and down at the blackjack table for weeks now. Probably not the smartest use of my parents' money, but the rush I get when I win, it's indescribable."

"Just be mindful of how much you're winning and losing. I don't want to hear about you missing a finger because you owed too much." Jason grinned, trying to lighten the mood. "But I'm sure you have everything under control."

Tyler stayed silent, opening a can of sauce. "I'm just having a little fun is all."

Jason fixed his apron. "Hey, random question, but have you seen a Thai food truck in the neighborhood we usually park in?"

"Food truck?" Tyler tilted his head. "Nope. That would be nice though—I like Thai food."

Jason drummed his fingers against the counter. "Well, there was one Sunday night set up next to my car."

"That is strange." Tyler clapped the flour from his hands. "Are you coming to my party tonight? My parents are on vacation until Monday and I've got the house all to myself. Sixty people, tons of girls—it's gonna be wild. Just like Thirsty Thursdays back in college."

"I'll let you know," Jason said as he sliced fresh mozzarella. "Might have to pass. I gotta help my grandparents with something tonight."

Tyler threw his arms up. "Come on, man! You can't miss this one. Everyone is going to be there. What are you doing, setting up paper cups for their Uno party?"

Jason laughed, shaking his head. "Exactly! I'll let you know if anything changes."

For the rest of the shift, Jason worked quietly, but his mind kept drifting back to the words of the Thai food truck lady.

That night, back at home, he sat on his bed in the dark listening to music, completely exhausted. Now that college was over, his usual weeknights were spent chilling in his bedroom, whereas before, he'd be partying, mostly because his roommate Tyler was always the one hosting the parties. He knew he always found excuses not to go out or do something new. Fear of failure, fear of getting started, fear of being judged—it all made it very easy for him to say no. Ultimately, he battled with low self-confidence, and he projected that into most areas of his life.

His phone vibrated and lit up. It was a message from Tyler. "You coming?"

Jason stared at the screen, his thumb hovering over the keyboard. He didn't want to disappoint his friend, but he didn't feel like partying.

He texted back, "Sorry, man, going to pass. Super tired, but next time."

He paused all notifications and placed his phone on the dresser. As he sat back on his bed, he turned up the music, which overpowered the voices of his grandparents' friends. He shut his eyes and forced himself to sleep.

Before his grandparents woke the next day, Jason threw on some clothes and walked out to the garage. He needed to get out of the house.

As he cruised in his Wrangler, the cool breeze flowed through the open windows, and the scenic turquoise ocean stretched for miles alongside him. Between the music and the views, he was so absorbed that he totally missed the pothole up ahead.

BAM!

The Jeep shook and rattled as one tire flopped around, but Jason was hardly fazed. His grandfather taught him a lot about cars, so replacing a tire was easy.

He climbed out and checked for cars before grabbing his tools from the back. He knelt beside the tire, realizing that it wasn't as bad as he thought. All he needed to do was plug the hole, which he had the tools for. Halfway through, his phone buzzed in his pocket.

It was Tyler. "You missed such an epic night!"

A photo came through showing people passed out all over Tyler's patio and some on top of inflatable pink flamingos in the swimming pool.

Jason shook his head as he wiped the grease from his hands onto a towel. He got back in the driver's seat, but when he turned the key, the engine stalled. He hit his hands against the steering wheel. "What now? I just got it inspected last week."

As he sat there trying to figure out what to do, a weathered postcard blew across his windshield and got stuck. He reached out the window and grabbed it, carefully unfolding the bent edges. The front depicted beautiful islands with mountains in the background and crystal green water. Printed across the front in white cursive text was "Koh Phi Phi, Thailand."

Turning it over, he read, "Dear Kathy, letting you know life is good. Your old friend is taking time away from her research to relax. I headed to the beautiful islands of Koh Phi Phi. I can't explain how lovely the people are here. There's something magical about this place. It evokes so much inspiration to keep traveling and exploring the world. I've island-hopped and spent time scuba diving. Please do visit one day. I would love to show you around beautiful Thailand. I miss the States and will try to visit one day. I hope all is well in San Diego. I know it's nothing like our beloved Boulder, but who could beat the weather? Give my best to Tom and the children, and we'll talk soon. With love, your friend, Maya."

Jason was enamored. He took a picture of the stunning islands on the front of the postcard for inspiration. He found a few travel blogs as he searched Thailand on his phone, skimming through travel insights and things to do.

After a while, he tried to start his car up, and this time the engine turned on. *Weird, why did it stall just a moment ago?* he thought. He planned to look into it with his grandfather. He placed the postcard under his visor and figured he'd stop by the post office and deliver it out of courtesy, hoping it would reach the right person.

When he arrived home and stepped out of his Jeep, his grandmother called from the window, asking for him to grab the mail.

He opened the mailbox. There were a couple letters and a thick manila envelope, tied up with rubber bands and covered in international stamps. It was addressed to him. He stared at it, wondering who could be sending him something from abroad.

Inside the kitchen, he tore open the envelope. Pictures, articles, magazine clippings, and brochures tumbled out—all about Thailand. He quickly stuffed everything back into the envelope and hurried off to his room, unknowingly leaving a trail behind him.

Jason sat at his desk, searching the envelope and its contents for a sender, questioning whether it could have been from his grandparents or even Tyler. Were they trying to help him make up his mind?

The repeated coincidences surrounding Thailand raced through his mind. It seemed like a big mystery he was supposed to figure out. He grabbed his MacBook and began searching for everything related to Thailand, such as "best places to visit" and "things to do in Bangkok."

He found himself going down a rabbit hole of endless blog links and photos of bustling cities and street food, Buddhist temples, and stunning islands. He was on a mini rampage, searching and absorbing all he could about this country and its culture. He understood that Thailand, in a weird way, was calling him.

Throughout the week, Jason's new obsession distracted him, and his curiosity only grew. He watched documentaries about Thailand, listened to podcasts, and explored Thai music. He read about its history and customs. No longer did he feel undecided on where he should take his trip; Thailand was a sure answer.

One evening after work at the insurance agency, he was sitting at his desk in his room, finishing up some last-minute research for this trip. After jotting down a few hotel names, he closed his laptop and exhaled slowly. It was all coming together. He was ready to tell his grandparents all about his plans. He stood and rushed over to the door, but suddenly paused as a thought came to mind, *Is it a good idea to go? What if something happens to my grandmother while I'm away?*

He shook his head, assuming he was overthinking things, and walked out of his room, down the hallway, and into the kitchen where he heard his grandparents chatting. He walked in and took a seat, resting his elbows on the table. "So, I have some really great news."

His grandparents placed their teacups down and looked at him in quiet anticipation.

A big grin formed on Jason's face. "I'm going to Thailand for my graduation trip. You can't even imagine all the research I did. It seems like such an incredible place."

His grandmother glanced at his grandfather, speechless, than back at Jason. "Oh, that's marvelous! I'm so excited for you. Now tell me, how on Earth did you decide on Thailand?"

His grandfather lowered his glasses. "That's great news, Jason! But I have the same question—are you sure it's Thailand that you want to visit? I don't know much about it, to be honest. Are you bringing a friend? You want to be safe over there."

"Well, it's funny you ask, because I never expected that I'd settle on Thailand. Honestly, my top three choices originally were Italy, Spain, and England. For some reason though, I kept coming across information related to Thailand and did my research, and the rest is history. It's a country filled with incredible culture, beautiful islands, great food, and tons of adventure activities like scuba diving, cliff jumping, and riding ATVs through the jungle. And yes, don't worry, I'm going to ask Tyler to join me."

His grandfather nodded with a smile. "You know something, Jason, I'd love to be young again. Good for you. Just be safe and mind your surroundings."

"You're young at heart!" Jason patted his grandfather on the shoulder.

Jason proceeded to tell them his dates, the cities he was visiting, and some of the interesting tourist attractions on his list. He could tell how interested they were by all the questions they asked. His grandmother noted down all the important details.

After chatting for about an hour, his grandfather left the kitchen to go rest in the living room, but Jason continued to talk with his grandmother at the table.

She moved her chair closer to him. "You get that adventurous spirit from me, ya know." She winked. "When I was your age, I went everywhere: dancing and trying new restaurants. I even went to the Bahamas once. Never went to Thailand though. Ya got room for one more?"

Jason wrapped his arm around his grandmother's shoulder. "Of course, Grandma, you're one hundred percent welcome to come on this trip. You're the life of the party. I'm a little hesitant to go though."

She tilted her head. "Hesitant? But I thought you were so excited. What's on your mind?"

Jason lowered his gaze and wrapped his finger around the tablecloth's loose threads. "Well, I am very excited—it would be a dream come true to go—but I'm also worried. What if something happens to you while I'm away? It's not like Thailand's around the corner."

His grandmother jerked back. "Is that it? You're worried about your dear old grandma?" She lifted her arm and flexed her bicep. "I'm a tough cookie. No need to worry about me, dear. Look, Jason,

I appreciate your concern, but I want you to go on this trip because I know how much you've planned and saved up for it. What do I always tell you? Go out there and live your life. It goes by fast. I will be just fine and waiting for you when you come home. Now, no more worrying about me, okay? If anything, I should be the one worrying about my grandson. I love you, Jason."

He stayed silent for a moment and nodded, hugging his grandmother. "I love you too. And you're right—I'm definitely going on this trip. I'm pretty lucky to have such a cool grandma."

She ruffled his hair. "That's the attitude. And I'm lucky to have such a cool grandson. Now, go get some rest. I'm sure you have a busy workday tomorrow. My goodness, it's eight o'clock, almost bedtime for me."

Jason went back to his room and flopped on his bed. He eagerly sent Tyler a message, "Yo, I'm going to Thailand for my grad trip. You joining or what?"

Tyler wrote back almost instantly, "I'll pack my bags tonight!"

The next day at work, Jason and Tyler decided to tell Art about their upcoming trip. To their surprise, he was more encouraging than they expected. "You two a' young. You need to travel the world. Don't do anything old Art wouldn't do."

Tyler snorted. "Trust us, Art, we wouldn't do anything that you *would* do, but we appreciate the encouragement. We'll be leaving in two weeks."

Art pointed his finger at Tyler. "Oh yeah? Don't bother coming back if you don't change that attitude."

Tyler laughed. "You know I'm just joking. But who knows—maybe we won't come back. We might just open a pizza joint in Thailand."

The evening before their flight, Jason could hardly stay calm, checking every area of his room and making sure he didn't forget to pack anything. He heard a soft knock at his door, and his grandparents walked in, asking if he was ready to go.

His grandmother's eyes glimmered. "We're so proud of you, Jason, and the man you have become. We're so excited for you, but we're going to miss you around the house."

Jason hugged them. "I love you both very much, but ya know I'm coming back. It's only for a month. Are you sure you still want me to go?"

"Don't worry about us, Jason," said his grandfather. "You have yourself a great time, and when you get back, I'll set something up again with Mr. Murphy."

Jason scanned his bedroom one last time, then headed out to the garage to load up his car. As he pulled out of the garage, his grandmother called out from the door, "Don't forget to send us a postcard. We love you, dear."

He froze for a moment, looking back at them in the doorway, trying to remember them just as they were. He'd always felt so grateful to have them in his life. Although it still felt hard to leave, he was excited for the adventure ahead. However, he couldn't shake the anxiety around the idea of his grandmother getting sick while he was away. But he knew that she'd be just as disappointed if he didn't go. He remembered the discussion with his grandmother at the kitchen table the night he told her that he was going to Thailand. With a smile, he clearly pictured her as she flexed her bicep and told him how she was a tough cookie. She insisted on him going on this trip. She was right—he needed to quit worrying about her and live his life.

His phone rang. It was Tyler. "Yo, where are you? Let's get this party started."

Before driving away, he made a promise to himself that he wasn't bringing along his fears, excuses, or anxieties on this trip. He was going to keep an open mind and do his best to step out of his comfort zone.

CHAPTER 6

THE LAND OF SMILES

"This is your captain speaking. We will be taking off momentarily. Please ensure that your seatbelts are fastened. We're looking at clear skies all the way through. Enjoy your flight and thank you for flying with ANA."

Jason exhaled slowly, his grip on the armrest loosening as he leaned back into his seat. The plane began to roll, and the vibration beneath him sent a nervous flutter through his stomach. The engines roared and the plane surged forward. His fingers tightened on the armrest again. As they picked up speed along the runway, his heart pounded. Then came lift-off and a smooth transition into the sky. He took a big, deep breath, smiling with relief as they ascended into the clouds.

He tried to distract himself during the first few hours by napping, watching movies, talking with Tyler, and listening to music. But he found it hard to concentrate on anything but the destination.

Jason pulled out a book, one of a few that he packed in his carry-on bag. It was about big-wave surfers and the power of *ho'oponopono*. He learned it was a simple prayer for self-forgiveness, a concept he'd been working on since the passing of his parents.

At the top of the first chapter, there was a quote about embracing the present moment: *"When you worry, you're stuck in the future;*

when you're depressed, you're stuck in the past. Stay present." Jason read it twice, remembering those words. Staying present was something he still hadn't mastered. Too often, he found himself stuck in the imaginary future where everything was perfect.

As the hours passed, Jason closed his eyes and tried his best to sleep. When the attendants lowered the shades and turned out the lights, most passengers dozed off, but he wasn't tired. Careful not to disturb Tyler or the other passenger sitting in his row, he slipped by them, standing to stretch. As he shuffled down the dark aisle, he tripped over someone's leg sticking out. "Sorry," he whispered to a woman whose groggy eyes blinked open, but she just waved him off and went back to sleep.

In the bathroom, after he'd washed his hands and wiped his face, Jason's eyes caught sight of a small beaded necklace hanging over the sink. He picked it up to take a closer look, squinting at the tiny beads that were mini jade tiger heads highlighted with hints of turquoise. At the end of the necklace hung a round golden medallion. Small characters were etched into the medallion. When he held it up to the light, his eyes widened. He gasped. They were the same characters from the strange text message he'd received a few weeks ago at the beach.

Jason jumped when he heard a knock on the bathroom door, almost dropping the necklace into the toilet. "Be right out." He quickly exited, trying to avoid eye contact with anyone.

He stopped abruptly, though, when a woman came walking toward him in a panic. It was the woman he'd tripped over—he recognized her cherry blossom scarf.

"Sorry to disturb you, but I left my necklace in the bathroom." She had a frantic look in her eyes. "Have you seen it?"

Jason held up the necklace. "I think I found it. Is this it?"

Her face lit up. "Thank you so much!" She clasped her hands. "It's so important to me."

Jason's eyebrows furrowed in curiosity. "If you don't mind me asking, what's the meaning behind it?"

Her voice softened. "It's from my village, Arhat—a place sacred to the Thai people."

"Sacred?" Jason said. "That's interesting. I did a lot of research about Thailand, but I don't remember reading anything about the village of Arhat."

The woman stepped toward him, placing the necklace around his neck. "I want you to have this, as my way of thanking you for finding it. It will keep you safe on your journey. The strength of my village lives within."

Jason blushed. "I appreciate this, but I can't take it. I can tell it means a lot to you."

She smiled, resting her hand on his shoulder. "It's okay. I want you to have it. We never truly own anything; we just borrow until it's time to pass them on."

Jason extended his hand. "'My name's Jason."

She reached out to shake it. "I'm Preeda. Please do enjoy my lovely country."

"Thank you, Preeda. Pleasure to meet you. Maybe we'll cross paths again in Thailand."

On the walk back to his seat, he tried not to trip over anyone this time, sliding back toward the window seat. He held the medallion up one more time, closely observing it, thinking about how kind Preeda was to give it to him. The characters, that text message, what the Thai food truck lady had said to him, even the postcard and the envelope—he contemplated the astronomical chances of those occurrences happening all around the same time. *And here I am, on a flight to Thailand, almost as if someone guided me here on purpose. Maybe it's all meant to be. Maybe I'm on my way to finding that special place.*

After a few hours, the captain announced that they'd be landing soon. The plane's descent sent a rush of nerves through Jason's stomach. As it approached the runway, he gripped the armrest again, holding his breath. *Boom!* The wheels hit the ground, jolting his head side to side as the plane landed. It rolled steadily down the runway toward the gate, and Jason turned his head toward the window, curious about his surroundings.

Once the plane came to a stop, he shot up from his seat, fingers tapping restlessly against his leg, impatient for passengers ahead of him to walk off the plane.

The inside of the airport was packed with people rushing past. Jason rubbed his clammy hands together as he took it all in. There was a pungent smell of flowers and spices in the air, and when they got outside to the pick-up area, he felt the chaotic energy of scooters zipping around and taxi drivers shouting, trying to gather tourists into their cars.

One of the taxi drivers waved them over, and before Jason could even speak, he found himself and Tyler already crammed into the back seat, taking off into traffic. Jason tensed as they drove on the opposite side of the road. *Right, that's normal here,* he reminded himself. Most of the ride was spent staring out the window, quietly becoming acquainted with his new environment. It was by far the worst traffic he'd ever witnessed. His heart pounded every time scooters dangerously cut in front of them, bobbing and weaving.

Once they pulled up to the hostel, they grabbed their bags from the trunk and paid the driver, who zoomed off in a flash, blending into a sea of cars and scooters. After checking in, they wasted no time in getting out to explore the city of Chiang Mai. The streets buzzed with life. Jason caught the spicy aromas of Thai curries mingling with sweet fruit from food stalls while wafts of incense trailed from people praying at small shrines. Vendors called out, trying to sell everything from snacks to trinkets.

Jason nudged Tyler. "Looks like we're about to become expert negotiators."

"How about a beer?" Tyler suggested, wiping the sweat from his forehead.

They stumbled into a random bar, which to Jason's surprise, was packed with expats. They pulled up a seat and ordered two beers.

A young guy sitting next to them who seemed around the same age introduced himself, "How's it going, mates? I'm Tom from Sydney. You guys also living here in Chiang Mai?"

Jason held up his beer. "Nice to meet you, Tom. I'm Jason and this is Tyler. We just arrived today. We're from California."

Tom tipped his hat. "No way! That's ripper, mate! You're going to love this city. Hope you get to explore the rest of Thailand—it's a gem."

Tyler stuck his thumb up. "We'll be here for a month, going north to south. How about you? You said you live here?"

"I've been here for about two months, but I'm heading back on the road now," Tom explained. "I'm traveling around the world for one year. Used to work for a fintech startup. Saved my money and quit. You're only young once."

Tyler's head jerked back in surprise. "That's awesome! We just graduated college, so we were like, let's take a grad trip before working. Who knows—maybe we'll stay longer."

Jason leaned in, resting his chin on his hand. "That's really cool! Any recommendations on things to do here?"

"Just get lost and embrace everything," Tom said. "Take some ATVs through the jungle and do a waterfall hike. My friend runs a tour business called GoGo Adventures—check 'em out. Anyway, guys, great to meet ya. Add me on Instagram. If you need any more recommendations or places to stay I have a ton of friends in this city."

After Tom left, Jason connected to the Wi-Fi and found the tour that he'd recommended. There was an opening for the next day, which they decided to book. After a few more beers, they wandered off into the streets to grab a bite, and then headed back to the hostel to rest. Jason sent his grandparents a message letting them know they'd made it.

"Jason, hurry up! We're going to miss our bus," Tyler yelled.

They ran as fast as they could, nearly missing it.

The rickety old bus lugged them two hours out of the city center and into a swarm of greenery along dirt roads where phone signals were nonexistent.

At the drop-off point, a man waved a yellow flag, encouraging everyone to gather around.

The tour guide took everyone by foot into the jungle to an area where several ATVs were lined up and ready to go. Jason and Tyler each took one and followed a line of others the rest of the way, running over sticks and dirt holes. Jason popped up and down during the bumpy ride, and the humid heat soon clung to his skin. The farther into the jungle they got, the more he could hear the powerful sounds of a waterfall. He also took notice of the birds and wildlife chanting rhythms.

They parked alongside a glistening waterfall, and Jason was captivated by the pristine pink foam forming as the powerful water crashed down, slightly splashing them. The guide gathered everyone to announce that whoever dared climb the waterfall must sign a waiver. For a moment he reconsidered, but Tyler nudged him on. "Come on, man, can't back out now. We didn't spend all those hours on a flight to miss this."

One by one, they followed the guide up the waterfall, ropes secured, digging their boots into the slippery rocks as they climbed. Jason made sure to have his GoPro attached to his helmet and found himself doing just fine going very slowly until suddenly, he slipped.

"You okay down there? I'm not catching you if you fall," Tyler yelled out from ahead.

Jason waved his hand. "Doing just fine. I'll race you to the top."

He paused for a moment to catch his breath and looked upward to observe the remaining distance. He squinted, trying to look past the mist, and what he'd initially thought was another guide was instead a mysterious stranger. Disheveled gray hair wrapped around the sides of his pale balding head, and a long wiry white beard rested just past his Adam's apple. Like a wild jungle creature, the man peered down at him as if reading his soul.

Jason shook his head and wiped his face. When he looked back up, the man was gone. He tried to ignore the shivers that ran up his spine and continued to climb until he reached the top where Tyler was waiting for him.

Jason and Tyler removed their equipment and found a nice spot to take a break before their jump. "Did you see him at all? That creepy old man?" Jason asked, but he could tell that Tyler had no recollection based on his confused expression.

They rested and replenished themselves for no more than thirty minutes before Jason heard the tour guide calling for the group. "For those brave souls making the jump, please listen carefully. If you are not, Edwin will guide you down by trail. Now, a couple of safety tips: take a big leap with your arms crossed, and please, no flips, dives, or any crazy Red Bull stunts. Once you reach the bottom, Tony will assist you. Okay, who wants to go first? How about you, Tyler?"

Evidently, Tyler was glad he got picked first because he didn't hesitate at all when the guide called him over. Jason knew Tyler was an adrenaline junky and not always the best listener, but he still admired his friend's fearlessness. Tyler ran at full speed, leaping off and doing a 360 spin before sinking deep below the water. Jason counted the time it took before Tyler resurfaced—only eight seconds. A guide safely led him to the side.

Jason then heard the guide call his name. He stayed put for a moment, trying to hide behind the others. His palms began to sweat, and he took short breaths to prepare himself. All eyes were on him as he timidly approached the edge. He looked down and then back at the guide.

"You don't have to jump if you don't want to," the guide reassured him.

Jason waved his hand, letting the guide know he was okay. He inched closer toward the edge and paused, clamping shut his eyes. He felt the warm jungle air on his skin, took a big exhale, and jumped. The vertical drop made his stomach flip and he flared his arms until he eventually broke through the cool water, sinking. When he opened his eyes, he looked up, realizing how far he had sunk. His heart raced and a tightness gripped his chest.

Then, a feeling of complete peace overtook him. *It's so quiet. Nobody is pressuring me to do anything down here. If only I could stay a while longer,* he thought. When he turned his head, he saw something coming toward him. It was difficult to make out at first, but when it came into focus, Jason let out a muted yell as a ghoul flashed before his eyes and a voice told him, "Leave Thailand forever."

He swam as fast as he could to the surface, feeling short of breath until he broke through, coughing and gasping for air. The guides helped him climb onto the bank, and he continued coughing up water, shaking with fright.

"Hey, man, what happened?" Tyler crouched near him. "I was ready to come in after you."

Jason dismissed him with a wave "I'm fine. I just sank too deep."

On the ride back, Jason remained silent, grappling with his thoughts about what he'd encountered. Whatever it was, he wanted to put it out of his mind.

CHAPTER 7

THE PENDANT'S POWER

When they arrived at their hostel, Jason wanted to rest, but Tyler suggested they have a few drinks to take his mind off today's incident.

Jason squeezed his temples. "I could use *several* drinks," he said. "Why don't we check out the club scene while we're at it."

Tyler rested his chin in his palm. "Wow. Never thought I'd hear you get so excited about drinking and clubbing. I like this version of you, Jason. See, travel brings out the best in people."

After a few beers from the bar across the street, they went back to the hostel to get changed for a long evening. Jason was determined to make tonight memorable.

He had messaged Tom earlier, who gave him some nightlife recommendations for the Old City, an area filled with lively crowds and all-night escapades.

When they got there, Jason felt they had walked into a circus. There were low-key bars with life-size Jenga sets, and no shortage of dance bars turned rabbit holes where the music seemed to never end and booze flowed from fountains.

They barhopped for the first hour, amused by interesting names like the Pickled Boot and Tiki Tahoes. Jason loved how kind everyone seemed. They even made friends with a cute Thai bartender who kicked their butts in Jenga, and then gave them a few rounds of free shots and suggested they check out Conchi Carlita, a cool speakeasy nearby.

After perusing the Old City, they took the bartender's recommendation and grabbed a tuk tuk over to Conchi Carlita. When they arrived, Jason followed his GPS down a barren, dead-end street, which struck him as odd. Most would never have known this place existed if they weren't told about it.

Tyler scratched his jaw. "Are you sure we're at the right place? I just see a green dumpster filled with trash and rats."

Luckily, Jason had taken the bartender's number and messaged her. His phone buzzed within seconds. "Behind the dumpster! There's a little blue door. The password is 'Banana leaves... bonanza.'"

Jason waved Tyler over. She was right. There it was. A small sky-blue door with a golden lion knocker and a little concealed opening above that.

Jason knocked, but there was no answer. Then Tyler knocked a few times. They stood back and both jumped when the little opening revealed a pair of suspicious eyes peering back at them. The ominous royal-blue eyes just silently watched, scanning them from head to toe.

Jason broke the silence by giving the password, "Banana leaves... bonanza."

When they entered, it was like something out of a movie. Jason passed through a wave of cigar smoke that dissipated like fog. Soulful swing music coursed through dancing patrons and people spoke loudly as they slapped cards on blackjack tables and the rapid clicking of roulette tables never ceased. Jason could see Tyler's eyes gazing toward the blackjack.

"Jason, after we grab a drink, I might play just one round." Tyler rubbed his hands together. "I can easily win in a place like this."

They squeezed through tons of people and inched toward the back of the bar.

Tyler snapped his fingers. "Now this is what I call a speakeasy. Bartender! An old fashioned for my friend and make mine with mezcal."

They grabbed their drinks and made their way over to the blackjack table. Tyler eagerly slid into a seat next to an intriguing gentleman who wore an eye patch and had a handlebar mustache. Tyler slammed a few thousand baht on the table and organized his chips. He was in his element—strategic about every move he made, always keeping his eye on his opponents, trying to read them. Tyler lost the first three rounds, but it almost seemed like it was on purpose because thereafter he was unbeatable. The others, including the dealer, ground their teeth and tapped their fingers in frustration.

Out of the corner of his eye, Jason caught sight of a man moving through the crowd. His charcoal sport coat and gray checkered pants seemed out of place in such a casual hangout. He pulled an olive fedora down low as he smoothly swayed through the crowd like a phantom. His cold stare and grim disposition gave Jason the creeps, and he became short of breath as the man got closer. Jason turned his gaze to the ground, hoping the man would ignore them and just walk past, but it was no use. The man stopped before them, his hands landing on Jason and Tyler's shoulders. "I think you boys had enough," he said, his voice low and deep.

Jason trembled. "Yep, sure, we're done. We can leave."

Tyler's eyes were glued to his cards. "No, we can't. I'm just getting started. Take a hike, buddy." He shoved the man's hand off his shoulder without even looking at him.

Jason nervously grabbed his jaw and held his breath as he braced for the man's reaction, but he did nothing. The man just stepped back, folding one hand over his forearm. He smirked, eyes locked on them like a mercenary eyeing up his target.

Chills ran up Jason's entire body. He even felt the hair stand on the back of his neck.

"Man, I think it's time to go," he murmured to Tyler.

Tyler didn't budge. His eyes stayed fixed to his cards, his fingers twitching as he reached for the growing stack of chips in front of him. He was so composed; nothing could break his focus.

When Jason turned back around, he noticed the man was gone. Relief washed over him, and he took a long sip of his old-fashioned, easing his nerves, as Tyler celebrated another win at the table.

In no more than a minute, Jason felt warm breath on the back of his neck, close enough to make his skin crawl. Then came the sharp press of a blade against his lower back. His body locked in place, frozen by fear. Behind Tyler, another thug pressed a switchblade against his back. Jason caught sight of the man in the olive-green fedora standing across the room. The man tipped his hat with a wink.

The thugs quietly escorted them away from the table. The crowd didn't seem to notice—or didn't care—as Jason and Tyler were shoved through a back door into a dark dingy alleyway. They were pushed up against a few rusty trash cans, stumbling but catching their fall. Jason read the confusion and anger on Tyler's face, but neither of them dared move.

Then the man in the fedora appeared, stepping forward with the same calm demeanor as his henchmen stood just behind him. "You boys didn't listen. Don't worry, they'll go easy on you. You'll still be able to do some sight-seeing—with a limp, of course."

He snapped his fingers, and the thugs walked forward with their sharp switchblades. Jason's heart raced at an uncontrollable pace as his adrenaline surged. Tyler seemed just as nervous. He breathed hard and clenched his fists, preparing to defend himself. As the henchmen moved in on them, Jason felt a sudden burning sensation against his thigh. He reached into his pocket, pulling out the necklace that the woman had given him on the flight. His eyes focused on its glowing intensity, pulsating with warmth. When he glanced up, all three thugs looked as if they'd seen a ghost. They were frozen as their mouths hung open.

The man in the fedora twitched. "Where did you get that?"

Jason didn't respond and the man's face turned pale, all his confidence stripped away. The three of them backed up, and the man continued to apologize until they slipped through the speakeasy's door. As soon as they left, the necklace's glow faded.

"What the hell just happened?" Tyler panted with his hands on his hips. "And where did you get that thing?"

Jason shook his head in disbelief, staring at the necklace resting in his palm. "I don't know what happened. That was insane. Did you see how they reacted?" He wiped his hand across his face, still trying to process it. "Some woman on the flight here gave it to me. She said it came from a sacred place called Arhat or something. I didn't think it meant anything."

Tyler exhaled slowly and nodded. "Well, it meant something to them. Let's get out of here before they change their minds."

Jason pocketed the necklace. "Yeah, let's go."

Without another word, they bolted from the alley and grabbed a tuk tuk on the street and sped off, disappearing into the night.

As they whipped past scooters and cars, rocking side to side as the tuk tuk cut through traffic, Tyler stamped his foot. "Can you believe those guys? I was on a roll!"

Jason shook his head. "I'm just happy we're alive. Are you not still freaked out a bit?"

"I was more freaked out about the necklace. I've played a ton of underground games before. Guys like that are all talk."

"Ah, okay—glad one of us is comfortable with having a blade against his back," Jason quipped.

The tuk tuk dropped them off in front of a row of clubs with thumping loud music. Jason could feel his body vibrating. They waited in line, which moved quickly, and were given bracelets to enter. It wasn't the biggest club, but it had a spacious dance floor and several tables for bottle service, which seemed to be the norm. The DJ's booth was positioned in front of the crowd and he was playing EDM classics by deadmau5. It was difficult to hear, let alone speak, but Jason made his best effort to chat up the cute Thai girl next to him. He was proud of himself for approaching her without hesitation. He even saw a surprised look on Tyler's face. He'd barely spoken when she grabbed his hand and led him onto the dance floor. They moved to the rhythm, their bodies intertwined, and locked lips. Jason felt alive, disconnected from everything he'd left back home in San Diego. Everything around him faded, and all he could feel was this moment.

CHAPTER 8

CITY OF ANGELS

In the days following, they relished the cultural vibrancy of Chiang Mai, then carried on with their trip throughout the rest of the country. The next stop was the buzzing capital, Bangkok, only an hour away by flight.

Bangkok was a different beast, Jason thought, as he could sense the liveliness and zeal from both the locals and tourists. It was a city that seemed to never sleep. He remembered from his research that sky bars were popular here and one of the tallest was called Ascend, atop the world-renowned Nakbu Hotel, where ambassadors and celebrities stayed.

It was their first night on the town. Jason hailed a cab for them. Arriving at Nakbu Hotel, they were escorted through the lobby by the concierge to an elevator. Their anticipation peaked as they smoothly ascended to the eightieth floor. Jason heard the music growing louder the closer they got to the rooftop. The elevator came to a sudden stop, "*ding*," and the doors opened to reveal a crowd of young expats and local socialites. They all appeared to be in their mid-twenties to early thirties, and dressed to the nines. The women wore black high heels that wrapped up their ankles, and their short, thin designer dresses came in various colors and patterns—some were all black, fringed and strapless, while others were solid white and bright purple, cut low to expose their backs. Most of the men wore dark dress pants with their chests peeking out through their fitted button-down shirts and sports coats that ranged in color and pattern.

Jason loved how stylish everyone was, and it didn't seem to be a stuffy or cliquey crowd as strangers greeted him and Tyler while others laughed and socialized. He got the vibe that everyone was just here to have a good time. Some were even dancing to the feel-good sounds coming from the DJ, who had spiky dark hair and wore a white-netted shirt, accessorized with silver David Yurman chains and bracelets.

Jason began moving his arms and body in time to the music as they made their way over to the well-lit bar situated on a square platform right in the center of the rooftop. People sat around the crafty bartender, who shook and poured a plethora of tasty concoctions. Jason and Tyler managed to grab two seats and were served refreshing lychee martinis without even ordering. Jason looked around, admiring the interesting characters that surrounded them, each seeming to have their own unique story.

The guy sitting to the right of him stuck out his hand. "I'm Chris. What brings you to Thailand?"

"Probably the same reason you came here—vacation." Tyler shook his hand. "Great to meet you, Chris. I'm Tyler and this is Jason."

Chris told them how he used to be an investment banker in New York but had recently quit his job to permanently stay in Thailand. He'd started out on vacation, just like them, and then claimed to have met the love of his life.

He rested his elbows on the bar. "A penthouse in this location only goes for six hundred bucks per month. I used to pay four thousand per month in Manhattan. Money, I got enough of it. Sucks when you can't spend it though. I was pulling eighty-hour workweeks. Being here, I've never felt so free."

Jason meditated on his words. *Never felt so free. Is that what it takes? Should I just stay here and become an expat?*

Throughout the night, they met many others like Chris, who they felt inspired by—those who'd taken a leap of faith, leaving all the stress of old jobs and problems behind. Jason was captivated because he figured that, like them, he too was a misfit back home and wanted to avoid being trapped in the rat race and status quo.

They walked the edge of the rooftop to marvel at the magnificent views. Below, cars the size of bugs whizzed down busy streets.

With two shots hoisted into the air, Tyler grinned. "Here's to the trip of a lifetime."

After another drink or two, they made their way back downstairs, eager to explore the next spot. Jason hailed another cab, and on their way, he asked the driver if he could recommend any good bars, despite not knowing if the man understood him. To his surprise, the driver took them to a place called the Iron Fairy Jazz pub. Jason never imagined ending up at jazz bar in Thailand, but after walking inside, the atmosphere spoke for itself, and it didn't disappoint.

Inside, it was dimly lit, and everything including the bar was carved from pure sequoia wood. Jason was almost immediately caught off guard when the lights went out and a voice as smooth as velvet began to sing. A spotlight shone on a rusted spiral staircase that was situated to the left of the main pub floor and ran up to an exposed balcony with seating. Down the dark metal steps, a young Thai woman moved with swagger to the rhythm of the piano, her voice untouchable. Jason was captivated as she sang Sinatra's "I've

Got You Under My Skin," her eyes seductively charming as she paraded around the bar, entertaining everyone. She jokingly sang, "I've got you, under my... skirt," while glancing over at Tyler, which garnered laughs from Jason and the crowd.

Toward the end of her song, she walked over to Jason and pulled him over in front of everyone and they began to dance. Toward the end of the song, she placed the mic beside his mouth. He leaned in and yelled, "*Buenas noches*," and the drums and piano faded.

Jason was surprised by how carefree he'd been on this trip so far. Even Tyler commented on several occasions how he'd been seeing a different side to him, in a good way.

After the jazz bar, they walked through the streets and night markets. Jason was enthralled by the food vendors, who seemed to be the pulse of the city. They were the electrical current that passed through the circuits of the streets, furiously cooking up first-class food. As Jason and Tyler squeezed their way through the crowd, they picked up delicious snacks along the way like satay skewers and pad kra pao. They dipped spicy pork spring rolls into delicious sweet sauces, and the instant crunch and grease provided euphoric highs.

It was a perfect first night in Bangkok.

They wasted no time sleeping the next day and were out early to see the sights around the city. The sound of busy streets didn't perturb them, but the humidity that hung over them like a wet blanket was unbearable. It was the type of weather that required multiple showers per day. Luckily, they found somewhere to stop off for some iced coffees, the jet fuel necessary to carry on with their day. It was a place called Clover Café—more of an upscale spot, Jason presumed by its vibe. As they sat back in white cushioned seats, giant plant-shaped mahogany fans slowly spun above their heads. Jason flipped through one of his guidebooks, having noted earlier that they needed to visit Wat Pho temple, knowing it was a must-see.

When they entered the temple, their expectations were blown away. Jason observed a sanctuary of magnificent multi-tiered roofs arching high over the entrance to sacred grounds. As they strolled through, they became aware of the tranquil vibes surrounding the chapels, each ornamented with fragments of colorful pottery and upturned stucco-topped brick roofs. Detailed murals with Buddhist symbolism lined the walkways. Jason gazed at two sturdy, fierce lion guardian statues. The plaque next to them said they stood as protectors. Off to the side, he tuned into a tour guide, explaining to Tyler how Wat Pho became the first public university in Thailand for science, religion, and literature.

Tyler wiped his sunglasses against his shirt. "Didn't you say there's a giant Buddha around here somewhere?"

Jason searched on his phone. "Yes! It's right over there, I think."

Before entering, they removed their shoes and bowed. It didn't take them long to discover the enormous golden Buddha lounging on its side, making them feel like ants. They took turns snapping pictures of each other in goofy poses until Tyler saw a sign hanging up that read, "Traditional Thai massage."

He pointed at it. "I could go for a massage. Should we try it?"

Jason adjusted his backpack. "I'm down to try everything. Let's go."

They followed the signs through the temple and across the courtyard into another small temple that was made specifically for Thai massages.

They waited until their names were called and followed a female masseuse dressed in a sky blue t-shirt and white linen pants into a quiet room with low-lit candles.

Jason observed the massage beds lined up next to each other, laden with firm but still soft cushions positioned within dark cherry wood frames. Relaxing aromas from eucalyptus humidifiers filled the room. The massage therapist handed Jason a pair of pajama pants and escorted him over to a changing area blocked off by a curtain. He removed his shirt and shoes and slipped into the soft pants. He placed his clothes into a cubby space and then walked over to one of the beds where the massage therapist was waiting. He lay down on his back, and the therapist started working on his legs and thighs, massaging them with strength until she reached his feet, squeezing and bending them.

Jason turned his head to see Tyler next to him, also mid-massage. He could see a confused look on Tyler's face.

"What's the difference between this and a regular massage?" Tyler asked him.

Jason didn't respond until he felt the therapist aggressively bend his legs and push his hips side to side. She then dug her elbows into his back and stretched his arms. He yelped.

Tyler looked over. "What?" He gasped. "Ouch! Okay, I see the difference now."

Toward the end of the massage, the specialists instructed them to breathe in, hold and release, breathe in, hold and release. They did this a few times and then sat silently before they were startled by the sound of a gong.

Jason glanced over at Tyler. "So, thoughts on the massage?"

Tyler rubbed his knees. "If you asked me ten minutes ago, I would have said I felt like a human pretzel, but now I kind of feel phenomenal. You know what we need to do next?"

Jason was all ears. "What are you thinking?"

"Suits—we need tailor-made suits, especially if we're starting jobs when we go home. The quality is supposed to be incredible here and at good prices."

Jason's eyebrows shot up, but he pulled out his phone to search for the best tailors in Bangkok.

The way Tyler was bouncing on his toes, Jason could tell he was excited. Tyler rushed out of the temple to the main street and waved for a tuk tuk.

They zoomed around Bangkok's crazy traffic, soon arriving at a mini-mall. Up a fancy escalator on the second floor, Jason spotted Peninsula Tailors, a shop with big white and blue letters. They walked in, then awkwardly stood around, wondering how this all worked. One of the tailors came toward them. He was an older Thai gentleman with salt-and-pepper, slicked- back hair. He wore light gray checkered slacks with black loafers and a white button-down shirt with the sleeves rolled up. He extended his hand. "Name is Albert. How can I help you both today?"

Tyler stepped forward. "Great to meet you, Albert. I'm Tyler, and this is my friend Jason. We need suits—we're starting new jobs."

Albert shifted his weight forward. "Well, you came to the right place. Let's get you two measured. Can I offer you a beverage—water, coffee, or maybe some whiskey?"

When Tyler said whiskey, Albert snapped his fingers and pointed back at him. "My kind of guy. Jason, you come with me. Patricia, please take care of Tyler."

Albert walked Jason over to the fabrics and he quickly became overwhelmed by all the patterns and styles to choose from.

Albert stood with his arms crossed. "So, what speaks to you, Jason? What's your style?"

Jason brushed his hand over the fabrics, thinking. "I honestly don't know where to start."

Albert placed a hand on his chin. "I see something sleek and sophisticated for you. Maybe a royal-blue three-piece with a vest, a white shirt, and a sapphire tie."

Jason envisioned a suit like the one Daniel Craig wore in *Casino Royale*. He loved the recommendation.

Albert clapped. "Hey, I learned from the best, kiddo. I spent several years on Savile Row in London before returning to Bangkok to open Peninsula. We worked with them all in my day—movie stars, politicians, you name it. I'll never forget, I was a young apprentice in London when Cary Grant walked in. There was no one around, so I greeted and helped him."

Jason's head jerked forward, his eyes wide. "Wow, no way! You met Cary Grant? I watch his films with my grandparents all the time. Albert, don't kill me, but can we also check out a few more styles? I'm just curious."

Albert smiled. "Of course, please, don't feel shy. When you ask for good service, you get good service. We've already planned all this out for you like a grand performance."

After Jason selected a fabric and style he was happy with, Albert walked him and Tyler over to the checkout area. They watched as he submitted their measurements, letting them know the suits would be ready for pickup in three days. Jason and Tyler thanked Patricia and Albert.

Before they left, Albert pulled a business card from his pocket. "Jason and Tyler, it was a pleasure serving you. Here, take my card, and remember, always live with style."

As they walked out of the tailor's shop, Jason pondered Albert's words, "live with style." It had a nice ring to it. He looked down at the card in his hand, flipping it over. A message on the back caused him to stop mid-step: "Arhat is waiting for you." Jason's hand shook, almost dropping the card. Simultaneously, the necklace in his pocket warmed against his thigh.

"Hey, Ty, wait here. I'll be right back."

Jason walked back into the shop, straight to the front desk. "Is Albert around?"

The woman barely looked up. "He just stepped out for lunch."

Jason nodded and walked out. It was another sign pointing to something he couldn't explain. The notion of Arhat was beginning to feel more real than ever.

He pulled the necklace from his pocket and hung it around his neck, deciding that's where it belonged.

CHAPTER 9

ECHOES OF ARHAT

For the rest of the afternoon, they walked the streets of Bangkok, exploring and getting lost, until they found themselves in another lively street market of vendors selling clothing, jewelry, and food. Jason thought the merchants were charming and true experts when it came to negotiating. From his experience so far, they seemed to know every tactic in the book.

Tyler came across a stall of fine pottery he thought would be a nice gift for his parents. While he looked at the different styles, Jason figured he'd visit some stalls nearby.

"I'll be back, Ty. I'm gonna take a look at this stall across the way."

Jason was drawn to the vibrant textiles and intricate crafts all around him. Just as he was sifting through some colorful silk scarves for his grandmother, he began to hear laughter, like children playing. It didn't faze him until he heard the steady beat of tribal drums that didn't seem to match the chaos of the bustling market. He looked around, searching for the sound of the drums, and even checked nearby stalls, but there were no drums being played.

Next, he heard chanting. The words were strange and unfamiliar, and they matched the rhythm of the drums. It was a language he'd never heard—far different than the Thai he'd grown accustomed to. Then came the sound of screeching animals and birds chirping. He felt like he was walking through a jungle. The sounds became louder and more intense, and his necklace began to pulsate. He grabbed hold of it against his chest and turned in every direction, searching for where the sounds were coming from until he paused, feeling frozen in place and helpless. He covered his ears with his hands and yelled, "STOP!"

The noise suddenly ceased, and when he looked around, people nearby stared back at him with confused expressions like he was crazy.

Then, through the crowd, he noticed her—a small girl standing still, her joyful eyes fixed on him. She was barefoot and dressed in tribal clothing with seashells on her wrists and larimar beads around her neck. One of the necklaces was almost identical to his. Jason blinked, unsure of what he was seeing.

He glanced behind him, wondering if she was looking at someone else, but when he turned back toward her, she shook her head and smiled. Then, with a wave, she beckoned for him to follow. Jason pointed to himself, mouthing, *Me?* She nodded and smiled again before turning and running.

"Wait!" Jason called, pushing his way through the crowd, bumping into strangers. Every so often, she would stop to wait for him, wave, and then run off again. Eventually he was led to an open square with fewer people, and he stopped, panting, and scanned the crowd. She was gone. He couldn't find her anywhere, as if she never existed.

As a few people moved out of his way, up ahead he saw a lonely old man sitting cross-legged in the dusty street between two vendors, swaying side to side. He looked to be playing a game, maybe dominos, Jason thought. He walked over and examined the peculiar stranger. The closer he got, the more familiar the man became. He knew he'd seen him somewhere before but couldn't put his finger on it. When he was only steps away, it became apparent. It was the old man who'd spooked him during the waterfall hike in Chiang Mai.

"It's you! I saw you that day at the top of the waterfall. Who are you?"

The old man ignored him and continued to sway with his eyes closed.

Jason spoke louder. "Hey, I'm talking to you. What game are you playing anyway?" He waited for a response but got nothing. "Maybe it's not you. Never mind."

As Jason turned his back, he heard the old beggar say, "*Mahjong!*"

Jason turned around. "Ah, you mean the Chinese game?"

Again, the old man didn't immediately respond or open his eyes, so Jason impatiently turned to walk away again.

"Juniper! Arhat is waiting."

Bewildered, Jason looked back. "Did you say Arhat? And who's Juniper?"

However, the old man did not reply, and Jason became frustrated. "Are you going to answer me or not?"

As soon as Jason began to turn, the old man reached out and grabbed his pant leg. Jason kicked his hand away.

"Jason! Please listen to me. You must understand the importance of your journey."

He felt the necklace warm against his chest. He stood speechless, staring back at the old man, who continued to sway.

"You see that necklace? It will guide you there. I'll make sure."

Jason was scared. "Look, what do you want with me? You're creeping me out. Who are you?"

The stranger opened his eyes. "It doesn't matter who I am—all that matters is that you find out who you are. Whether you decide to pursue Arhat or not is up to you. I leave you with this map, the key to your happiness."

His hand shot out like a snake and gripped Jason's forearm, bringing him to his knees. Jason let out a yelp of agony and tried pulling away but the man's grip was too strong. In horror, he watched the old man's eyes roll to the back of his head. Jason continued trying to break free, but it was no use. He sensed himself getting lightheaded, and then a vision entered his mind.

He was soaring across an open ocean, piercing through thick clouds, the wind rushing through his hair until he slowed down and all the clouds dissipated. He witnessed tall cliffs surrounding a vast jungle island, and whatever force had taken hold of him moved him down to the island. At rapid speed, he moved past dense, unending trees. Faster and faster, he raced through the lush green jungle until he was met with a blinding white light. When he opened his eyes, he was hovering over a village. Everything was blurred, but he could make out crowds of people laughing and conversing with one another. Some looked to be fishing, and others were dancing alongside colorful huts. What he noticed in particular was the energy that surrounded him. It was intoxicating. He felt so alive, so free. No worries bombarded his mind, and he felt content and happy, but before he could investigate further, the blinding white light flashed again, returning him to the Bangkok market. When he opened his eyes, he quickly pulled away, rubbing the sore spot on his forearm.

Tyler's voice from behind caught him off guard. "Jason, where did you go, man?"

Jason turned and walked toward Tyler, rubbing his temples and trying to comprehend what just happened. "I'm sorry, I was just talking to that old man."

Tyler looked at him with an odd stare. "What old man? You seeing things again?"

Jason turned around, searching for the old beggar, but he was gone. "What? He was just here. I swear." Jason looked for him in the nearby stall, but he was nowhere to be found.

Tyler walked up to him, patting him on the back. "Sounds like you need a drink, buddy. Maybe the heat is getting to you. Let's go find a bar to cool off in."

They ended up at a small dingy dive bar across the street from their hostel. Entering, they stepped across creaky old wooden floors. A jukebox off to the side was playing The Rolling Stones. It was filled with middle-class expats down on their luck, slinging back shots and beers. Jason covered his ears as the seats made screeching sounds when they were pulled out from under the tables.

They ordered beers at the bar and sat down at a table. Jason couldn't get the strange vision out of his head.

"What's with the fixated stares? Earth to Jason. Can you hear me?" Tyler waved his hand in his face.

Jason just concentrated on the coin he spun on the table, lost in deep thought.

Tyler slapped his hand on the table. "Hello! You barely touched your beer. You okay?"

Jason looked up at him with a serious face. "Ty, would you believe me if I told you I knew where to find paradise?"

Tyler sat back and took a swig of his beer. "Well for starters, I'd tell you that you're batshit crazy, but if it's a place where I'm the richest guy on Earth surrounded by chicas, then sure."

Jason smirked. "It wasn't by mistake. The woman on the flight, the way those thugs got scared when the necklace glowed. Arhat, man, it's a real place."

Tyler tilted his head. "Come again? What's not a mistake? Arhat? Buddy, you're scaring me a little right now—you've been acting weird."

Jason whispered, "Look, Ty, I know I sound crazy, but as your friend, I'm telling you the truth. Arhat is real. It's a sacred village and it's paradise. I saw glimpses of it, but that's not what drew me in—it was the feeling I got from being there. I felt invincible, like I had the power to accomplish anything, and even more, I was at such peace with myself. I felt fulfilled and completely centered. It's hard to describe, but look, check out the necklace." Jason took it off and slid it across the table, watching as Tyler looked around and then grazed his fingers over the tiger head beads. He saw him gasp, and then a natural smile formed on Tyler's face as his eyes grew larger and fixed on the medallion. It seemed as if the necklace was also speaking to him.

Tyler pushed the necklace back toward Jason. "Dude, what was that? That feeling I got from the necklace? Here, take it back."

Jason leaned in. "That's what I'm talking about. Maybe this Arhat place will turn out to be a bunch of bull, but why wouldn't we at least try to find it?"

Tyler looked up as he thought. "I mean, I was hoping to catch a Full Moon party and hit up some of the islands in the south, but who knows, maybe we'll end up finding vast amounts of treasure if it's really that special of a place."

While Tyler was clearly still on the fence, Jason was convinced. Especially after the vision he'd seen when the old man grabbed his arm. If Arhat was anything like he envisioned, then all his worries would be gone.

They spent the rest of the day and night slinging beers. Tyler kept the rounds coming while Jason started researching the details of their upcoming journey. They would have to take a few trains, a boat, and maybe even a flight. He suggested they stock up on supplies and food the next day because who knew what they might encounter along the way.

Finally, Jason said, "So, we have two options: fly or take a train down to Songkhla. It's close to the Malaysian border. It's a fifteen hour train ride, but we'll get to see most of the country along the way. Then we'll need to somehow get a boat to take us to this island here." He pointed on the GPS map.

Later that night, back at the hostel, Jason phoned his grandparents from the lobby to check in on them. His grandmother picked up.

"Hey, it's your grandson. Morning! I can smell the famous French toast from here!"

Rapid-fire words came through the phone. He could picture his grandmother's face glowing. "Jason, how's my grandson doing? It must be late there, huh? One minute—let me call your grandfather. It's Jason, pick up the other phone."

His grandfather's voice immediately came through. "Hiya Jason, we're so happy to hear from you. How's your trip? You two must be having a ball."

Jason slightly moved the phone away from his ear because of how loud his grandfather was and smirked. "It's been an adventure, to say the least. I miss you both very much. How is everything? What have you both been up to?"

He could hear his grandmother exhale. "Just taking it easy. And we miss you even more. We're still hosting our weekly parties, and I do some gardening, and your grandfather works on his car. Nothing new around here, Jason."

He let out a sigh, feeling relieved that they were doing well.

"You're staying safe?" his grandfather asked. "Have enough money? Everything's okay?"

Jason slightly stammered, as he didn't want to mention anything about Arhat. "Ahh, yeah! All good. We're seeing a lot of cool things, going to sky bars, trying great restaurants. It's such a cool country. Speaking of, I wanted to talk to you both about something. Tyler and I are planning to extend the trip. There's just so much we want to see, and we figured this is the best time to do it."

He could hear his grandmother's smile as she responded, "I think it's a great idea. You two should do it. You're only young once. Go have fun. Just be safe and keep us updated on all your trip details."

Jason shifted his weight, anticipating his grandfather's response.

"Thanks for letting us know," his grandfather said. "Send us your new dates and the names of the hotels and places you'll be visiting next. I'll give Art and Mr. Murphy a heads-up about your change of plans."

Jason leaned his back against the wall in the lobby. "Thanks, Grandpa. I'll make sure to email you all the details. We're heading south. There're tons of beautiful islands down there. Anyways, how are you feeling, Grandma?"

He gripped the phone after a long silence. He could hear his grandparents talking to each other. His grandmother's voice lowered in the background. "I don't want to spoil his trip. Maybe when he comes home."

He pushed the phone against his ear, trying to listen in on their conversation. He made out his grandfather's elevated reply, "We should tell him; the boy deserves to know."

Jason began to feel himself sweat. "What? Tell me what? What's wrong?"

His grandmother's words couldn't have come out slower. "Well, Jason... I don't want to you to get concerned, but I've found out the cancer has come back. Now don't get all worried. I've been to the doctor, and we have it all under control."

Jason dropped the phone and jolted back. He started breathing heavily and shook his head a few times.

He picked up the phone. "I'm sorry, I needed a moment. Are you sure? That's what the doctor said? How though? I thought you beat it."

His grandmother exhaled. "Yes, the doctor confirmed it. But you listen up, Jason. Don't worry about me. I'm as tough as nails. You know that. I don't want this to spoil your trip now."

Jason pounded his fist against the wall. "Ahh, I know, Grandma. You beat it once, and you'll beat it again. It's just, I hate hearing that. I just want your cancer to go away forever. What are the next steps in treating it? I can cut my trip short and come home to help out."

His grandfather cleared his throat. "They have your grandmother on some type of cancer therapy pills. This is meant to slow the progression. She may need to undergo chemotherapy at some point. We don't want you to worry. I'll be taking care of her."

"Listen to us, Jason," his grandmother said firmly. "You need to enjoy the rest of this trip, and I want you to. You wouldn't want to upset your grandmother now, huh? Go have fun. I promise I'll be here when you come back."

Jason remained silent for a moment, contemplating what to do. "You really are something, Grandma. I admire how positive you can be even during the most challenging times."

He heard her chuckle. "You know me well enough, Jason, and that strength lives in you too. You are my grandson after all. Anyways, you have a good rest of your trip."

"Alright," Jason said.

"Your grandfather and I are going for our walk now. Don't forget to send us your details. We love you."

Jason smiled. "I love you both as well. We'll talk soon."

After the call, he thought about the vision he'd had when the old beggar grabbed his arm. Although he only saw faint and somewhat blurry images of the village, he could still recall how full of life it was. However, it was the feeling of being there that he remembered most. He felt weightless. All his worries and depression disappeared. He had no anxieties. He was at complete peace with himself. All he could feel was this lust for life and an urge to love and help others. Arhat seemed like a place where miracles happened. He had the strongest feeling—he didn't know where from—that there had to be some cure there that could permanently heal his grandmother.

Suddenly, he was more desperate to find Arhat than ever.

CHAPTER 10

BLINDED BY TRUST

On the day of their departure, they arrived at the train station around 6:30 am, early enough to spare some time for a quick bite since the next train didn't leave until 7:00. As they waited on the platform, the mechanical beast screeched along the tracks until it came to a halt. The doors opened, and the conductors waited for passengers to board. After a few minutes, they waved their arms, signaling to each other that all passengers were aboard and it was time for the train to leave.

Tyler and Jason moved through the train car, securing two window seats facing each other, and lifted their luggage overhead before settling in. Once the train doors shut tight, the conductors collected tickets, and Jason felt the engines come to life beneath them, hissing and chugging as the train slowly pulled away.

They passed the first hour talking about sports, stocks, and other random topics, like whether cold plunges boost the immune system. As Jason stood to use the bathroom, Tyler said, "Yo, don't forget," and tossed him some travel toilet paper.

Row by row, Jason pulled himself forward, fighting against the train's momentum until he reached the nearest bathroom located at the back of the train. On the way out, he heard a bunch of chatter in the vestibule next to the bathroom. It sounded like laughing and cheering. He walked over to see what all the commotion was and discovered a few teenagers shooting a harmless game of craps.

He watched a few rounds as they took each other's money and got competitive. One of them shook his hand from side to side, getting ready to roll, until Jason realized that they had all paused, turning to look at him. One of the teenagers asked if he was lost and where he was from. Jason told them that he was just on vacation and that he was from California.

The one shooting craps waved him over. "Nice to meet you, California, come play a round with us."

Jason thought it comical that they'd nicknamed him "California," but he appreciated their invite. He crouched down in the center, listening to the eager kids throw coins around like candy, betting on him and against him. He picked up the dice and shook his hands, then launched them against the train door.

He watched intently as the first die dropped. It was a three. The second spun and rocked, building anticipation. A couple of the kids threw their arms up in victory, while the others were subdued. He played a few more rounds, feeling motivated as he kept winning. Roll after roll, they cheered, "California! California! California!"

Jason then heard Tyler, who had come to find him. "Gambling without me?"

"He's winning us a lot of money," one of the kids shouted.

"Well, count me in." Tyler pointed at Jason. "That's my best friend."

From time to time, Jason looked around to ensure their fun was not disturbing passengers, but they must have because he suddenly heard loud footsteps that pounded like an earthquake as the conductor walked toward them. His face was red and his nostrils flared.

Jason couldn't understand the conductor because he yelled at them in Thai, but it was obvious they were in trouble.

Two more conductors ran over. As the rowdy kids mocked and teased them, Jason realized the next stop was coming up. He and Tyler tried to go back to their seats, but they were instead pushed and pulled by the conductors, who mistook them for punks and threw them off the train along with the kids. The train departed, leaving them behind, stranded and distraught.

Jason paced with a hand on his forehead. "All of our supplies and our bags are still on that train. And we can't just stay here!"

One of the kids overheard him and responded, "Not your lucky day. No trains until tomorrow. I'm Cetek. You can roll with us. That's Bakka and Dusit over there. Those old fools did us a favor—we live here."

Jason and Tyler walked away from the group for a moment to discuss what they should do since getting kicked off a train was not part of their plan.

Tyler whispered, "Let's ditch these guys. They just got us kicked off the train."

Cetek called out to them, watching as Jason shifted his weight. "You won't find any places to stay. This city doesn't get tourists."

Jason quietly contemplated Tyler's idea about ditching them until Cetek yelled, "Don't worry, guys. You're in good hands. It's a small city, but we'll show you around. Just lighten up—we'll give you a true local experience."

Tyler leaned toward Jason, covering his mouth while watching the group of teenagers. "You sure about these guys? I don't trust them."

Jason stared at the ground, thinking. "I don't either, but we need a place to stay. We can leave in the morning. At most, we're going to grab a drink and a bite to eat. We could always ditch them if things get weird."

Tyler shook his head. "If you say so!"

Jason and Tyler walked over to where the kids were standing near the train tracks. Jason nodded. "Thanks, Cetek, we appreciate that. Sure, we'll crash just for the night. We have to be up very early tomorrow to catch the next train out of here. "

The group took Jason and Tyler for a late lunch at one of their favorite noodle shops in town, but their raucous behavior caught Jason off guard. Cetek and his buddies drove customers from some of the tables so they could push them together for themselves. They harassed the owner and waitress with outlandish requests. Like hungry hyenas, they slurped their soups, burping and talking loudly while Jason and Tyler looked at each other with wide eyes. They even began throwing noodles around, making a mess all over the floor and table.

What annoyed Jason most was that after lunch, they left without cleaning or paying. Jason and Tyler again glanced at each other in silent disbelief, then helped the poor waitress clean up and paid her.

From outside of the restaurant, Cetek called out, "Let's go, California! Don't tell me you guys are helping them."

Jason walked out. "What was that back there? You guys trashed the place and you didn't even pay."

Cetek placed his arm around Jason. "Relax, California, we meant no harm. It was all in good fun. I talked to the guys, and we're going back tomorrow for community service."

Jason threw off Cetek's arm and stood back, pointing a finger in his face. "Who the hell do you think you guys are? You're a bunch of punks. You don't treat people like that. You better get back in there and help now."

Cetek was inches away from Jason's face, staring him down. "What are you going to do about it?"

Jason could feel Cetek's breath against his cheek, and instead of looking away, he stood his ground and stared right back at him. He watched as Cetek's angry expression turned into a sinister grin. "There's no problem here, California. We're all friends, right? Guys, do California a favor and go help clean up."

Jason backed away, watching as Cetek's goons went inside. He and Tyler had already done the work, but he still appreciated their efforts, and on top of that, he was proud of himself for standing up to someone for once.

Tyler patted Jason on the back. "Well done, man. I'm impressed."

After sunset, they stopped off at a local bar. Since he wasn't really in the mood for drinking, Jason passed on most of the shots offered to him. Cetek and his friends got loaded. Jason noticed that even Tyler didn't drink much, making it obvious that he didn't like these guys. They stayed for about two hours until Bakka and Dusit walked outside. Jason grew curious as to why they seemed so excited, to the point that they could barely control themselves.

Cetek, still sitting at the table with a girl in his lap, leaned over. "You guys ready to have some real fun?"

He shoved the girl off his lap and got up, waiting for Jason and Tyler to follow them. All the while, as they moved toward the exit, Jason kept thinking, *these guys are trouble*, but deep down, he was intrigued, and he knew Tyler was too.

Dusit and Bakka hailed a few tuk tuks. Riding in these things had always been exhilarating to Jason, but this time he felt nervous apprehension, especially as the drivers traveled down some dark roads, wrapping around bends that took them up into the hills overlooking a well-lit city. The views were magnificent, but what caught Jason's attention most was the neighborhood they'd been dropped off in. Dusit told Jason and Tyler to keep quiet as they hid behind a few bonsai trees. All the while, Cetek peeked out at a well-decorated Thai mansion just in front of them. Bakka explained that this home belonged to the richest man in Thailand, the largest distributor of Apple products in the country. Jason looked over at Tyler, who shared his troubled expression.

Tyler turned toward the group. "Guys, sorry to cut this party short, but we're out of here." He pushed past them but was held back.

Dusit grabbed hold of his arm to stop him. "Where the hell do you think you're going?"

Jason held his breath, and his body locked up when he saw Bakka pull a gun from his pocket and step forward to place it against Tyler's forehead.

Cetek patted Jason and Tyler on the shoulders. "You're either with us or against us."

Tyler stood completely still. He didn't make a sound. Jason could hardly hear him breathe. He just stared down the barrel of Bakka's gun.

Jason held his hands up. "Everything's good here. We'll go with you—right, Tyler?"

Tyler nodded, and with his gun, Bakka waved at them to walk toward the house, following behind to ensure they didn't try to run away. Jason thought about finding a way to ditch the group as soon as they had the opportunity.

As they approached the mansion, Jason realized that this was not their first time as Bakka and Dusit slipped through the window with ease, opening the back door. Then Cetek and his cronies turned the man's home into a zoo. Expensive bottles of whiskey were opened and passed around like cheap sodas. Artifacts and collectibles were juggled and became slingshot targets. Dusit and Bakka even grabbed two ancient-looking swords off the wall, battling each other and slicing up furniture. Jason quickly assumed a neighbor must have heard them and called the police as he heard loud sirens out front, causing them all to hide.

Cetek cut the music and killed the lights. Dusit and Bakka escaped out of the back door while Jason and Tyler hid behind a kitchen island with Cetek. Jason began to tremble as flashlights glared through the dark home. Cetek shoved Jason into Tyler, and they fell while he sprinted toward the side door. Before Jason and Tyler could react, they were surrounded and handcuffed. As the police dragged them out of the house, Jason spotted Cetek staring at them with a sinister smirk and shrugging his shoulders before running off.

CHAPTER 11

A FAITHFUL FRIEND

They were pushed roughly into the back of a truck, and after what seemed to be no more than a fifteen-minute drive, the vehicle came to a stop and they were ripped out. The dreary concrete police station was down a barren alleyway with no sign of life. There were no windows, and some graffiti and several roaches decorated the outside walls. They were shoved through the metal doors into the station and past several messy desks, then thrown into two firm gray seats. Jason panicked as he witnessed two officers pointing at them during a heated conversation in Thai. He and Tyler sat with their hands shaking in fright. One of the officers walked over, grabbed them by their necks, and brought them in front of a camera for mug shots before placing them in a barren cell.

It was hot, dark, and damp. Mold was growing on the walls, and the pipes overhead leaked onto the dirty stone floors. Rats and roaches scurried through the cell and spiders danced up the concrete. The smell was repulsive, a mix of mothballs and farm animals. Jason sank against the hard wall, staring off as Tyler argued with the officer sitting at a small desk facing the cell.

Jason barely slept that night. The early morning dew stuck to his dehydrated skin. He wasn't hungry at the sight of the rice porridge served for breakfast. He knew as well as Tyler that this was no time to think about food. What discouraged him most was that they hadn't even been given the chance to phone anyone or contact the US embassy.

Tyler pounded his fist against the wall. "This is all a mistake—they gotta realize that."

Jason was lost in his thoughts, replaying how they'd gotten themselves into this mess.

"It's my fault. I never should have gotten us mixed up with those kids."

The afternoon heat rolled in like death, and they sat, marinating in their filth. Jason was quietly meditating, battling negative thoughts and trying to stay positive. *How many days will they keep us here? Will anyone ever know that we're here? What if something happens to Grandma?*

Jason started shouting desperately at the officer, "We demand to speak to somebody! This is a mistake. Let us out at once!" But since the guard didn't understand what he was saying, he just shot back angry words in Thai, hitting his club against the bars of the cell.

Jason sat back and, for a moment, lost hope. "Ty, man, what are we supposed to do? Who knows how long we'll be locked up? Nobody knows we're here."

Tyler placed his arm around Jason and pointed toward the little opening above them. "Jason, look at the lights. Look at the lights, man. That's all I want you to focus on right now. Forget everything else. I'm scared too, but we'll figure this out."

Jason heard someone enter through the front door of the station, and the officer rushed off in a hurry to greet them. Peeking out, he could partially see that all the other officers and administrative employees were saying hello to the woman who had just walked in. *Is she someone of importance?* he wondered.

He saw the woman speaking with the captain, but she was fixated on her phone. The captain's eyes shifted toward Jason as they spoke, and he handed the woman a file that she took to what he assumed was her office, closing the door behind her.

Jason leaned back. The overwhelming heat made him feel drowsy. He wrapped his arms around his knees and lowered his head, trying his best to disconnect. Shortly after, he heard footsteps coming toward the cell, but he figured it was just the officer who had been keeping an eye on them. When he lifted his head, he saw the woman standing before the bars, flipping through what he assumed was his profile as she glanced down at it and then back at him multiple times. It didn't matter much to Jason. The heat and lack of water had caused his throat to dry out and the room felt like it was spinning. The cell door screeched as it swung open, but he paid little attention as he kept his head down, feeling too dehydrated and hungry to look up. He heard the desk officer yell at them in Thai, banging his baton against the cell, but he didn't bother to react until the woman spoke.

"That's enough! Jason, do you remember me?"

He lifted his head, staring at her.

"Jason, do you remember my necklace?" she said in a soft voice. "We met on our flight to Thailand. Do you still have it?"

He slowly pulled the necklace out of his shirt, holding it in front of her face, and then took it off and rested it in her outstretched palm. Still delirious, he found himself staring at her for a moment, unsure if it really was her. "Is it you? Preeda?"

"Yes, Jason, it's me," she confirmed.

He tilted his head. "But how? Why are you here?"

She placed her hand on his shoulder. "I'm the director of this station. The real question is, why are you here? Let's get you out right away. We'll go to my office to talk."

Jason carefully stood, waking Tyler, who jumped up in a flash once he saw that they were leaving. After getting cleaned up, they sat down in Preeda's office.

"Now, how did you end up in the home of the richest man in Thailand?" she asked curiously.

Jason shrugged. "We honestly had nothing to do with the break-in. We got mixed up with some local gang who got us kicked off our train. We were on our way to Songkhla."

Preeda folded her hands on the desk. "The leader of this gang, is his name Cetek?"

Tyler almost left his seat. "Yes, Cetek is his name! Like Jason said, he got us kicked off our train—that's how we ended up in this city. They invited us to stay with them, and before we knew it, we were forced at gunpoint to break into that man's house."

"I see. No explanation needed, boys," Preeda said. "We've been watching those guys for a while now. They were picked up today for theft."

Jason's mouth hung open. "You weren't kidding about the necklace keeping me safe. The chances of us meeting like this are nearly impossible."

Preeda nodded. "Let's just call it fate." She picked up her phone and called for someone to come into the office. Soon, the captain entered. He stood in the corner with one arm crossed over the other.

Preeda returned her gaze to Jason and Tyler. "On behalf of our department, we want to extend our sincerest apologies for the mix-up and would like to offer you suites at The Rankow, our finest hotel. We'll have you escorted there immediately. Feel free to utilize all amenities offered."

Jason felt an indescribable swell of relief. Cetek must have been lying about there not being places to stay.

Emerging from the dark of the station, Jason shielded his eyes from a blinding light. As they settled in the back of a police car, the soft cushion seats brought a smile to his face. Preeda came to the window.

"I would like to invite you both for dinner tomorrow night at my home. Here's my number if you need anything at all. We are truly sorry for the mix-up."

On the ride to the hotel, they found themselves falling asleep.

Tyler slapped his forehead and shook himself. "No one is going to believe this story back home."

Jason exhaled. "I know. And she's from Arhat."

"You're kidding." Tyler's face lit up.

Jason showed his palms as he shrugged. "I know! Now you see why I'm so keen to get there. It feels like too much of a coincidence."

Tyler rested his head back against the seat. "Yeah, I see that. To be honest though, I'm just glad to be out of that rat hole cell."

When they arrived at The Rankow, they both stuck their heads out the window as they were left quite speechless by its architectural brilliance. It reminded Jason of Wat Pho, one of the largest temples in Bangkok. Its chedis were heavily ornamented with white marble sculptures of dragons, horses, and elephants, and several windows were stained glass.

Jason noticed a man walking toward the car to greet them. He was slender and dressed in a black striped three-piece suit, and had slicked-back dark hair. He opened the car door with a bow, extending his hand to guide Jason out of the car. "Hello, gentlemen, we've been expecting you. Welcome to The Rankow. I'm Tet, the general manager. We have prepared two suites for you."

Jason and Tyler followed Tet up to their private suites, where he showed them in and assured them they would want for nothing during their stay.

Tyler disappeared into his suite and Jason went into his own. He marveled at its elegant interiors: a plush sofa, king bed, views of the park. The bathroom was next level, with a white marble vanity and walk-in shower. It reminded him of a picture he once saw of a room at the St. Regis Hotel in New York City. He snapped a quick picture, sending it to his grandparents and checking to make sure they were doing okay. After a long, soothing shower, he dragged himself over to the cozy bed and crashed into a coma-like sleep.

When evening rolled around, Jason was woken by the rumbling of his stomach. Still tucked away under the covers, he thought, *Room service!* He scanned through the menu, picking out a variety of things he craved: blueberry pancakes, spare ribs, chicken lettuce wraps, coconut mussels. He phoned room service and ordered all of them as well as a pitcher of fresh watermelon juice. Thirty minutes later, a knock at the door caused him to sit up with excitement.

"Room service," a voice called from outside. The room service attendant, dressed in a white cocktail jacket with black pants and black bow tie, rolled a cart of food into the room, and Jason waited in anticipation as he left it by the window. Jason wasted no time digging in.

Just as he swallowed his last bite of spare rib, he received a call from Tyler.

"Dude, can you believe this? I just woke up. I'm literally feasting on scallops right now and drinking champagne. This is exactly the life I plan to be living one day."

"I'm right there with you. Hang tight, I need to take a bite of these blueberry pancakes." Jason took a big forkful and washed it down with watermelon juice. "I think there's a spa here."

Jason heard Tyler chewing before he exclaimed, "We're definitely hitting the spa!"

They spent the rest of the evening taking full advantage of all the spa amenities, such as full body massages, a variety of saunas, and cold plunges.

The next day, Jason received a call from Preeda confirming dinner around 5:00 pm at her house. Tet also assured him that he would have a taxi waiting for them out front at 4:30 to take them there.

On the short ride over, Jason stared out the window, observing people as they passed by until they reached a charming little off-white cottage. The driver let them out at the end of a winding path of rustic stepping stones that led to a dark cherrywood door. Both sides of the path were filled with green plants mixed with full bushels of blue, white, and lavender hydrangeas.

As Jason and Tyler walked toward the home, they approached what seemed like a gateway. A wooden arbor was covered in green ivy that blended with yellow daisies and purple irises. Jason spotted a woman walking past the window and the front door opened.

Preeda greeted them with a big smile, standing at the door in a white cooking apron and a light blue pair of chinos with black flats. Her thick hair rested on her shoulders and swayed as she moved.

When they stepped inside, Jason could smell the wonderful aroma of delicious food being cooked. The living room, where two little girls played, was decorated with two cozy couches, a single chair facing a rectangular wooden table, linen curtains, and beautiful red and gold chindi rugs. To the right of the main entrance, two sliding doors had been pushed back, revealing a small dining room with a table at the center. Six chairs surrounded it, each before a place setting.

Preeda motioned toward a tall, lanky man with dark hair brushed neatly to the side, who stood facing the entrance. He wore an off-white apron over a black T-shirt and dark green cargo shorts. Standing beside him were two small girls, one on each side, their black hair tied up in short, high pigtails. They wore matching yellow pinafore dresses layered over long-sleeved white shirts, each patterned with tiny black floral shapes.

"Jason and Tyler, I'd like you to meet my husband, Chakan, and these are my two girls, Kanda and Malai."

Her husband did his best to communicate while their girls blushed and hid behind their mother.

Preeda extended her arm. "Please, make yourselves at home. Take a seat in the living room."

She poured Jason and Tyler each a glass of fine German Riesling and served them a few small pieces of cantaloupe wrapped with prosciutto. She also plated mini Thai shrimp lettuce wraps for them. It didn't take Jason long to understand that tonight's dinner was a fusion of Thai and Italian cuisine, but he wondered why. It started to make more sense after he noticed tons of pictures around the house of Preeda in Europe.

She sat down on the couch in the living room with a glass of wine. "I spent two years living in Italy, mostly in Rome and Florence, studying art. It wasn't until I returned to Thailand that I met my husband. Although I love art, my true calling was to join the police force. As a young girl in my village, I was always strong, looking out for my people. Now I get to protect and instill justice in my city."

Tyler sipped his wine and glanced up at the wall in front of him. "Preeda, did you paint these?"

Preeda's husband uttered a few words in broken English, "Don't let her fool you, she great artist."

As they sat at the dinner table, her husband placed the first course on the table. He removed the lid, exposing a coconut curry stew with rice and fresh fish. In addition, the girls brought out a large plate of seaweed salad with an assortment of clams, mussels, shrimp, and squid in a light lemon-garlic-peanut sauce.

"Save room for dessert," Preeda warned.

After dinner, she invited them to sit out back on the wide cherrywood deck. Preeda brought over slices of lemon cake and cups of hibiscus tea, setting them down on a large circular wicker table. Her yard was mostly enclosed by woods and tall arching trees. The deck faced a charming little yard with a narrow dirt trail that led to a beautiful wooden pavilion that had a roof covered with tons of green plants. Her cottage garden was full of colorful flowers and sweet scents. As her daughters played in the yard and Tyler tried chatting with her husband, Jason silently walked with Preeda down the path toward the pavilion. Although Jason appreciated her having them for dinner, he knew in the back of his mind that there was a bigger reason for the invitation.

He listened intently as she brought up the necklace.

"Keep it close to you, Jason. You will need it on your journey to Arhat."

He strolled with arms behind his back. "But why me?"

"I wish I could tell you, but the Ancestors chose you."

Jason paused for a moment. "Ancestors?"

"You will understand when you get there."

"But what if everything goes wrong trying to find it?"

"The fear of taking risks should never stand in our way when we believe in something," Preeda explained as they continued walking. "When I was called to leave Arhat, it was a big sacrifice. I had to ensure that the spirit and strength of my village lives on in all of us. Arhat is much more than a place—it's a mindset. It's a representation of happiness and a life untethered from the world's darkness. Most importantly, it embodies love and kindness. Just like you, the Ancestors also chose me. They are of a higher power. Arhat will always be my home, and although I may no longer be there, its meaning will always live within my heart. Please don't lose faith, Jason."

He took a breath. "Ah, Preeda, I just wish I understood, but I don't." He paused for a moment, then continued, "I guess I have to find out for myself. Between you and me, my grandmother has been battling cancer for a while now, and I'd do anything to help her. Could Arhat help her?"

They stopped and Preeda faced him. "I'm sorry to hear that, Jason. A cure, I cannot guarantee, but I as well as my people will surely keep her in our prayers. Don't lose hope."

On the taxi ride back to the hotel, Jason thought about what Preeda said to him.

"So, are we back on the road tomorrow?" Tyler asked.

"Yes, we can hop on the earliest train and finally make our way to Songkhla. Preeda has a cousin up there who can fly us to the small island off the coast."

Tyler stayed silent for a moment, then spoke, "You sure you still want to find this place? We just got locked up in jail. This was never even our plan to begin with. Think how cool it would be to just hit the islands and go to a Full Moon party."

Jason stared back with a straight face. "Look, I'm going find this place. I'm convinced that it exists, but we won't know for sure unless we try. If anything happens to us, it's on me."

Tyler laughed. "Man, you really don't give up once you got your mind set on something. I admire that about you. Let's do it." He held out his fist for a bump. "Let's find this place!"

CHAPTER 12

FISHING FOR PARADISE

The train they took the next day passed several small towns and grassy landscapes. After many hours had passed, Jason eventually heard a whistle blow and saw a sign for Hat Yai. After departing the train, they grabbed a taxi to Songkhla.

They checked into a nearby hostel, then ventured out to explore the beach city. Jason became mesmerized by the colorful colonial architecture and its bustling food stands and markets. He was pleased to see the palm trees that swayed in the cool ocean-scented air—a faint reminder of home.

Up by the beach, Jason took out his phone to call Paul, Preeda's cousin. Initially, Jason was taken aback by his response. "If you're trying to sell me something, I don't want any."

Jason quickly clarified who they were, and Paul's tone instantly changed. "Why didn't you say so? Meet me at KenYa's—it's a bar—in half an hour."

Jason placed his phone back in his pocket. "He told us to meet him at some local bar in thirty minutes."

Tyler shrugged. "Cool, let's head there now."

At the bar, Jason anxiously checked his phone, wondering if Paul would show. When he heard a rumbling scooter pull up, his doubts faded. It rattled and stalled, and its black exhaust leached through the bar's windows. A middle-aged man walked in, accompanied by a wiener dog. The man wore black sunglasses, old cargo shorts, a wrinkled button-down with a palm tree pattern, and worn-out flip-flops. His dark, greasy hair was slicked back, and the scent of cigarettes and booze wafted over. Jason thought he looked like a messy celebrity being hounded by TMZ.

The man approached, lowering his shades. "Hey guys, how you doing? I'm Paul, you must be Jason. Sorry I'm late, I lost my watch. This is my dog Ella. Say hi, Ella."

Jason extended his hand, but Paul gave him a casual high-five before signaling the bartender. "Hey what's happening? I'll take the usual: a beer, a doggie bowl for Ella, and two cold ones for my friends Jason and Tyler."

Paul rubbed a hand through his hair and lit a cigarette. "So, you know Preeda? If you're a friend of my cousin, you're a friend of mine. We're not biological cousins, but we're longtime friends."

"Yes, we're friends of Preeda. She mentioned that you could fly us to Perka Island," Jason said.

Paul smiled. "She's got a great family. And of course I can. It's a short ride."

"So, how long have you been flying?" Tyler asked. "That's pretty cool,"

Paul took a swig of his cold beer, which was covered in condensation. "I've been a pilot for twenty years. I was in the military... Air Force. Now, I just run my own charter business and give flying lessons. So, when you guys looking to go to Perka Island?"

Jason leaned over. "As soon as possible. We're prepared to pay as well, so just let us know what works best for you."

Paul kicked back with a laugh, slapping Jason on the back. "Pay? I'd never take money from my cousin's friends. It's a thirty-minute ride. I can get you there tomorrow morning."

Jason held up his beer to cheers with Paul. "That would be amazing. Are you sure? Thank you so much."

Paul lifted his bottle, simultaneously patting his dog on the head. "Of course I'm sure, and I'll even throw in some flying lessons on the way there, if you guys are up for it."

Jason's eyebrows shot up, followed by a grin. "Yeah. Sure. Tyler, you always wanted to fly, right?"

Tyler pushed his empty beer bottle forward. "Hell yeah. Did it once a long time ago at a local airport, but I'd love to try it again. But you're the one who's a bit scared of heights."

Jason looked at the bartender. "Ah, I'll take another, please." He turned back to the guys. "Anyway, what time and where should we meet you tomorrow, Paul?"

Paul lifted his dog up onto his lap, then grinned at Jason. "Afraid of heights, are you? Ahhh, you'll be alright. You're flying with one of the best. Isn't that right, little Ella Fitzgerald?" He pet his dog on the head. "Okay guys, meet me at Hangar Eighty-Seven at seven am. I'll send you the address." Paul finished his beer and stood up, sticking his hand out to shake theirs. "I gotta get going now. Jason and Tyler, it was a pleasure meeting you. I'll see you bright and early tomorrow." He pulled a few crumbled baht from his pocket and tossed them on the bar, then gave the bartender a salute before walking out and driving off on his noisy scooter.

Outside the bar, Jason was drawn to the beach by the sound of music. He and Tyler removed their sneakers to feel the warm sand between their toes and watch locals playing soccer and dancing.

They sat back in the sand and chilled out until the sun began to set. Down by the ocean, a strange-looking character dressed like a genie caught Jason's attention. The genie spun and sprinkled dust, humming to himself. Most people ignored him, but Jason found his antics amusing. He kept moving closer to them until he eventually walked by.

The genie tripped over Jason and muttered, "To trip and fall, we all trip and fall, but never forget to keep climbing the wall."

Jason laughed, but the genie startled him by saying, "Oh, it's you... almost there now, aren't you? Don't lose focus, don't give up—you're nearly there."

"I'm sorry, what are you referring to?" Jason asked.

"I hope you both can swim. Don't be afraid—it will guide you there."

A surprised expression formed on Tyler's face as they watched the man dance away into the crowd. "What the heck was that? We didn't eat anything bad, did we?" he joked.

Jason chuckled. "You're not crazy because I saw him too. That was weird."

"This whole journey has been weird, man, but I'm here for the ride!" Tyler exclaimed.

Jason and Tyler arrived at Hangar 87 on time and found Paul running inspections on a single-propeller plane. "Are you guys ready to rock and roll? Let's get this baby fired up, and I'll show you what flying really means. Hope you don't mind little Ella joining. I never fly without her."

Aboard the plane, Jason tried to focus as Paul explained the different meters and gauges. "Now, who wants to take off and fly her for a bit? How about you, Jason?"

He hesitated. "Paul, um, I've never done this before. It's probably better if you fly."

"Nonsense, it's like riding a bike," Paul insisted. "It's landing that's difficult."

Tyler chimed in, "Come on, bro, once in a lifetime experience. Just don't crash!"

As Tyler sat in the back with little Ella on his lap, the plane started up. Jason watched the propeller whirl as the engines roared, causing him to grip the wheel nervously.

"Slowly bring her out," Paul instructed, "and steer her onto the runway."

The plane rolled forward, ready for takeoff. Rock music blared as Paul guided Jason, who was shaking at the wheel.

As the plane slowly made its way down the runway, Jason kept looking over at Paul, awaiting his instructions. "When should I pull up?"

Paul turned up the music and drummed his hands against his lap. "Not yet. Almost! Wait on it. Okay, now! Time to fly like a bird."

Jason closed his eyes, gently yanking back on the yoke, and he felt the plane lift.

"You're a bird, Jason," Paul said. "You just took off for the first time."

Jason was astonished to be soaring through the clouds. Eventually, Paul took over and flew the rest of the way.

Outside the window, Jason could see Perka Island up ahead, a small secluded landmass. Paul took the plane lower until the runway appeared and the wheels touched down smoothly. Ella squirmed and barked in Tyler's lap, and Paul looked back at them.

"She always gets uneasy during landings." He handed Tyler a treat to give to her.

Out on the runway, Paul shook their hands. "Jason, Tyler, it was a pleasure meeting you. I hope you find what you're looking for. If you need anything, you know how to find me. There's a few motorbikes available to rent by the hangar. Take those inland to the fishing village. The island is about a square mile, so it shouldn't be hard to find. The villagers will help you."

They watched as Paul boarded his plane and took off with little Ella. Jason felt the weight of their journey as Paul's plane disappeared into the sky. There was no turning back now.

Tyler pointed to the hangar, and Jason saw a couple vintage motorbikes and a man in a hut nearby. The keys were already in the ignitions, so after paying the man, they hopped on and rode off in search of the fishing village.

Jason noted the absence of cars, and locals gave them strange stares, suggesting to him that they rarely saw outsiders. Tyler stopped up ahead, so Jason yelled out, "What is it? Did you find something?"

Tyler waved him over. "It looks like another road leading into the jungle."

Jason proceeded cautiously. "Should we? I don't want to get lost."

"Come on, man, don't be scared," Tyler insisted and drove onward.

Jason followed, swerving around mud pits and branches until the trees thinned, revealing a small village. He guessed that it must be the one they were looking for.

A young teenager came to greet them. "My name is Lou. Nice to meet you."

Jason parked his bike and walked up to Lou. "Nice to meet you, Lou. I'm Jason. We're just passing through and need a boat."

"No boats available now," Lou explained. "But I can have one for you tomorrow morning."

Jason and Tyler agreed to stay the night, following Lou through the village. Jason was captivated by the small community, and their diligent work ethic centered around fishing. Outside bamboo huts, people cleaned and carried baskets of fish and supplies. At the docks, boats pulled up and sizable fish were offloaded onto carts to be taken into the village.

That evening at Lou's home, Jason couldn't sleep. He leaned against the wall, staring at the necklace Preeda had given him and twirling it in his fingers.

Neither he nor Tyler really knew how to drive a boat, let alone navigate the ocean. *Is this still a good idea? It's not too late to turn back.*

Tyler was sleeping off to the side, and Lou came over and sat down next to Jason. "You're going to find it, right? Many have tried, but I believe you will be the one to reach Arhat."

Jason tucked his knees into his chest. "So you know about Arhat too, huh? We'll see about that, Lou, but thanks for the encouragement. Why is Arhat so important?"

"It's important to all of us," Lou explained. "It gives us hope and strength in our lives. You should get some rest now—we'll wake very early."

Before the sun rose, Lou led them to a boat at the docks, fully stocked with amenities. After thanking him, they departed into the morning fog. Jason felt a mix of excitement and uncertainty.

As Tyler drove, Jason got some shut-eye. Vivid dreams of Arhat slid into his mind as his imagination ran wild. Scenes of green jungles, sparkling waterfalls, and pink sandy beaches filled his thoughts. Pineapple plants and coconut trees were planted everywhere, and the sounds of various birds created a sweet therapeutic harmony. Blurry flashes of a woman came in and out. He couldn't determine who she was or why he thought of her. Puffs of smoke formed in white letters: *Juniper, Juniper, Juniper.* He woke in a panic, drenched in sweat, only to see a calm ocean. He thought of the old man and the vision he had, how he too said the word *Juniper.*

Tyler glanced at Jason. "Alright, sleeping beauty, your turn."

Jason drove, and as the day passed quickly, the darkness soon encapsulated them. He looked to the sky, accepting that all they had were the moon and stars to light the rest of the way.

As they cruised on course, he said, "It's crazy to think that mankind has only discovered five percent of the ocean floor. I listened to a podcast on the flight about Thailand's mythological creatures. Legend has it that a giant koi the size of a whale has inhabited these waters for centuries. Fishermen far and wide have searched for it, but it's uncatchable."

Down in the small cabin, Tyler said nothing as he lay back, relaxing.

"Ty, do you ever get worried about the future or just feel... lost?"

Tyler continued to lounge with his hands behind his head. "I have my doubts here and there, but I'm not too worried. I'm going to be super rich either way. The gig with my dad is just to get me started. I plan on being my own boss, so maybe I'll take over the tequila business one day or just start my own thing."

"How do you have so much confidence and faith in yourself? I have so many doubts about what I'm supposed to be doing with my life."

Tyler yawned. "You think too much. Look at where we are now. Take it in for a moment and forget those worries. It all works out. I wake up every day knowing that I'm about to run the show, and I'm going to have the best day of my life. As competitive as I seem, I've always made it a priority only to compete with myself. When you hold more respect for yourself, others do as well, so kill the outside noise and be the boss."

Suddenly, Jason saw something in the water and yelled.

Tyler emerged from the cabin. "Why did we stop? Don't be messing with me."

Jason pointed out into the ocean. "Did you see that? Get up here."

Tyler ran up as Jason kept his eyes peeled. The moon was so bright that it provided enough light for him to see a giant teal tail erupt from the ocean and splash back down. For the next few minutes, nothing more happened. Then, Jason locked in on what looked like a submarine missile coming straight toward their boat. They braced themselves and dove for cover. He watched as it came within inches of their boat before disappearing into the black ocean. Before they could think, he felt their boat rumble.

"What the hell was that?" Tyler wiped his face with his hand.

Speechless, Jason shook his head. "I don't know, but I saw its tail, whatever it is. Could be a whale. Let's just hope it doesn't come any closer to us."

Just when he thought everything was calm, Jason felt something latch onto their boat. He lost his balance when the boat shifted aggressively left, then right. The front of the bow dipped slightly into the ocean, bringing water on board. He couldn't figure out what it was or where it was taking them.

Waves splashed them head-on, and Jason's lungs filled with seawater, leaving him gasping for air as he desperately tried not to fall overboard.

"Ty, hold on, man!" he shouted.

The boat finally settled, and all was calm again. Jason and Tyler rushed to the side of the boat, looking all around for whatever had grabbed them, but there was nothing out there. Suddenly, something burst through the water. They wiped their eyes, staring up at a mighty koi suspended in the sky, high above them. It was only seconds away from falling on top of them. Jason and Tyler yelled at the top of their lungs, scurrying around the deck until it crashed down, collapsing their boat. All went dark and quiet.

CHAPTER 13

THE WATERFALL OF COLORS

A warm yet cooling sensation, like menthol, invaded Jason's body, causing him to wake. His eyes fluttered open, and he realized it was daytime and they were sprawled face down in a pool of clay that smelled pleasantly like sweet candy apples. He didn't know how they'd arrived here—all he remembered was that they were on a boat out at sea, and then he'd blacked out at some point. He hoisted himself up, adjusting, still dizzy from the accident, trying to remember what happened. Soon, he felt stronger, and his mind was sharper.

When he faced Tyler, they shared a silent expression of confusion. He could tell they were both wondering, "Where are we?"

Jason tried stepping forward, but immediately slipped back. He extended his arm to break the fall, but realized his efforts were helpless as the stream of clay carried him and Tyler off through the mysterious jungle.

Jason's heart pounded, yet he felt an exhilarating rush as he was pushed along in various directions like a waterslide. Up ahead, an incline appeared. Although he dug his hands and feet into the clay to slow down, he braced for the inevitable. He shot up the ramp and launched off the end, flying through the air and splashing into a natural hot spring.

When he surfaced, he noticed he was surrounded by pink foam, like a warm bubble bath. He looked up. Tyler came hurtling toward him, crashing into the hot spring. After Jason caught his breath, he ran his hands through his hair and planted them on his hips, surveying his new environment. He noticed the familiar scents of orchids and jasmine like the ones his grandmother grew in her yard.

Tyler stumbled, then caught his balance. He placed his hand on his head, squeezing his temples. "Dude, where are we?"

Jason stayed silent, looking around in astonishment, feeling as if he'd been here before. He took in the crisp air and watched as colorful kingfishers and pittas flapped their wings.

Did we make it? Is this Arhat? he asked himself.

They climbed out of the hot spring and trudged through the roots and warm dirt. Jason became awestruck by the bright fireflies that zinged past them, shedding light on the shaded spots by the trees. They pushed big green leaves out of the way and stepped over thick vines laden with light green moss. With every step forward, he felt tiny vibrations in his feet, and he tried to rationalize why this island made him feel like energy was benevolently surging through his body.

"I feel so euphoric—I can't explain it!"

They stopped to drink from a stream, and Jason found it to be some of the purest water he ever tasted.

"Are we dead?" Tyler touched his body. "All I remember is being out at sea."

Jason scanned his surroundings. "I don't know, man. Is this Arhat?"

"We're in the thick of the jungle. We couldn't have capsized."

Jason yelled, "Ty, look out! Duck!"

Tyler narrowly dodged a small lychee ball hurtling toward his head. Jason saw another coming his way.

"Who threw that?" Tyler called out. "Where did that come from?"

With a smirk, Jason pointed. "I think I found our sniper. He's more like a fur ball."

A smile grew on Tyler's face as he discovered the little monkey in a tree. "Hey, little guy, come down. I'm not going to hurt ya."

The monkey swung down toward them. It had fluffy dark-brown fur with a long white stripe under its belly and tiny pink paws. Its little tail waved back and forth as it carefully observed them. Then it jumped on Jason's shoulder before hopping over to Tyler, pausing to play with his hair. It leaped off Tyler's head and stood in their path screeching as if it was waiting for them to follow. Tyler lowered his brows and looked at Jason.

"Does he want us to come with him?" Jason asked.

Tyler shrugged, and they walked in its direction.

"How about we give him a name?" Tyler suggested. "I was thinking Tonka."

Jason examined the creature closely, agreeing that the name suited him since his dark fur resembled a tonka bean. "So, where to next, Tonka? Are you going to be our little guide?"

They followed Tonka until reaching what seemed like a cozy place to rest as night started to fall. Jason thought this little spot a safe haven, surrounded by streams and shielded by lots of trees that provided ventilation. When it was time to sleep, he found an area to kick back with his hands behind his head. He gazed up through an open patch in the vast trees at a clear star-filled sky.

Jason stood to stretch, having thought it was morning already, but when he looked around, he saw that Tyler and Tonka were sleeping. He stumbled over something, but caught himself, only to become startled by what he'd tripped on—it was his own body. *Is this a lucid dream?* He wiped the sweat from his face. Nearby, he heard the intense pour of a mighty waterfall, so loud that it overpowered any other sound around him. As he stood listening, he felt a cool puddle of water around his feet, and looking down, he noticed how the puddle came from a glistening pink-tinged stream. Its sparkle was so hypnotizing that he followed it into the dark jungle, noticing how the sound of the waterfall increased the farther he tracked the stream, as if it was leading him directly to the falls.

He pushed through tons of trees, assuming he was getting closer as the sound of the falls intensified. *Finally,* he thought, as he parted two giant banana leaves to discover a colossal waterfall pouring down onto a black slate rock. This was no ordinary waterfall—the streams reminded him of violin strings in vibrant lavender and powdery red.

Jason dove in, feeling a sense of calm as he swam around to cool off. As he neared the falls to observe their colors, he noticed something behind them. He climbed out and walked around to the other side of the falls, entering a cave.

Inside, he marveled at the rocky walls filled with glistening diamonds. Ahead, he saw a flat surface filled with engravings depicting a tribe—caveman-like images of hunters and gatherers, a big celebration, an entire community. Suddenly, he heard them. Turning toward the falls, he saw shadows of people dancing and chanting like spirits moving through the cascade.

"Hello, is someone there?" he called out, but the mystical beings he saw vanished, and he was left alone, wondering. A few minutes passed, and another shadow appeared in the waterfall—this time, it was the outline of a young woman dancing and laughing joyously. He tried to keep quiet so the shadow wouldn't realize he was there, but it was useless. She stopped and looked in his direction.

"Hello, umm, I'm sorry if I interrupted you. My name's Jason."

She took her time to respond, "You're not interrupting me. I'm just dancing. Where do you come from?"

He walked toward her. "San Diego, but, umm, I'm in search of a place called Arhat."

"Why are you looking for Arhat?" She put her hands on her hips.

Jason didn't have much of an answer but told her about the necklace.

The shadow shifted her weight. "Can you describe the necklace?"

He detailed everything about it and the shadow went silent. He sat on a rock, facing the falls. "How are we communicating right now?"

She laughed. "With words, of course. And that necklace is from my village."

Jason smirked. "Of course with words, but you speak English?"

She traced her finger along the falls. "English? Is this your language? I only speak my native tongue, which is Arhatian."

Jason tapped his index finger against his chin. "Then how are we communicating?"

"Well, it's simple. As long as you are on this island, your language will be translated into mine and vice versa. The power of the island allows us to speak."

He stood up. "Interesting! I kinda understand. But why can't I see what you look like? I can only see your shadow. Can you see me?"

The shadow twirled. "Same. I can't see you either. Only if you reach Arhat will we see each other."

Jason scratched his head. "This isn't Arhat? This island?"

He waited for an answer, wondering why she wasn't responding.

"Hello, are you still there?"

He stood for a moment, perplexed, before realizing she was gone. He left the waterfall. Arhat remained a total mystery, but he knew that if he had the chance to meet the young woman again, he might finally learn how to get there.

They spent the next day exploring the jungle. Tonka helped them collect food and showed them where they could drink fresh water. He even pointed out which fruits were safe to eat, screeching at the ones they should avoid.

"So, if this is Arhat, that means we made it, and if we made it, then there has to be treasure somewhere, right?" Tyler asked.

"I honestly don't know! Last night I had a strange dream. I woke up and I was detached from my body, then I found a colorful waterfall where I met a girl. I mean, I don't even know what she looks like. She was just an outline of a girl. I asked if this was Arhat, but then she disappeared, so I'm thinking we're not there yet. Behind the waterfall though, I saw depictions of people. It was a whole community, so Arhat's gotta be close."

Tyler stopped in his tracks. "No way, dude! You gotta meet that girl again and ask how we get to Arhat. Hell, I can already envision the treasure waiting for us."

Jason knew Tyler loved money, but finding treasure was the last of his concerns. Finding a cure for his grandmother was the real treasure, and that meant finding Arhat.

Tonka took them back to camp as the sun was beginning to set, and helped them prepare the foods they'd gathered during the day. After a sufficient meal, they drifted off to sleep. Jason tossed and turned until he woke to the sound of the waterfall of colors.

Upon arriving, he sat and waited, wondering if she would appear. Finally, he heard a soft, playful voice.

"What took you so long? I was waiting for you to come back."

Jason scrambled to his feet. "Umm, yes. I'm here. You left last night."

"Yes, my family called for me. I'm Juniper, by the way."

Jason's breath caught in his chest. "Um, what did you say?"

She began to dance. "I'm Juniper!"

His mind raced. *What? Was Juniper a real person after all?*

"Jason, are you still there?" Her voice broke him out of disbelief.

"Umm, yes. I'm still here."

Juniper ran her hands across the water. "Last night you asked if this is Arhat. It is."

Hearing this reassured Jason, considering how far he had come. "So I made it! Where's all the people?"

"Arhat, the place you seek," Juniper explained, "is a direct lineage to the love that circulates in the world. It is a place of renewal and exists to instill peace in the hearts and minds of humanity. We face a great struggle though, Jason, for as time goes by, the younger generations, many our age, are forgetting Arhat. It's become a bedtime story—a myth rather than a real place. The power of my village is not based on physical existence. Faith is the true strength of Arhat."

Jason tried to understand what she meant, but was still puzzled. "Umm, okay. But this island is Arhat? Am I here now?"

Juniper sat cross-legged. "Yes, this island is my home, but I'm not sure you'll reach the village where my people live. It is up to our Ancestors, those who guide us through life's journey. It is said that the only way to reach my village is to sacrifice something significant for the good of another person. You must be selfless in your actions, and your motives must be pure, backed by love. Only then will the Ancestors make their decision."

A pit of anxiety grew in Jason's stomach. *What does that mean? And if I don't make it there, how would we get home?*

He placed his arms behind his head. "I'm sorry, but I don't understand. What sacrifice? There's a chance I might not even reach the village? Why was I led all this way?"

"Remember, a sacrifice for the good of another person, out of love. You'll know it when it comes to you. I'm afraid that's the only way, Jason," Juniper declared.

While waiting for the Ancestors to decide, Jason continued getting to know Juniper. Over the next five nights, he returned to the waterfall of colors, and each morning, he excitedly updated Tyler, awestruck by all he'd learned about Arhat. He became hooked on his conversations with Juniper, sensing that their intrigue for each other was growing. How odd it was to grow close to someone he'd never physically seen before. He enjoyed the effortless flow of their discussions. They were stimulating and authentic, about family, special talents, and their biggest fears. Juniper taught him some of Arhat's customs, and he felt it only fair to also tell her about San Diego. He could sense Juniper's intelligence—she seemed to be a wealth of information, witty, and quick. He liked that she was sarcastic and humorous.

All the while, he kept his grandmother in the back of his mind, unsure how to ask Juniper, and instead danced around his real question about whether there was a cure or not. "Does sickness and death exist in Arhat?"

"Of course. We are human after all, so we get sick too, but it's rare, and our healers often have antidotes. Our medicines come from various plants throughout the jungle. However, our souls live on forever in the form of our spirit animals in the next life."

Jason's head drooped for a moment. It wasn't the most reassuring feeling knowing that there might not be an exact cure for his grandma, but he wasn't convinced all hope was lost. Maybe he could speak to one of the healers if he ever made it to Arhat.

The next night, Jason came back and waited for her to show up as usual. He waited for what felt like an hour without her appearing. Disappointed, he left. For three consecutive nights, he returned, expecting to see her, but she never showed up. This made no sense, he thought. Why would she just disappear? He wondered if something had happened to her.

CHAPTER 14

THE ULTIMATE SACRIFICE

"Look, Tonka wants to play!" Tyler shouted. "Race you to wherever he goes?"

Jason rolled around in the soft bed of green moss. He stretched his legs and arms and took a big yawn then jumped up. He splashed some cold water on his face from the nearby spring and turned toward Tyler with a big grin. "You're on! But I hope you can keep up. I was running six miles twice a week before this trip."

Tyler grabbed one foot, pulling it behind him, stretching his quad, then switched to the other. "Ha! Do you know who I am? I'll run circles around you. Let's go!"

They chased after Tonka, keeping pace with each other, until they found themselves at a large spring with two pieces of ivy hanging over it.

Tyler grinned at Jason. "You thinking what I'm thinking?"

He ran full speed, grabbed onto the ivy, and did a backflip into the spring. Jason followed, launching himself and crashing into the refreshing water.

As they swam around, Jason updated Tyler on his recent interaction with Juniper.

Tyler swam on his back. "Great! So you spoke to her again, and now we're going?"

Jason leaned against the moss outlining the spring. "Well, it's complicated."

Tyler lifted his head. "What the heck does that mean"

"She told me that I'd need to make a sacrifice for the good of another person, and only the Ancestors, some higher power, would decide if we're permitted to reach the village."

"That's... not what I was expecting to hear. You're gonna have to spell it out for me."

"Juniper said the sacrifice would come unexpectedly."

Tyler was slightly disgruntled. "So you're saying there's a possibility we may never reach the village? Well, that's great. Guess we'll be stranded here forever. It's not like we have phones to call for help. Everything I had was on the damn boat. How long have we been here?"

Jason wiped water from his face. "I have no clue! I met Juniper our first night here, then spoke with her every night for the rest of the week. Then she disappeared for the next three nights. So, ten days, I guess?"

"Yeah, give or take, but we have no damn clue. On top of that, who knows how long we'll be stuck on this island searching for Arhat. It's the craziest feeling not knowing what day of the week it is. It makes ya think, time really is just a construct." Tyler turned his head toward Tonka. "Hey, what's up with him? Where's he trying to take us now?"

The monkey, who was a few feet away from the spring, screeched and waved them over. They got out, shaking the water off their bodies, and ran after him. Suddenly, Tyler stopped and let out a loud yell, startling Jason. When he turned to look, Tyler had grabbed his left foot, revealing a puncture. A sharp, thin plant stuck out from the ground, which looked like a needle that he must have stepped on. Tyler slowly lifted it, pulling it clean from his heel like a syringe out of a vein.

"Ouch! Look out for any of those sharp, pointy plants around you."

Jason figured it was nothing severe as Tyler popped back up and continued walking like nothing had ever happened. However, Tonka seemed concerned, jumping up and down and making loud noises.

They ignored Tonka's antics and carried on until Tyler asked if they could pause for a break. Turning, Jason noticed that Tyler looked winded. "What's wrong, getting old?"

Tyler sat and rubbed his foot. "I don't feel right. I'm really tired for some reason."

In no more than a minute, he collapsed.

"Ty, what's wrong, man?" Jason knelt by his side and inspected him, deeply concerned when he saw the color of Tyler's skin change.

He didn't answer. Jason paced back and forth, trying to understand what happened. What had he stepped on?

He struggled to figure out how to help him. It all became too much, and Jason dropped to the ground, grabbed his knees, and rocked back and forth, hyperventilating.

He started talking to himself. "What am I supposed to do? I don't want my friend to die, but I don't know what to do to help him. I need to find a way. Come on, Jason, think. Think. This is no time to be a coward. You need to figure this out."

He hastily looked over at Tonka, who was screeching again. Jason scrambled for a solution, and out of desperation, asked, "Tonka, how do we help him? What do we do?" He turned back toward his friend. "Ty, hang in there, buddy. It's going to be okay."

Tyler was barely able to speak—he just lay there, stiff and paralyzed, sweating profusely. Jason checked his pulse. His breathing and heart rate had slowed. Green liquid oozed from the puncture wound, and at the same time, his veins dilated and turned green.

Jason didn't want to leave Tyler alone like this, but Tonka continued to call him over, so he decided to follow. "I promise I'll be back, Ty. Hang in there, buddy."

What Jason feared most was that his friend might be dead by the time he came back from wherever Tonka was leading him to. Still, he chased after Tonka, his heart pounding, sweating with fear, until they stopped in front of a tall unique-looking tree. Its canopy was vast, thick with green bristles that extended like an umbrella. Smooth twisting branches the color of ginger root ran narrow into the earth. Beneath the crown of the tree, groups of small dragon-fruit-like orange pods dangled, each one pulsating.

Tonka climbed it hurriedly, shaking a branch until a pod fell, splitting open before Jason. He picked it up and examined the inside, finding a spot of green gelatinous substance no bigger than a penny. He looked at Tonka, who was jumping around and screaming, pointing at it. Jason got the notion that this substance might save Tyler. What other option was there?

He ran back toward Tyler at full speed, feeling adrenaline kick through him. "Come on, Ty, hang in there, buddy. I'm almost there."

Jason reached his friend, finding him pale as a ghost but still breathing. Just as he stepped forward, a sharp pain shot up his leg. He fell back, squeezing his foot, and looked down to inspect it. He had also stepped on one of the poisonous plant needles. He peered into the distance, feeling hopeless. Soon, he would be in the same condition as Tyler, with only enough antidote to save one of them. He was already feeling woozy, leaving no time to go back for another pod since he'd likely collapse along the way. He took a deep breath, trying to make what he believed to be the most difficult decision of his life. Jason breathed heavily as tears fell down his face. He held the pod and scooped out the jelly-like gunk, looking at it, then at Tyler. He sighed, took one more deep breath, and limped over to him.

"It's going to be okay, Ty," Jason said, feeding Tyler the jelly, hoping it would save him. After ensuring Tyler ingested every bit, Jason sat back, watching and praying. All the while, he grew increasingly exhausted. As he felt himself fading out, he caught glimpses of Tyler becoming healthy again. Tyler's breathing regulated, and his body began to move. It was enough for Jason to know it had worked. Then, his body went numb.

Faintly, he saw Tyler stand, grabbing his temples and looking around. Jason became too weak to stay upright and sank onto his back. In a blur, Tyler rushed over to him, and tried to perform CPR. Jason couldn't understand why Tyler was pounding the ground and screaming in agony. He could vaguely hear Tyler saying things like, "This can't be happening! Come on, Jason, stop playing games and wake up. Just another one of your jokes, right! Jasoooon!"

Jason tried to call out to him, but he was too weak, and completely paralyzed. Tyler rested against a tree with his head in his lap, repeating, "My friend is dead."

Jason couldn't understand. Maybe he was dead, but he didn't feel it. He heard a voice, although it wasn't Tyler; he didn't recognize it. "Have faith, Jason!"

A sweeping wind brushed over his body and several leaves flew up and circulated around him until a translucent spirit drifted toward him. He felt scared and wanted to run, but he was immobilized. The closer the spirit got, the calmer he felt. It took the form of a woman with fine hair running almost the length of her body. She was dressed in a long white gown with flowers stitched onto the shoulders and around the collar, and a beautiful crown of white feathers lay upon her head.

She stared into Jason's eyes before hovering directly over his body and sinking into him. Every cell in his body reawakened. He could feel his strength coming back. His heart pounded, and he took deep breaths while moving his arms and legs. The spirit became so bright that it almost blinded him and the energy in his body intensified.

CHAPTER 15

THE TEMPLE OF ARHAT

"Jason!" Tyler yelled.

"Ty, where are we?" Jason rubbed his eyes.

Tyler's hands shot up. "You're alive!"

"Well, of course I'm alive." Jason squeezed his pounding head.

Tyler tried to help him up. "I don't think you realize, you were a straight stiff."

Jason thought for a minute, trying to figure things out. "Wait, we're still here on the island, aren't we?"

"Yeah, we never left. Well, I mean, you did."

Jason began getting flashbacks. "The poison! I chased Tonka, who led me to a tree that had all these orange pods with some jelly substance inside. I assumed it could help you, but then I stepped on one of the spikes. I didn't have enough time to go back for another, and there was only enough for one of us. After that, I just remember becoming weak. I saw something so strange, though. There was this flash of light that nearly blinded me, and then all of a sudden, I felt my body grow stronger. Then I woke up."

Tyler shook his head. "What are you talking about, man? I don't know anything about bright lights, but now you're alive and that's all I care about."

They drank from a nearby stream. Jason still felt faint, but as he rested, he sensed a strong presence nearby, not communicating in words but in feeling. He became attuned to its calling, a deep intuitional tug that he couldn't ignore. He stood up and followed the pull, wherever it was guiding him.

"Yo, Jason, where you going, man?"

He jerked his head. "Just follow me. Something's happening. It's telling me to follow."

Eventually, they arrived at a stone wall covered in ivy. Jason slid his hand along it. The wall seemed like it stretched for miles until they came across the entrance of a temple in the shape of a giant pyramid. Carefully, he stepped inside the cold, murky space. His foot bumped into some rocks sticking from the ground, and looking down, he discovered a circle of tiny flat-topped stones with characters carved into them. He crouched, studying them before he pulled out his necklace. It shared the same characters, and the gap in the middle of the stones seemed to fit perfectly with the necklace's circular medallion.

After placing the medallion in the center, the floor began to rumble, and neon blue light radiated through cracks in the floor. Each stone character shone brilliantly.

He looked at the walls, where fine neon blue lines shot out like spiderwebs through every crevice, illuminating the temple. The dark eerie den transformed into an awakened sanctuary.

Jason discovered etchings on the walls that seemed to depict Arhat's entire history, its inception, and developments. The first image showed a giant star that fell vertically from the sky, causing a splash as it crashed into the ocean. Two enormous waves formed into the shape of human hands. The burning red sun existed between them. As the palms came together, the sun cooled, and enclosed in the hands was life.

Jason looked inquisitively at the next image: a giant lotus blooming from the ocean. Its white layered petals faded to pink at the edges, encapsulating a bright yellow center. As the petals lay against the water like lily pads, they grew, building in volume and length for miles, forming a pod-like shape that resembled the island.

Jason pointed out, รักทีสมบูรณ์แบบ. See that, Tyler? It translates to 'rebirth.' Juniper said that Arhat is a place of renewal and built on love. My grandmother told me that lotus flowers symbolize 'rebirth and new beginnings.'"

Tyler placed his hand on the wall. "So when did you start learning how to read Thai?"

Jason wasn't sure how to explain. "Trust me, it's not going to make sense. Just know that when we speak, our language is translated into theirs and vice versa. The same goes for reading. Give it a try. Focus on that symbol there."

Tyler focused in on it, and then his face lit up. "This is wild!"

In the image, what looked like human life emerged from the soil, which was healthy and abundant. "They prevail as the first among them all, named the Elders, according to the writing on the walls. Here, it refers to the Ancestors that Juniper mentioned."

As they scanned the rest of the temple, they came to an etching that depicted the progression of Arhat's society. It showed people coexisting together, laughing and hunting. A big portion was dedicated to villagers making crafts. There were musicians and countless celebrations. What Jason found most interesting was that there was nothing signifying rulers, kings, or slaves. Instead, he read something that said the Elders were the chiefs of the village, meant to provide direction to the people, but everyone was equal.

Tyler read one of the Arhatian characters. "Strength lies in those who seek it."

Following that was a picture of people being praised and rewarded for their accomplishments. Villagers meditated intensely, nourishing their minds. Family, friends, health, and wellness seemed most important. Everyone looked happy, engaged in hobbies and tasks. Then there was a ceremony where villagers praised Earth, and people left Arhat to spread its love and kindness to the world.

Jason remained completely enthralled while Tyler wandered through a corridor. Jason continued following the images until he saw a depiction of a foreign man.

Before he could read further, Tyler called out to him, "Jason, I just found a chamber."

Jason left the picture, but his thoughts stayed behind, wondering who that person was and why they came to Arhat.

He searched for Tyler, following his voice through gloomy corridors.

"I'm down here—just keep walking straight."

When Jason walked into the chamber, he felt a trembling sensation in the ground, which startled him. "Ty, you feel that? Something is happening underneath us."

Before his eyes, the stone walls melted away as if they were nothing more than an illusion, exposing vast amounts of wealth hidden within. Tons of gold and diamonds shone with gleaming brilliance. Precious rubies were embedded into necklaces, bracelets, and rings.

He looked over at Tyler. *Why is he acting so calm? Does he not see it?* he wondered. Immediately, he heard the voice that had guided him to the temple, and it told him to grab Tyler's hand.

Tyler looked at him strangely. "What are you holding my hand for?"

Jason waited, watching Tyler's expression, as if by holding hands, his friend would gain the power to see all the wealth in front of them. Tyler's eyes shifted toward the walls, and when he saw it, his mouth dropped open and his legs trembled. He began hyperventilating.

He took a few deep breaths, and closed his eyes, then opened them again, looking over at Jason, speechless. His body twitched as he turned to his left, his right, and then behind, taking in the gold that surrounded them.

Grinning, Tyler ran over and flopped down onto the treasure, rolling around in it. "Jason, we found it, man. Everything we'd been searching for on this trip. We're rich, buddy, rich."

Jason joined the celebration by grabbing some coins and dancing, but then stopped to think. *Wait! Is this the only reason we came here? Is this the only reason he wanted to come here?*

Tyler's fixation reminded him of Gollum from Lord of the Rings. Jason recalled his grandmother's words, "*Never touch or take what does not belong to you.*"

He let the gold coins fall from his hands. "Ty, hold up! I'm just as excited as you, but none of this is ours."

Tyler gave Jason a blank stare. "Not ours? Finders keepers!"

"Yeah, but remember we're here to find Arhat. This belongs to its people."

"*Yeah*, but we can do both. First, we gather all this treasure and then try to find Arhat. Or we can just go home."

Jason tried to reason with him. "It's just not right to take it."

Tyler swatted the mountain of diamonds in front of him and faced Jason. "Not right! Was it not right when Art didn't pay us for a whole month, or when my bike got stolen? Look, it's a dog-eat-dog world. I don't know how to get home from here, but we're not leaving without all this. Anyway, truth is, I can't go home without it or else I'm screwed."

Jason gave him a baffled look. "What do you mean, can't go home without it?

"I owe money—like, a lot of money."

"Like student loans? I thought your parents covered that."

Tyler exhaled, glancing at his feet. "I'm only telling you this because you're my best friend, but I never told my parents I was getting scholarships, so I took their money for tuition and gambled it all away. And I got involved in a few underground blackjack games."

"Why didn't you tell me that?" Jason said, raising his voice. "Is this the whole reason you came in the first place? How much do you owe?"

"I don't want to tell you." Tyler shook his head. "Let's just say, it would take most of my life to pay back, and the people from the blackjack games want it now. I'm dead if I don't return with a way to pay these guys back. Why do you think I came on this trip? Yeah, I wanted to travel, but I also needed to get out of town."

Jason turned away from him. "And you waited until now to tell me all this? That's totally not cool! Can't your parents help you?"

Tyler sighed. "I'm sorry. I should have told you the truth about why I wanted to join you in the first place. It's not like I didn't want to go on this trip, it's just that I'm in a really bad situation right now. Leaving San Diego seemed like the most logical solution. And when you mentioned Arhat, my imagination ran wild. And no, my parents can't know. If I go back without that treasure, I'm dead, plain and simple. I'm really sorry."

Jason turned away and slammed his fist against the rock wall. He then faced his friend and pointed at him. "I understand where you're coming from, but you should have told me about your gambling situation a long time ago. I could have tried to help you." He rested his hands on his hips and paused. "Your apology means a lot, but going forward, I just want you to be honest with me. I know you love money and all, and I'm not saying it's not important, but it's not everything. We'll figure out another way to help you pay back the debt. I promise."

Tyler paced back and forth, still trying to stuff his pockets. "Did you not hear me? I can't go back without this. We'd be the richest people in the world."

Jason paused for a moment. "Did you feel that? The temple rumbled again."

Tyler rolled his eyes. "I felt it. Don't tell me we're gonna have to leave all this behind."

Worry appeared on Jason's face. "If you want to live, we should probably leave right now!"

They ran out of the chamber and back to the main room, where Tonka was jumping around and calling for them. Jason saw the entrance closing and darted toward it.

"Ty, let's go."

"Right behind you, buddy!"

Jason grabbed the necklace from the center of the stones, and they dashed for the opening. Tyler and Tonka rolled through, and then Jason dove headfirst. The stone slab clamped down on his shirt, but Tyler pulled on him and ripped him free.

They sprinted from the temple back toward the jungle, then turned to watch as the entire structure shook like it was about to break apart, but instead, it flickered and froze, then zapped out of existence. Jason just stood, trying to process it all.

Tyler raced toward where it used to be. "Gone! All that wealth is gone. We were so close."

Walking back through the vast jungle, neither spoke a word. Thoughts of Arhat still pervaded Jason's mind, while Tyler bit his nails, distraught over the lost treasure.

Once they reached their camp, Jason got a fire going, roasting some fish they'd caught on the way after Tyler cleaned them out.

As they sat eating, Tyler admitted, "I kind of acted like an animal back there."

Jason patted him on the back. "Judgment-free zone, man! We're all dealing with our own obstacles, but you know I'm always here for you. To be fully transparent, my reason for coming on this trip was not really for vacation, but to escape a lot of grief I've been carrying."

Tyler glanced over. "Escape? What are you trying to escape? Yeah, maybe there are things about yourself that you can work on, but that's normal, bro."

"Maybe I don't always show it, but I get pretty depressed from time to time. I think much of that has to do with losing my parents at such a young age, but it's a culmination of a lot of things, I guess." He stared at the ground and threw a few stones that he'd been juggling in his hand. He then looked over at Tyler. "Coming to Thailand was a chance to run away from all my fears and anxieties. I dread working for that insurance agency, you know that, but I do it because it makes my grandfather proud, and I have no clue what else I should be doing with my life at the moment."

He exhaled and slapped his knee as he continued, "I hate that I put up with Art's excuses about never paying us on time, and how I often let others take advantage of me and take me for granted. I've always had trouble setting healthy boundaries for myself. It's hard to say no most of the time. Though I made a promise before boarding our flight that I was going to leave all that behind."

He stood up and began pacing before turning back toward Tyler. "I've tried to step outside of my comfort zone, and I guess you've seen that a bit on this trip so far. When the opportunity came up to find Arhat, it was a no-brainer because it was a chance to prove to myself that I was brave enough to find it. A place that sounds so great that I might even find a cure to save my grandmother."

Tyler dropped his fish and turned toward Jason. "Man, I never knew you were going through all that. You could have talked to me about it, ya know. I'm a better listener than you think. I guess neither of us was honest with our intentions, but like you said, we're all dealing with our own obstacles. You know I always got your back too."

"Thanks, man." Jason extended his hand for a fist bump. "So now what? You still want to try to find this place?"

Tyler stood. "Now what? Brother, we didn't spend a night in jail, capsize in a boat, step on poison, and almost get stuck in a vanishing temple to sit back and say, 'now what!' We're going to find this damn place, and we're going to find a damn cure for your grandmother, and who knows, maybe a little treasure. What do you say?"

As he stood beside Tyler, Jason was confident that they were on the same page. Everything was out in the open now—there was nothing to hide. Having the support of his best friend gave him the conviction he needed.

After dinner, they walked over to their sleeping spots and Jason lay back with his arms behind his head, staring up into the night sky, feeling the vastness of the universe consume him. He listened to the sounds of the jungle, but all he could think about was Arhat and Juniper.

CHAPTER 16

THE OTHER SIDE

As Tyler and Tonka slept, Jason stayed up, staring into the sky. He was suddenly disturbed by a loud noise. "*Binggggggggggg, bingggggggggg,*" a blast of sound rang out. He looked around to see if Tyler and Tonka had woken up, but to his surprise, they were still fast asleep. He covered his ears, cringing as the ding pierced his eardrums. The jungle's volume rose dramatically. Hundreds of monkeys screeched, tigers roared, elephants blew their trunks, birds squawked. Jason shook, yelling, "Stop! Stop! Stop! I can't take it anymore."

Then silence—he heard nothing but his breath.

Through the trees, he noticed two mystical and entrancing eyes. Unsure if they were animal or human, he grabbed a sharp stick that he used for fishing just in case, ready to defend himself. They looked more like human eyes, he thought. The leaves parted, revealing several yellow butterflies bunched together to form the shape of two eyes. Jason sighed, rubbing his hand down his face and dropping the spear. He watched the butterflies intently as they formed into something else, an angelic woman levitating and waving at him to follow her. He couldn't understand why he wasn't afraid. "Why do I feel so safe with you? Was it you guiding me all this time?"

He followed her into the jungle and then through what looked like a botanical garden. He was awestruck by the rare and glowing species of flowers everywhere. Toward the end of the garden, she led him to a giant boulder stuck in the ground and pointed to it. The spirit hovered over the boulder, her brightness causing him to cover his eyes. When he removed his hands, he saw carefree yellow butterflies floating away.

He stepped forward to inspect the boulder and discovered several Arhatian characters carved into it with a place to fit the medallion of his necklace, just like the stone circle in the temple. *Another key*, he thought. He removed his necklace, fitting the medallion into place, and stepped back as neon blue lights shot out through every crack. A passageway opened. He pulled his necklace from the stone and put it back on.

Hesitantly, he stepped inside and began his descent down a dusty staircase, dodging rubble and debris. For a moment, he stopped to look back, wondering if he should go any farther. He took a deep breath and continued. Several torches along the walls guided him through the cave. As he followed them, his anxiety grew, realizing how far he had walked into the cave with no idea of where it would exactly lead him. But he felt reassured when he saw a few yellow butterflies just up ahead, which guided him the rest of the way. As he crept along a rocky wall, he peeked through some of its holes, noticing an open area. The ground was covered in sand and crushed pebbles and in the center was an elevated stone platform.

Through the rocks, he spotted a young girl quietly meditating. He hid, observing her. Long chestnut-brown hair flowed down over her shoulders. Her upper body was covered in traditional gold Thai silk, and her stomach was exposed like a belly dancer's. A sky-blue silk cloth hung around her hips with larimar jewelry adorning her arms and neck.

As he moved, the girl's eyes opened instantly. He tried to stay quiet, but sensing she knew someone was there, he smiled nervously. "Didn't mean to disturb you. I'm kind of lost."

She stayed where she was, and speaking softly, she said, "You didn't disturb me. I'm just meditating to clear my head."

Jason moved closer, but as he got a better look at her, something started to happen to him. He found himself fixated on her, and she stared back at him with the same fascination. He noticed her long eyelashes that made her hazel eyes sparkle. Natural blonde streaks ran through her hair. Tiny brown freckles rested on her cherry-blossom-colored cheeks, and she had the cutest dimples. Her smile alone, though, under a set of full lips, was enough to make Jason faint. She stood and walked over to him, her hips swaying with each step.

Jason broke the silence. "Why do I feel like I know you?"

She took her time to respond, caressing his face with her soft, gentle hand. "I don't know, but I feel that as well. Where do you come from?"

Jason stood still with his arms by his side. "San Diego. I'm looking for Arhat."

She ran her fingers through his hair, observing him intently. "Jason, is it you?"

Jason knew it was her—it had to be Juniper. They hugged each other tightly in disbelief. Their cheeks pressed together as he whispered, "You're even more beautiful in person. But what happened? You disappeared? I thought something happened to you."

Juniper pulled back, still holding him, and looked into his eyes. "It pained me to be apart, and I hated the thought of never talking to you again. Our fate separated us and brought us back. The Ancestors only allotted a certain number of nights to speak to each other before it was up to you to make a sacrifice. Only then would there be another chance to meet. Will you come to my village? Tonight is our moon festival, and we will celebrate loved ones who have passed. They exist in the form of their spirit animals, like I told you. You must join."

Jason was slow to respond. He stared back. "Yes, let's go. I mean, wait, Tyler is still on the island. Can I bring him?"

Juniper nodded. "Of course, you must not leave him. Get him and come back. I will be waiting for you."

He continued to process everything—how close he was to reaching Arhat, the chance to find a cure for his grandmother, and how he had finally met Juniper, someone he never thought he'd talk to again. "Is there a faster way back to the jungle?"

Juniper extended her arm. "Yes, just take this path."

Jason stopped to embrace her once more, and then he darted off up the path. Relief washed over him as he found himself back in the jungle, only minutes away from camp. He saw Tyler and sprinted toward him, eager to share his discovery of Arhat, but just before he reached him, the sky opened, and massive raindrops fell, resulting in a monsoon. Tyler and Tonka woke, and he tried calling out to Tyler, but he knew they couldn't hear him as the torrential downpour overpowered his voice. Instead, he signaled for them to take cover under a giant banana leaf nearby.

Once shielded from the rain, Jason was too excited to speak and found his words coming out jumbled.

"Slow down, man," Tyler told him. "What are you trying to say?"

Jason took a deep breath and calmed himself. "Ty, I found it! We need to go right now. Come on, let's go before it's too late."

Tyler held his hand up. "Wait! Hold your horses. Found what? The village?"

Jason didn't need to explain further. His necklace began to glow a bright turquoise against his chest.

Tyler stared at him. "You're not joking, are you? You found it, didn't you? Arhat! You found Arhat! Come here." He pulled him in for a hug.

"We're nearly there, Ty! Juniper's going to take us."

"Then what are we standing around wasting time for? Let's go!"

They ran out into the monsoon. Jason led Tyler and Tonka back through the botanical garden until they reached the boulder. Tyler looked at Jason. "So, now what?"

He watched as Jason removed his necklace and fit the medallion into the boulder. When the cave revealed itself, Jason saw the shock in Tyler's eyes.

As they walked inside, Jason noticed that Tonka was missing, so he left the cave, finding Tonka standing in the rain. He watched, confused, as Tonka ran in the opposite direction. *Where is he going? Is he scared?* Jason thought.

He tapped Tyler on the shoulder, telling him to wait, and sprinted back into the rain for Tonka, but the closer he got, the farther Tonka scurried away.

Jason stopped. Tonka stared back at him.

Tyler walked over. "Where is he going? We're not going back into the jungle."

Jason just watched Tonka. "I think he's saying goodbye."

"What!" Tyler's brows shot up. "Why would he be leaving now?"

"I guess sometimes people or things only come into our lives for a moment to teach us or guide us in some way."

Jason and Tyler waved to Tonka and watched as he disappeared into the jungle.

"Thank you, little buddy," Tyler called out. "We'll never forget you!!"

Leading the way into the cave, Jason occasionally checked to ensure Tyler was following. The torches along the walls helped them navigate.

When they arrived, Jason felt a sense of ease on seeing that she was waiting for them. Tyler wasted no time in introducing himself to her. Jason knew Tyler was never shy or hesitant when he saw a beautiful girl, but this time, he noticed something different. Juniper greeted Tyler like an old friend, but her gaze quickly return to Jason with a look of infatuation and love. Tyler understood right away who Juniper was interested in, and looking back at Jason, he realized their rare connection.

She placed a hand on each of their arms. "You're just in time for the moon festival."

It was too surreal, Jason thought, and as they followed Juniper, he noticed the environment around him transformed with every step. The rocky cave walls filled with green moss and the surface beneath their feet shifted into warm pink sand, dotted with thousands of little pieces of sea glass in various colors. He could feel a gentle breeze. The farther they walked, the brighter it became as light pierced through the end of the cave. Even his emotions began to change, and he felt a surge of positivity—more like a state of absolute bliss. He could hear the cheerful sounds of people and music, which caused a smile to form. Some magnetic force began to take hold of him. When he stopped, he felt himself being gently pulled forward. At what had initially seemed like the end of the cave was a swirling sky-blue vortex.

Before passing through, Jason asked, "And once we enter, can we leave?"

Juniper grabbed his hand. "Yes, you can leave, but you will not be able to come back. The Ancestors have allotted you only this one opportunity."

Jason held onto Juniper's hand and all three stepped through the vortex.

CHAPTER 17

THE VILLAGE OF ETERNAL JOY

On the other side, as Jason's eyes adjusted, he was struck by the beauty before him. He fell to his knees with his hand covering his chest as he tried to slow his breathing. He couldn't believe they had finally made it to Arhat. He was completely enthralled by his surroundings.

Blue pittas and Indian rollers rested on trees, while purple orchids and white jasmine sprouted along the path where they stood. The sound of a nearby waterfall blended in with people talking. There was life all around them—artists lost in their work and musicians playing soulfully as dancers moved their hips harmoniously to the music. The sun shone brightly, casting a youthful glow on everyone in the village. Jason surveyed the people. The women wore colorful headscarves with their hair draped down their backs. Rosy cheeks contrasted against their warm brown skin, and all of them wore halter tops and coin belts that dangled from their hips. The men were marked with tattoos of various symbols and wore red garments wrapped around their waists. Everyone was covered in larimar stone jewelry.

Tyler was the first to snap out of it, jumping up and down. "Man! We made it! Can you believe it?"

Jason felt sensory overload as he continued to observe the unfolding festival. Children ran around with noisemakers. Villagers were dancing, covering each other in paint, and preparing baskets of food. Coconuts were scattered all over the ground. Some of the villagers stood on them, competing to see who could keep their balance the longest while others kicked them around like hacky sacks. Jason watched curiously as several people also wiped their bodies down in coconut oil, making them glisten in the sun. Nearby, he saw a group of women with hair that was long, black, and untamed. They laughed loudly as they gripped their hands around big halved pomelos and squeezed so that the juice streamed down their wrists into a carved wooden bowl. One woman picked up a bristly brush and dipped it into the bowl of pomelo juice. She then began painting long streaks down the hair of the woman next to her. Jason wasn't exactly sure what they were doing, but he had heard once that certain citrus juices could create natural highlights.

He wished his grandparents were here to witness such beauty alongside him. *Problems don't exist here*, he thought.

A massive conga line formed, and Tyler was the first to jump in. Jason and Juniper soon followed, and it led everyone out of the village and into the jungle.

Through the trees, Jason could hear the animals going crazy. Monkeys were screeching, elephants blew their trunks, and tigers roared loudly. He was passed a tusklike flask filled with juice, which he sniffed before sipping. It tasted like sweet pears.

He swirled it around his mouth before swallowing. "What is this?"

Juniper took a sip. "It's tazwack. We extract the nectar from the tazwack vines and ferment it. We usually drink this during celebrations."

Tyler grabbed the tusk, exclaiming, "Well, don't hog it!"

As they danced their way to the top of a mountain, Tyler slowed. "Jason, do you feel out of breath, or am I just out of shape?"

Jason placed his hand over his heart. "I guess I am too because I can barely breathe."

Juniper wrapped her arms around their shoulders. "It's the altitude. You're not used to it. Here, chew on these. It will help." She passed them what looked like mint leaves.

As they chewed on the leaves, Jason felt his entire body tingle and his eyes widen. He took deeper breaths and felt his energy return. He looked over at Tyler, who started dancing the rest of the way up the mountain with the others.

At the top, Jason was amazed when he peered out into the open sky, witnessing a blood-orange sun transitioning into a cool moon. Atop the mountain cliff, he looked over at a flat, wide-open space that was mostly enclosed by the jungle. A towering fire was at the center, and the villagers started dancing around it. Three overly excited dogs ran toward Jason, and he knelt to greet them, laughing as they licked his hands.

Juniper bent to pet one on the head. "Don't mind them, they love people. This one is Sol. You can remember her because her right ear falls over her eye. The one next to you is Manana—her eyes resemble blueberries. And that's Anoche—he loves to swim.

Jason massaged his left palm, revealing a cut he got from accidentally grabbing a thorny branch in the jungle. Noticing the cut, Juniper took hold of his hand. "You want to know what really makes these little dogs special?" Juniper held Jason's hand up to the three dogs and they came forth, licking his wound, which miraculously healed in an instant.

Tyler's eyes shot open. "Say what! Talk about magic!"

Jason rubbed his hand where the cut used to be. "How's that even possible?"

Juniper stroked Anoche. "It's their saliva. It contains a special healing property."

Jason thought about his grandmother and finding a potential cure for her cancer, but before he had the chance to ask Juniper, laughter erupted a few feet away, and Juniper turned toward the group who were laughing and dancing. "Jason and Tyler, come with me, I must introduce you to my friends."

They followed her over as Jason wondered what Arhatian people his age were like.

"What's all this fun you're having without me?" Juniper teased the group. "Everyone, meet my new friends Jason and Tyler."

Jason quickly noticed how touchy-feely people were here as Juniper's friends hugged and kissed them like they had been long-time friends.

He listened carefully as Juniper introduced them, "Okay, that's Lala, over there is Hoko, and that's Nela. Lala is bubbly and has the cutest chubby cheeks. Her intuition is freakishly accurate. Hoko is more like the big brother of the group, and by far one of the tallest people in the village. He's an extraordinary navigator and can even chart directions based on changing weather patterns and constellations. Nela is very friendly and loves to talk to everyone, and she is a genius mathematician. She also loves good luck charms—as you can see, she wears many of them around her neck and wrists."

What caught Jason's attention were their eyes. Everyone in Arhat had brilliantly colored eyes. *How is it possible to have light purple eyes like Nela's or creamsicle orange like Lala's?* he wondered.

Jason continued to observe, noticing Nela and Tyler exchange flirtatious looks. He became distracted, as did the rest, when a strong voice emerged from the darkness. The man the voice belonged to was well built, yet his age was apparent by the withered texture of his skin. He looked to be someone important, prominent, and strong, maybe a leader of some sort. His facial expression was poised and content. His red skirt had yellow gemstones attached to it, and his chest and arms were painted with white tribal symbols. Atop long salt-and-pepper hair sat an astonishing headdress, a true masterpiece made of feathers with yellow being the most abundant color. His wrists and ankles were covered in bracelets that looked like little tambourines. Beside him stood a strong woman, equal in presence. Jason admired her elegance and style. She had soft reddish tones powdered on her cheeks. A fine white silk cloth wrapped around her body, and a red scarf adorned with sapphires was tied snugly around her forehead. The black lines at the corners of her eyes reminded him of Cleopatra. Her lips were lightly stained oceanic green. Her skin, like everyone else's, was warm and tan, and she had seductive dark blue eyes that appeared lighter as the moon's brightness reflected off them.

The man began to speak, "My people of Arhat! I welcome you with open arms, as does my wife beside me. We are a people of love and strength. We serve as a light in a dark place, and we strive to give hope and faith to the world. Tonight, we celebrate our past loved ones, those who contributed to the good of our village and this world. Their spirit animals live among us as our guardians and protectors. Let us celebrate as one."

The man picked up a large halved coconut shell. With both hands, he extended the shell to the sky, and as he closed his eyes, he made a prayer offering. Jason looked around, noticing that everyone else, including Juniper, closed their eyes, but he decided to watch as the man took a sip from the substance in the shell and poured the rest over the fire. As everyone opened their eyes, a stream of green light shot up into the sky like some type of aurora borealis, and spirit animals began to form. Their translucent, blue-tinted appearances soared through the sky.

"All souls are connected," Juniper whispered into Jason's ear with a smile.

He stared at her for a moment. She pointed toward the sky. "Look! That's our spirit moon. It gives each of us our personalities when we come into the world."

Jason admired how the moon was an unusual color, showing faint hints of blue and purple while glimmering meteors showered just behind it. The spirit animals, though, captured his attention the most as they pirouetted through the sky like ballerinas.

Tyler moved close to Juniper and Jason. "What are those things flying around?"

"They're our loved ones, those of Arhat who have passed into their next life. Their spirit animals live on and look after us all the days of our lives."

While they listened, Jason and Tyler caught glimpses of leopards, tigers, bears, eagles, and elephants.

Then everyone began sitting on the ground. Even the music softened and the surroundings became darker as the fire went out.

As Juniper and her friends sat down, so did Jason and Tyler. The crowd looked up at the sky as if they were waiting for something to happen. It was pitch-black at this point, and as Jason sat next to Juniper, he felt her hand hold his.

Finally, he thought, as something happened in the sky—the spirit animals looked as if they were about to act out a story.

Juniper whispered into his ear, "This one is about my grandfather."

Jason watched as the spirit animals told a story about a man named Bodhi.

Late one night, Bodhi woke to the sound of a fierce animal. Stealthily, he grabbed his spear to inspect it, circling the panther that had its eyes on his sleeping baby boy. The hungry beast waited to pounce, finally jumping toward the child, but Bodhi leaped in front, deflecting its sharp claws, and pierced it with his spear. Respectfully, he prayed over the panther's body before giving it up to the heavens, and removed its claws, which he wore around his neck to remember that night.

Jason was entranced as the spirit animals told a few more stories of courage, bravery, and faith, which inspired him to embody those traits. With his grandmother always in mind, he wondered if they had the ability to heal others. As the stories came to an end, Jason appreciated the peace in the darkness because he knew once the flames of the fire were reignited, the party would roar on.

Something through the trees caught his attention though, causing him to wonder what was lingering out there and if anyone else sensed it as he did. As he grew fixated, it revealed itself, which made his palms sweat. A pair of glaring red eyes stared through the trees. They blinked and focused on him. They were the most wicked eyes he'd ever seen. He heard a voice in his head. *Leave Arhat forever or die.* His heart skipped a beat and goosebumps formed up his arms.

Juniper rubbed his skin. "Everything okay, Jason?"

He didn't answer because he was far too disturbed by what he'd seen and heard.

The music started back up. Juniper pulled him toward the rekindled fire to dance with the others. After a while, he forgot the voice. He must have just been hearing things.

Jason saw the chief and his wife making their rounds and greeting everyone.

Juniper held his hand and intertwined her arm with his. "The one who gave the speech is Mongurt. His grandfather was one of the founders of Arhat. He is not a king but an equal, and that's his wife, Katalan."

As the party continued, Jason and Tyler were among the first to fixate on the copious amounts of food circulating.

Nela waved her hand in front of their faces after they tasted some of the fresh boar. "Hello, boys! Can you hear me? I know it's tasty, but come back to Earth."

Tyler licked his fingers. "That's last meal status."

Jason saw something that looked like mashed potatoes, so he dipped his finger into it to try it, but he was blindsided by the unexpected texture and taste. It reminded him of yogurt with the airiness of a piece of angel food cake.

He pointed out some wispy, fluffy substance that floated right past their faces. "What is that? It looks like cotton candy."

Juniper reached out for a piece, handing it to him and Tyler, and when Jason tasted it, flavors of strawberry gelato came to mind.

Juniper suddenly gasped with excitement. She walked toward an older couple heading in their direction. "Madra! Father! Come and meet Jason."

As her parents walked up to them, Juniper's father extended his hand. "Jason, call me Tiko. It's a pleasure to meet you. I hope you're enjoying Arhat."

Her mother followed, "And I'm Jahira. Very nice to meet you, Jason. If there is anything that you need in Arhat, we'll always be here for you. Did you come alone?"

"Thank you both so much, and it's truly a pleasure to meet you as well. I came with my friend, who's just behind me, I think." He wondered why Tiko and Jahira were looking past him, and when he turned around, he saw Tyler and Nela kissing over by the fire.

Tiko smirked. "I think your friend is settling in just fine."

They all laughed as Jason folded his arms and shook his head, unsurprised at the familiar scenario.

Before Juniper's parents left, they invited him and Tyler for dinner the next day. *Is everyone here this nice to strangers?* he thought.

When her parents walked away, Juniper and Jason strolled off, side by side. "I hope my parents didn't intimidate you at all. They're very friendly."

Jason stopped and faced her. "Not at all. They seem super sweet."

Their moment was quickly interrupted as they felt arms placed around their shoulders. It was Tyler, shirtless and covered in necklaces. "Jason, you're right—this is paradise. Juniper, I love your village. Like, I might never leave."

As the three laughed, Jason heard a sarcastic voice. "Hey, new guys, ever play Ring of Fire?" They turned around to see a young punk standing before them with his friends. Jason observed his crossed arms and devilish grin. The young man, tall and fit with tribal tattoos, seemed overly confident.

Jason's eyes widened in surprise when Juniper ran over and hugged him tight. *Does she have a boyfriend?* he wondered until he heard her say, "Brother!"

A smile grew across the young man's face as he hugged his sister, swinging her around. He introduced himself, "I'm Titi, Juniper's older brother."

Jason and Tyler strode over to say hello, but Jason felt discouraged when he realized Titi was more interested in trolling them than making introductions.

Titi looked him up and down. "So why are you guys here? You can't just show up. You have to prove yourselves. Can you beat us in Ring of Fire?"

Juniper smacked him on the arm. "Always trying to compete. Leave our guests alone."

Tyler whispered into Jason's ear, "Is this guy for real? I will kick his ass if need be."

Jason moved away. "Chill out, man. I don't want to make a bad impression."

Tyler rolled his eyes, and they followed Titi to the playing grounds, which had two long rectangular sandpits running parallel to each other. At both ends were blue flaming stakes that Titi called "ocienes" or "holy flames."

He explained the game, "The objective is to get the guta or metal hoop around the ocienes to earn pearls. Each person gets three turns. A ringer earns three pearls; the closet guta earns one pearl. The first to fifteen pearls wins."

Titi demonstrated effortlessly, getting three ringers in a row. Jason and Tyler felt confident, having played similar games back home. Tyler eyed up Titi's friend, his opponent, while Jason prepared to face Titi.

Before they began, Titi suggested a bet. "Alright new guys, listen up. If you beat us, you've proved yourselves. If you lose, you have to face me in a full day of competitive games. If you lose the games, you have to leave Arhat."

Jason stared blankly back at him, watching as a grin formed on his face. It was not a good feeling because Jason knew if they left, they couldn't come back.

Tyler walked forward. "Is that supposed to scare us? You're making it too easy."

Jason's hands shook before he spoke. "Look, why don't we just enjoy the festival?"

"Titi, what are you doing?" Juniper asked. "Stop acting like this toward our guests."

Jason tried to find reasons to avoid this confrontation, but Tyler nudged him on. "Come on, man, you can't back down. Tell this idiot we agree to his bet."

Titi began mocking them. "Figured you two would be too scared."

Juniper tried to reason with her brother, but he ignored her.

Tyler tapped Jason's arm. "Come on, man!"

Jason swatted him away. "The last thing I want to do is go home after we just got here."

"Who says we're losing? This game is just like horseshoes. If we back down now, no one is going to respect us."

Jason exhaled. "I'd rather not risk losing. Who cares what people think?"

Tyler rolled his eyes, then looked over at Titi. "Challenge accepted!"

"What did you just do?" Jason said, frustrated.

"Don't worry, man, we got this!" Tyler grinned. "Believe in yourself."

They walked to their separate playing fields and the games began.

Halfway through one of his matches, Jason heard cheers coming from where Tyler was playing, and then out of nowhere, he saw his friend running toward him with his hands in the air.

"I won! I won!" Tyler screamed.

Jason paused for a moment, getting nervous as everyone surrounded him and Titi to watch their last match. Jason needed one match to win. He launched his guta, which came up short. Then Titi scored a ringer. It was Jason's last chance—if he didn't get a ringer, it was over for him. Everything around Jason moved in slow motion, but as he was in a winning position, he remained composed. He saw Juniper, Tyler, and others cheering. Focusing on the blue flame, he tossed the guta and closed his eyes, hoping for the best.

Instead of cheers, he heard Titi's haunting voice, "Nice try, new guy. You're better than I thought. Anyway, a bet is a bet. See you for the games in three days."

Jason's heart sank as disappointment overwhelmed him. He found himself slipping into a hole of "what-if" scenarios until he felt something pulling at his leg.

He looked down and a child stared up at him. "Don't worry, big bro, you're going to be fine."

Jason smiled. "Well, thank you, little guy. I'm Jason. What's your name?"

The child waved his little hand at him. "I'm Osito and you're my big bro, right?"

Jason chuckled. "Sure, nice to meet you, little bro."

Mongurt came over, clapping loudly. "What a match—best I've seen in a long time."

Katalan approached too. "Excellent, Jason. Who were you just talking to, may I ask?"

Jason looked down and saw that little Osito was gone. He shook his head without an answer and thanked them for their compliments.

Mongurt stood before Jason. "Welcome to Arhat. How are you enjoying the festival?"

Jason looked around and then back at them. "It's amazing! This is our first day here. Juniper has been showing us around."

Mongurt nodded. "Ah, Juniper, she's a brave girl. You're in good hands."

Jason noticed tears falling from Katalan's eyes as she stared at his necklace. Before he could utter a word, she said, "Preeda gave that to you?"

Jason shot her a strange look. "She did. She's from here, right?"

Katalan wiped away her tears. "Our sweet daughter was a chosen one."

"Preeda is your daughter?" Jason stepped closer and lowered his voice. "She helped us find Arhat."

Katalan hugged Jason, and Mongurt expressed his happiness for Jason and Tyler's arrival, making it known that they were welcome.

Tyler walked over with two cups of tazwack. "Don't worry, buddy. We'll be fine. Don't let Titi get you down. Here, drink this. Let's have fun tonight."

Nela ran by and pulled Tyler away to dance, leaving Jason alone until Juniper came up to him. "Sorry about my brother. He sometimes takes things too far. I'll speak to him again about stopping his nonsense. You don't have to play these games, you know."

Jason felt that if he backed down in front of Juniper it would make him look like a coward, even though he didn't want to face Titi.

Juniper smiled, and Jason stared, entranced by her beauty, forgetting the bet for a moment. He felt so safe with her, a person he barely knew. Juniper suggested they find a quiet place away from the celebration to relax.

They walked just a few feet from the music and dancing, and sat against a tree.

Juniper placed her hand over his. "So are you tired from all the dancing and meeting all my friends and family?"

Jason glanced at her. "Not at all. There's something about this place that makes me feel so alive. It's been a great night."

She rubbed her hand over his. "I just want to make sure you're having a great time is all."

Jason inched closer. "I'm having a great time because I'm with you right now."

Juniper blushed and they gazed into each other's eyes, then exchanged a small kiss.

The kiss felt different from others Jason had experienced. *There's some innocence to it*, he thought. Not like the run-and-gun party girls that he was more familiar with.

"Do you see it, Jason?" Juniper said, trying to catch something in the air.

He could see a bunch of little neon purple insects floating past them.

She caught one in her hand. "Those are the village's night lights. Look over there, it's their mating season." Thousands of them glowed at the edge of the jungle.

Jason placed his arm around her, and she rested her head on his chest. He lost track of time as they spoke until their eyelids grew heavy, mumbling to each other. He could no longer hear the music, and the fire that he felt from afar must have fizzled out.

CHAPTER 18

AN OUTSIDER'S INTRODUCTION

Jason's back slid off the tree he had slept against, and as he felt himself falling, he woke. A misty fog covered the lively festival grounds.

Is this all just a dream? He looked around. *It can't be, because here I am, and there's Juniper next to me.* When he looked over, she was still fast asleep.

He stood to stretch, and felt his body expand, letting out a big yawn. He embraced the cool air on his face and even found himself inhaling deep breaths of the fresh, warm jungle. All around, he saw villagers sleeping, couples curled up, and a few stragglers wandering around.

As he walked around the quiet grounds, an invigorating thought came to his mind, *It feels so nice to be disconnected from the world. No phones! No social media! They just don't exist here.* One thing that bothered him, though, was that he had not spoken to his grandparents in weeks and he still didn't know if he was going to find a cure for his grandma.

As he continued to walk, he saw the remains of the giant fire from last night, now nothing more than burnt logs and ashes. He tried his best not to step on anyone, including Tyler, who was passed out with Nela under his arm.

He walked up to the mountain's edge and gazed into the distance. A deep voice knocked him from his trance, "It's breathtaking, isn't it?"

When he turned to see who it was, Jason was startled by the sheer presence of the man. His height alone was intimidating. His hair was long and gray, and his scraggly whiskers fell just past his chest. A pair of beady green eyes seemed to peer into Jason's soul. His face was stern and serious, and he wore a charcoal shawl over his shoulders with a turquoise amulet around his neck.

"I'm Eshin. It's nice to meet you." Smoke drifted from his pipe.

Jason still felt a bit overwhelmed by his presence as he extended his hand to shake. He was baffled not only by the size of Eshin's hand but also by how mangled it appeared.

They casually strolled the grounds to a more peaceful area. Jason could hear the birds beginning to wake as they flew through rays of sunlight. Their soothing whistles, both high and low, blended into a rhythmic harmony.

He didn't recall seeing Eshin last night at the celebration, but maybe they just hadn't crossed paths.

Jason looked up at him. "Were you at the party last night?"

Eshin puffed on his pipe. "Three hundred years of dancing gets repetitive."

"You're three hundred years old? That's a lot of years."

"It's also a lot of pain." Eshin waved smoke from his face.

Jason pondered that comment. "You must have seen some interesting things."

"Indeed. I've been worldwide and witnessed wars being fought and starving villages. I have also experienced great acts of love and kindness."

Jason was speechless for a moment.

"Why though? Why is there as much evil as good in the world?"

Eshin remained composed. "Why is it that the sun is certain to rise and set each day? Unfortunately, my boy, this is the way of the world, but we all have a choice to love."

Jason studied Eshin's mangled hand as he used it to smoke his pipe. "Your hand," he said awkwardly. "What happened?"

Eshin rotated his wrist. "I'm happy you asked. The dichotomy between my hands, as you can see, is that one is perfectly fine, while the other is distorted. My right hand, the one that is tortured, represents humanity's growth and advancements. Most would think that my left hand should represent that, but it doesn't. Growth is gained through imperfections and failures."

Jason again pondered Eshin's words as they walked in silence.

Eshin pulled a small apple from his satchel. "You traveled a great way to be here, Jason. Surely it was not by accident."

"But why?" Jason fretted. "Why was I chosen to come here?"

Eshin blew out a ring of smoke. "That you will find out in time. I'm only a messenger between the Ancestors and Earth. My vision is only as good as the past and the present, everything that has ever existed and does now. Everyone has their own destiny to fulfill."

Jason was confused. "To be honest, I mostly came here hoping I'd find a way to help my grandmother. She's sick with cancer. Is there anything in Arhat that could cure her? I'm also concerned about the bet that was made with Titi because if I lose, then I have to leave Arhat."

Eshin paused for a moment, and then continued strolling. "I'm afraid, young Jason, that only the Ancestors have the power to determine life and death. Your grandmother's fate will be left in their hands. As for the bet you made, do not doubt yourself. You may be more surprised by your abilities than you think."

Jason had so many unanswered questions. Since last night, he had carried the anxiety of facing off with Titi, knowing that if he lost, he would have to go home. What if he had to leave Arhat without fully understanding the true reason he was led here? The fact that nobody could guarantee a cure also made him second-guess himself. He wondered if coming here in the first place was such a good idea after all.

Jason didn't bother to ask Eshin any further questions as he tried to process all that they had spoken about, and as he saw the villagers waking, he thought it best to go find Juniper.

As Jason walked back to her, he puzzled over his interaction with Eshin, not quite sure what to make of such a mysterious character. When he reached Juniper, he felt happy knowing that he'd made it back before she woke, slipping into place and pretending to sleep beside her.

He listened to her cute yawn as she stretched. He could hear the music start back up along with the voices of Arhat's people as they woke to greet each other and converse. He was surprised that he didn't see a single soul who was groggy from the night before. In fact, everyone looked full of energy. He recalled that Hoko mentioned how tazwack hydrates the body as you drink it.

He watched as Juniper opened her eyes, rubbing them. She smiled at him, and all he could think in that moment was how everything, for once in his life, felt perfect. He looked up, watching as everyone began to make their way back to the village, but nobody was in a rush. Instead, they took their time. Jason particularly admired how clean the festival grounds were.

"It's like we were never here. We partied so much, but everything is just as it was before we arrived."

Jason and Juniper regrouped with her friends including Tyler.

Traveling through the jungle, the group bantered and joked. Jason mentioned to Juniper that he'd met Eshin earlier that morning.

Her face brightened. "Ah yes, Eshin. Mysterious but harmless—we love him."

Once they made it back to the village, Jason and Tyler followed Juniper and her friends, excited about where they'd go next. Jason became infatuated with the talent around him. Along the sandy trails, he admired the painters who doused their fingers in various bowls of paint, switching between brushes and their hands to create. He also was captivated by the sculptors, jewelry makers, dancers, and musicians. He noticed children helping their moms dye beautiful garments.

Juniper brought their attention to a woman sitting against her home. "You see her, over there? That's Chanthira, one of Arhat's finest jewelry and clothing makers. She harnesses Earth's elements in all her work. When you wear her items, you feel positive and uplifted. That necklace you have, Jason, she made it. She makes them all for the chosen travelers."

Jason scanned Chanthira, a petite older woman wrapped in red cloth with thick wavy black hair resting on her shoulders. She wore many pendants and bracelets. He could sense her strong independence as she sat alone, vigorously working on her jewelry, unlike the other artists who talked to one another as they worked.

Jason and Tyler turned their attention to Nela as she pointed out another artist. "Hey, do you guys see her, the older woman painting? That's Mariposa. She loves painting rumba flowers, as you can see. They're painted along every home in Arhat."

Jason nodded toward another character. "How about him, over there?"

"That's Alden," Lala told them. "Arhat's best architect and designer. He has a keen eye for beauty and detail. Many of our temples and statues were made by him."

"You know how Alden gets his inspiration?" Hoko added. "He spends hours skipping stones. He never knows what he's going to create until he begins, and then it all comes together."

"Damn, I gotta rethink my life," Tyler blurted.

Jason agreed. "It's inspiring and intimidating at the same time."

"Well, I'm sure you're surrounded by talent every day where you're from too," Juniper said. "Maybe you just don't always see it. I'm sure you both have your unique gifts."

Tyler crossed his arms. "True, I'm great at sports. I'm competitive, and I rarely lose. Jason, on the other hand, is good at hanging out with old people."

The group laughed at what they thought was an innocent joke, but although Jason appeared to find it funny, he felt uncomfortable. Juniper smiled at Tyler's joke, but Jason could tell she didn't find it as funny as the others did.

The delicious smell of some baked goods swept past them. Juniper led the group over to a small hut from where it came. When they stepped inside, Jason recognized a woman over by the oven from the night before.

Juniper ran up and wrapped her arms around her. "Auntie."

This woman squeezed Juniper back. "Hey, Juni, how's my favorite niece doing?"

Juniper turned back toward the group. "Jason and Tyler, meet my amazing auntie, Zaza. She's also a phenomenal baker—just wait until you try her umberry bread."

Jason observed Auntie Zaza. Her permanent smile, flickering oceanic eyes, and the way she constantly shifted her weight made her appear energetic and even a little quirky. Her skin was glowing and radiant, likely from exposure to the sun. Her reddish-brown hair was bunched up in a ponytail, frizzy and out of place. Freckles were scattered across her cheeks, and fine crow's feet lined her eyes.

Auntie Zaza rested her hand on a chair next to her. "Come here and give me hug, Jason and Tyler. Welcome to Arhat."

After receiving his hug, Jason was taken back as she picked up a conga drum and started beating it as she danced around them—presumably her way of welcoming them to Arhat.

He heard a man say, "Knock, knock! Is that my Juniper I hear? I was just bringing over some freshly picked ingredients from the jungle to give to your aunt. "

Juniper's face it up. "Uncle Jesepa! You're here just in time to meet my friends. Guys, this is my Uncle Jesepa, one of the best cooks in the village. Most of Arhat's recipes came from him."

Jesepa rested his hands on his hips. "I never discourage a good compliment. Wonderful to meet you both."

Auntie Zaza held out a cloth containing baked goods, and Jason's eyes darted toward the bread. She broke a few pieces apart for them to try.

Jason picked up a piece, and the hot berries stained his fingertips dark purple. Just before taking a bite, he inhaled its intoxicating smell. The texture reminded him of a scone, light and crumbly, with slightly burnt corners.

After his first bite, Jason felt transported to another dimension, fully in tune with every flavor. He felt Hoko give him a light tap on his cheek to wake him up and saw him do the same to Tyler, who looked at the group, satisfied. "I'm ready to die now—my life is fulfilled."

"I could live off this bread forever," Jason chimed in.

Everyone began to laugh, including Auntie Zaza, and Jason could tell by her expression that she appreciated their compliments. "You boys just made my day. Give me another hug."

As they left Auntie Zaza's hut, Juniper whispered into Jason's ear, "Can I take you to one of my favorite places?"

Jason smiled. "Of course. Are all of us going?"

Juniper giggled. "Just you and me."

She dashed over to her friends gathered nearby to tell them that she and Jason were heading off to explore and spend some time together.

Nela went up and kissed Juniper on the cheek. "Of course, Juni, you show him a good time, and Jason, don't worry about Tyler, he's in good hands."

Before they left, Tyler waved Jason over. "Man, can you believe it? We're in paradise, bro. Okay, here's the plan. You stick with Juniper, and I'll stick with Nela for now. She's so hot—totally blew my mind last night, but more on that later. Maybe if we get close enough to them, they'll give us that treasure. Juniper is a total catch, so don't blow it. Try not to overthink things and just play it cool."

Jason placed his hand on Tyler's shoulder. "I appreciate your advice. Honestly, I've never felt a connection like this before with anyone else."

Tyler took a step back. "Damn. Well, if that's how you're feeling, go after her."

They fist-bumped, and Jason followed Juniper into the jungle.

CHAPTER 19

A LEAP OF FAITH

As they walked along winding trails, their hands intertwined. Jason was filled with questions. "I guess Preeda was a 'chosen traveler'?"

"Yes, and Katalan and Mongurt's daughter," Juniper said.

"So can chosen travelers ever come back to Arhat?" He looked at her hopefully.

"The chosen ones are selected by the Ancestors to fulfill a higher purpose. Although they leave the village, the spirit of Arhat never leaves them. They form a new home among people of the world who are in need, forever helping them."

He didn't realize how high they'd climbed until he felt out of breath. He wondered where he could get those minty altitude leaves so he could always have some in his pocket. They stood in front of a cliff's edge. He was captivated by the beauty of the jungle ahead.

Out of the corner of his eye, he saw Juniper walking along the cliff edge.

He called out, "I don't think that's such a great idea."

She laughed while balancing on one foot. "Follow me, we're almost at my secret spot, but you've got to follow me alongside the cliff to get there. What are you waiting for? Come on!"

Jason went silent, shaking his head. His mouth partially hung open and he stared at her.

"I'm fine right here."

She did a handstand. "Can you imagine all that you'd try if fear didn't exist?"

Jason could barely watch her. "I would do a lot of things, but this is reality, and I have lots of fears, including this."

Juniper returned to her feet. "Our situations are a result of how we perceive things. Change your story, and you change your reality. Come on, Jason. I'm waiting for you."

He looked up to the sky, nervous. "Thanks, but not enough to convince me."

She laughed as she shimmied back toward him. She grabbed his hand. "Look at me, Jason. I promise I won't let anything happen to you."

He looked into her eyes and oddly believed her, feeling safer than ever before. She guided him over to the edge, and he hesitantly reached out his foot while Juniper strolled ahead. He tried hard not to look down, feeling his stomach turn.

As they moved along the cliff, she remained in front, causing him to panic.

Juniper looked back. "I know you're braver than you think."

Jason exhaled deeply and mumbled, "I have to at least try to look brave in front of her." He moved forward, carefully traveling along the cliff edge. As he saw himself progressing along the narrow path, he gained confidence, moving faster until he planted his foot on a patch of rocks that shattered, causing him to slip right off the path's edge. He dug his hands into the side of the cliff, hanging by his fingertips as he shouted, "Juniper, help!"

She calmly moved back toward him, seeing his eyes fill up with tears and hearing his intense breathing. He tried to hoist himself up but felt too weak, waiting for Juniper, who knelt before him. Then, suddenly, he saw a vision of those haunting red eyes from the previous night and heard someone cackling. The voice came into his head again. *Die, Jason.*

Juniper's voice and smile brought him back. "Trust me when I tell you, let go!"

"Let go?" he yelled. "Are you going to just let me die?"

"Jason, I know you're scared, but let go. Remember, I promised I wouldn't let anything bad happen to you."

Angry and confused, he looked into her eyes, saying to himself, *why do I trust you so much?*, and then he let go. He let out a yelp and closed his eyes, preparing for impact, but when he opened them, he saw Juniper still smiling at him. His body felt airy and light—he was floating.

Juniper smirked, arms crossed. "So, how's it hanging?"

Suspended in mid-air, Jason looked around. "What is happening right now? Am I dead?"

"You're very much alive," Juniper assured him. "Probably should have mentioned the altitude particles. We have a species of plant in Arhat called KaRas, mainly found on the sides of cliffs. They're yellow plants, each with four arms containing a layer of powder, which circulates the sky at these altitudes. Those are the particles you're sitting in right now."

Juniper leaped off the cliff and floated next to him.

He shook his head at her. "You probably could have mentioned this earlier."

She moved over and hooked arms with him. "I could have, but how would you have learned to face your fears and trust? Like I said, while you're here, I won't let anything bad happen to you."

Together, they floated back toward the cliff's edge and shuffled the rest of the way around until they reached a wide-open cave. As they walked inside the cave, Jason felt her hands covering his eyes. "Another surprise? Can we please stay grounded this time?"

When they stopped, she removed her hands, and Jason shuddered in awe. They had emerged from the cave and were standing on the edge of another cliff. Thin smoky clouds dissipated, unveiling Arhat cradled in the hands of high-arching mountains within a vast jungle, surrounded by a body of water that glistened, clear as glass. It reminded him of pictures of the Bolivian Salt Flats. Eagles and rare birds spread their wings wide and soared. The people of Juniper's tribe rowed on small boats and fished. He had never seen sand so pink. He could spot several little trails that led into the village, and the powdery white homes stacked on top of one another.

Jason's knees buckled at the sight, and Juniper grabbed him to prevent him from falling. He took a seat, hanging his feet over the edge.

"This place, it really is perfect."

Juniper sat next to him. "It's one of my secret spots."

Jason gave her a kiss. "Thank you for this—it's incredible. And what is that lake called that surrounds Arhat?"

"That's Humtay Lake." She leaned her head on his shoulder. "It's where we sail, race sea turtles, fish, and free dive. It's one of Arhat's most sacred places. I will take you there too." Jason opened his mouth to speak, but Juniper held up her hand. "Hold your questions. We're going for a swim."

Jason was baffled yet intrigued. "But didn't we just get here?"

She stood and pulled him up. "Yes, but there's only so much time. Come on. I'm so excited to show you everything."

Jason followed her into the jungle, pushing past lush trees until they arrived at a hot spring. Juniper ran forward, removing her clothes. All Jason could see was her naked back, tan and smooth, and her free-flowing hair.

Shaking his head, he ran after her, also removing his clothes, and dived into the hot spring. Juniper climbed on his back and they floated around, enjoying the lukewarm water. When she let go and swam around to face him, no words were exchanged.

Just as Jason felt confident enough to go in for a kiss, Juniper splashed some water in his face with a smile. When she tried to swim away, he grabbed her arm and guided her back. They stared at each other, and Jason gently kissed her soft lips. She lingered for a moment before getting out of the water, covering herself, and dressing.

Jason followed, dressing as well, and watched as she wrung out her long thick hair.

"So, Jason." She slung back her wet hair, splashing everywhere. "What's the real reason you decided to come to Arhat?"

He thought carefully about his response. "What fueled me most was my grandmother. She's sick, and the doctors said she doesn't have much time. When I decided to find Arhat, I did it hoping that I might find a cure for her here."

"I'm very sorry to hear that, but I am not sure what cure can be offered. We shall leave this in our prayers to the Ancestors."

Jason placed his hand over hers. "Thank you, I appreciate that. I'd do anything to help her, so if it means praying to the Ancestors, then I'll do that and whatever else as well."

Juniper walked over and kissed him on the cheek. "Was there another reason that brought you here?"

"I guess I was just tired of always being afraid. I don't usually take risks like this, ya know. I mean, you saw me back at the cliff edge. I only did that because you motivated me, and luckily, I'm still alive."

Juniper played with his hair. "I believe you're braver than you think you are. Don't be afraid to let it shine. Back there on the cliff, you changed your story of doubt into confidence. If you can face fears head-on, they become as small as a pebble. I see that confidence inside you, Jason." She smiled. "You seemed pretty confident when you kissed me at the moon festival and just now."

Jason grinned and pulled her in for another soft, slow kiss.

Afterward, Juniper and Jason walked back to the village, where her parents were expecting them for dinner. They stopped on the street to wait for Tyler, who had spent the day with Nela, and after he kissed her and came over, Jason patted him on the back.

"Looks like someone had a great day."

Tyler grinned. "You could say that. And you? Wonder what you did in the jungle."

Juniper smirked. "Your friend Tyler, he's a nosy one."

As Juniper walked ahead, Tyler and Jason trailed behind, recapping their day.

"Okay, man, spill the beans. Give me all the juicy details."

Jason walked with a smile, his head facing the ground. "Not much. Just a great day."

Tyler rolled his eyes. "Ha! Please tell me you guys went all the way."

Jason laughed. "Is that all you think about? We're getting to know each other."

"Please!" Tyler exclaimed. "When's the last time a girl that hot was into you? You can take all the time you want, but don't be afraid to make your move."

"Don't worry. She's pretty amazing. I want to see where this goes."

Tyler stopped for a moment. "Where this goes? You think we're staying here forever?"

Jason carried on walking. "Who knows, but for now I like how things are going. And you and Nela—what's up with that?"

"We're obviously hitting it off. She's making me work for it though, but it's only a matter of time. There's something about her. She's so much fun."

Jason raised an eyebrow. "Well! Well! Is Tyler catching some feelings? Surprising that she hasn't succumbed to your seductive powers yet. You still think of Jessica at all?"

"Please, man," Tyler retorted. "It'll probably happen tonight or tomorrow. Funny you mention Jessica. I do think of her often. She's probably moved on by now."

"Maybe so, but I'm sure she misses you too," Jason pointed out. "She's probably a little worried and even confused since we've been away for so long."

Tyler shrugged. "Who knows? I was starting to feel something for Jessica too. We just seemed to always be on the same page, like she weirdly understood me. What if she thinks I moved on?"

"Wow! That's the first time I've heard you speak about a girl like that," Jason said. "That's how I feel with Juniper. You feel anything similar with Nela?"

Tyler looked up ahead, then glanced at Jason. "Honestly, not the same feeling I got with Jessica. But Nela is really cool and super beautiful. Plus, she's totally into me, so it's fun to spend time with her."

CHAPTER 20

GROUP THERAPY

As they approached Juniper's home, Jason heard her mother calling, "Juniper! Darling!"

Juniper hugged her mother, who then expected hugs from Jason and Tyler as well.

Jason asked if they could help with any of the preparation and Jahira almost took that as an insult.

"Help! Oh no, my dear. No guests of mine will help. You make yourselves at home. I'm making my famous kalatucka."

"It's a banana seafood stew," Juniper elaborated. "Cooked unripe banana with lots of shrimp, clams, scallops, and pieces of shredded white fish. It has coconut, onions, and many different seasonings and spices that come from the island."

Tyler stopped dead in his tracks. "Wow, sounds amazing!"

Juniper's two little sisters excitedly ran up, tugging at her skirt.

He patted them on the head. "This is Lotusa. She's ten, and she loves hiking and climbing big trees and mountains. She's very independent and fearless—never afraid to stand up for her beliefs. Jasmina, on the other hand, is a little ball of fun and eight years old. She is equally smart, but far less organized. She's a free spirit like all of us, and she can speak to animals."

Jason knelt to compliment Lotusa's jade necklace.

"It's her favorite," Juniper said. "It brings her luck."

Lotusa held it up for Jason to see. "I don't believe in luck. I believe in myself."

Juniper patted her on the head again. "I know, little sis. You're the strongest of all."

Tyler laughed, his hands on his stomach. "Sounds like me and Lotusa are similar."

Juniper looked over at Jasmina. "Are you wearing makeup again?"

Jason thought it was cute that Jasmina wanted to be like her mother and older sister.

"You're already beautiful without all that makeup," Juniper assured her. "Now go wash."

Juniper's father walked in. "Mmhhhhhhhh, is my honey cooking kalatucka?"

Tiko went up behind his wife, kissing her on the cheek, a gesture that faintly reminded Jason of his father and mother. While everyone else was chatting and laughing, he noticed Juniper watching him. Her soft, empathetic gaze gave him the notion that she could feel what he felt in that moment, a slight sadness at the reminder of his parents. She didn't know about their passing, but regardless, she was very intuitive. Her strong emotional intelligence made it feel like they were deeply connected. By no means was she a mind reader, but it was like she understood him without him always having to explain himself.

"Girls!" Tiko called, and right away, Jasmina and Lotusa ran over to hug him.

Jason could tell how much he loved his family. *But where's Titi?* he thought. *Hopefully, he doesn't bring up the bet.*

Tiko greeted Jason and Tyler. "Boys! It's great to see you again. Take a seat."

He poured them a cup of tazwack and sat beside them, catching up and drinking together.

Jason occasionally looked around. The girls played on the floor, and Juniper helped her mother prepare dinner. Their small home resembled a hut with thin walls of animal hide, bamboo, and a cone-like roof. Inside were animal skin rugs, and a private area out back for resting, preparing food, and working on projects.

"So how is Arhat treating you both?" Tiko took a sip of his drink.

"This place is perfect," Jason said.

Tiko laughed, resting his arm on his leg. "We're far from perfect, but I'm happy you like it here. And you, Tyler?"

Tyler leaned in. "Best place I've ever been."

Jahira carried over a basket of ingredients for the stew. "My love, did you bring the fish?"

Tiko walked out to the private area and called for Jason and Tyler to join him as he prepared the hanging fish for the stew. The stew was slowly cooking in a large clay pot dangling over an open fire. Jason offered to help again, but Tiko insisted it wasn't necessary. Lotusa eagerly ran over to aid her father, while inside, Jasmina pushed between her mother and Juniper to assist them.

Jahira looked down at Jasmina. "Dear, please go pick your mother some spices and call for your grandparents."

Many villagers passed by their home, and each of them thanked Tiko for fixing their homes and other things around the village. Aside from valuable carpentry skills, Jason assumed that most people flocked to Tiko because of his friendly disposition. He seemed to be a guy who could always be counted on.

Jahira called, "My sweet, how is the stew coming along? Do we need more time?"

Tiko leaned in, stirring the stew. "Only a few minutes more, my love."

Jason and Tyler helped Tiko carry a few things inside, where they found Juniper's family ready for dinner, sitting around a rolled-out blanket on the floor. Jason recognized Juniper's grandfather, Bodhi, the man from the story told during the celebration. It felt honorable to be in his presence. *He's the man who saved his son from the panther*, Jason recalled.

Next to him sat Juniper's grandmother, who Jason found to be a sweet woman, on the quiet side, yet proud of her family.

Tiko hoisted the pot of stew, setting it right in the center and filling each of their bowls. Before they began, he prayed, "We honor this meal to our Ancestors, our spirit animals. Blessings are upon us today, our people, our family, and Arhat. Thank you to my lovely wife, my children, and my parents. Let us enjoy this great meal together."

Jason picked up his spoon and dipped it into his bowl, releasing irresistible aromas.

Juniper watched his reaction and teased, "It's not that bad, right?"

Jason found himself speechless—the flavors of the stew were mind-blowing.

Tyler got a kick out of his reaction, trying not to spit out his food from laughter. "Trust me, he gets that way all the time. I don't blame him. The food here is amazing."

A small burst of anxiety overtook Jason when he saw Titi walk through the door, hoping that he wouldn't join them. Titi didn't say anything to Jason, making him feel uncomfortable as he just smirked and maintained eye contact with him until he'd sat down.

Across from him, little Jasmina was covered in food while Lotusa remained prim and proper without a drop on her. Unexpectedly, two dogs ran into their home, sniffing around. It was Sol and Anoche. They went straight over to Jasmina, licking her and nosing her bowl of stew. Jasmina whispered something to them, calming them down and making them walk away after eating.

From time to time, Titi purposely messed with Jason by "accidentally" elbowing him when he was about to take a spoonful. Jason could see that Tyler was also annoyed and waiting for him to say something, but Jason stayed calm, trying to justify it as Titi vetting the new guy.

Later that evening, when Juniper and her family had gone off to make prayer offerings, Jason and Tyler hung out at the back of the house, chatting and drinking tazwack until they were dizzy.

Tyler rested his right leg over the other. "So, when you gonna stop taking shit from Juniper's brother?"

Jason drank from his cup. "Look, man, he's being protective. We're the new guys. He'll eventually lighten up, and hopefully he'll forget the bet."

Tyler leaned forward. "You think a guy like that is going to forget the bet? We're walking targets, man. Well, you are. You're flirting with his sister. Look, what really matters is that you never let anyone walk all over you. Remember how you stood up to Cetek and those punks who got us in trouble? You need to respect yourself just as much as any other relationship. Would you let someone devalue your grandmother or your girlfriend? Of course not, so treat yourself with the same respect or else people will always find a way to mess with you."

Jason took another sip and looked up to the sky. "This is different though."

Tyler held his cup high for a toast. "We'll figure something out. We always do."

The following day was filled with the sounds of people preparing for what appeared to be a big day in Arhat. Juniper informed Jason and Tyler that everyone was congregating down by Humtay Lake for one of the village's largest group meditations. The celebration happened each year, two days after the moon festival.

Tyler looked at Jason. "Damn, these people like to party."

They walked with Juniper and her family down to the lake. When they arrived, Jason got the impression that there were more people here than there were during the moon celebration. Nela, Lala, and Hoko rushed over to them in excitement. Tyler immediately put his arm around Nela like she was already his girlfriend. They all joked around as they neared the edge of the lake. Jason watched in amazement as hundreds of villagers walked, not swam, out onto the lake, creating tiny ripples with every step. Juniper and her friends ran ahead of him, doing cartwheels and gliding on their stomachs across the surface. Jason tried to process how walking on water was possible, but he quickly gave up and just joined them.

Jason and Tyler ran out, sliding and running across the water with everyone else, splashing and chasing each other around until they heard a loud and powerful clap. Jason took it as thunder at first, but when he looked around, he saw everyone's attention on one person.

The crowd began to widen into a giant circle, and in the middle stood a spiritual guide or shaman, which Jason assumed based on his appearance. He was old and stood about five-foot-five, and his face and body were painted with various blue symbols. Deep crevices marked his face. He held his arms up and looked to the sky, appreciating the sun that shone down on him.

As the crowd watched in silence, Jason felt a mysterious gust of wind blow through. Everyone grabbed the hands of the people next to them and waited for the spiritual guide to lead them. First, he instructed them to shut their eyes, and then together they inhaled deeply, letting out powerful breaths while expanding their stomachs. Jason began to feel rejuvenated and energized.

Next, they lowered to the surface of the water and sat in a cross-legged pose while still holding hands. The spirit guide then recited a prayer, "*Tekkka neeee shaalaawaaaa.*"

Tyler whispered to Nela, "What does it mean?"

"It means we collectively give all things to those in need—our possessions, wealth, everything."

The shaman repeated this prayer three times and then became so silent that one could hear a pin drop, Jason thought. After a long pause, they let out a giant "*Ommmm*" together. Jason could feel tiny ripples across the water, then peeked his eyes open to see that they extended for miles like tiny tsunamis.

Juniper squeezed his hand. "Close your eyes, Jason." When he shut them, something felt off. When he tried to open his eyes again, he couldn't. It felt like they were glued shut.

She squeezed his hand again. "Relax, you'll be okay. Let us now send our prayers to the world, for those in need and for your grandmother."

The air began to change, and the weather conditions shifted. The bright sun felt as if it was replaced with dark clouds. Fat droplets of rain drenched them, and then suddenly stopped. Freezing temperatures swept in and Jason even felt snow flurries on his face. A light, crisp air then passed through, like a perfect spring day, and he felt his body heat up. He sensed that they were passing through the forces of nature, and he could do nothing but be completely aware and present.

Loud claps rang out in three-second intervals while drums played in the background.

"Juniper! What's happening?" Jason nervously asked as he felt himself levitating.

She held his hand tight. "Shhh, you will see. Focus now!"

They all sat in silence for a few moments, suspended in the air. So many forms of positivity came flowing through Jason's mind. He was forgiving himself, forgiving others, and envisioning the healing of his grandmother. He thought of romantic moments, exciting moments, and spiritual moments from his past and present as well as great moments to come.

Jason's positive images felt endless until something unexpected interfered. All went dark, and he could no longer see anything until a thick fog appeared. The haunting red eyes loomed from the mist. Then they turned black, so evil and demonic that Jason started to breathe heavily and the hand that held Juniper's shook.

A deep whispering voice warned him, *Leave Arhat. Leave or everyone you love will die.*" Then he saw gruesome images of his grandmother, Tyler, Juniper, and others mangled and decapitated. He started shaking aggressively until a powerful clap woke everyone up.

They all fell through the water, which felt as warm as a bath. Jason opened his eyes under the water and could see other people doing the same. When he emerged, the villagers were swimming, splashing, and laughing. It reminded him of a giant pool party, but still he was a little distraught by what he'd just witnessed. *Was I the only one who saw that?* He wanted to keep it to himself for now, since everyone was so joyful—it was truly a sight to be seen. Juniper hugged him, and Jason was surprised to see Tyler hugging everyone in sight.

Juniper gave him a big kiss, bringing him back to the moment. "The purpose of this meditation is to bind us together and release a collective surge of positive energy up to our spirit animals, who carry it throughout the world."

Jason had felt those positive emotions and seen wonderful images before the darkness overtook his mind. He wanted to completely forget it and just be in the moment with the others.

Tyler swam over. "Yo, that was crazy. Man, I had some insane thoughts. At first, I saw a ton of poverty around the world, like slums and hungry people everywhere. Then I started crying. I saw images of people around the world helping one another. There was no hatred, no wars or division between countries and cultures. The whole world was at peace. I was even one of the people helping, giving all my money and possessions away. It felt great! And bro, I literally saw some of the happiest people in my life in some of the slums. The crazy thing is, they weren't rich, yet they were still so content."

"Is this the same Ty talking to me right now?" Jason hugged him.

He spotted Titi and his friends swimming over, thinking that they were also coming to express warm gestures of friendship, but instead, he heard Titi announce loudly, so everyone could hear, "Hey, new guy, hope you didn't forget our bet. See you tomorrow."

A stone formed in Jason's stomach, uneasy about the bet he'd agreed to. *Can't he just back off?*

Juniper shook her head at her brother. "Titi, can you please leave my friends alone?"

"Just having a little fun, sis." Titi smirked. "A bet is a bet."

She turned toward Jason. "You don't have to do this. Don't let him get to you."

He glanced at Tyler, who nodded, as if to say, "Stand up to him like we talked about."

Jason swam closer to Titi. "Oh, I didn't forget," he said.

Titi kept his usual grin. "Sounds good, new guy. See you tomorrow—be here at sunrise." He swam away with his friends.

Juniper rolled her eyes and swung her arms around Jason. "We have a lot of work to do, but don't worry, you've got me to help you." She kissed him on the cheek. "My brother might be a great athlete, but I can still beat him in most games."

"Proud of you!" Tyler said. "You're going to be fine tomorrow, but... it's a good thing you have Juniper to train you. You're going to need it."

Juniper pulled back to look at Jason. "Ready to begin?"

He took a deep breath, throwing his arms up in the air. "Let's do this!"

CHAPTER 21

RISING TO THE CHALLENGE

The crowd around Humtay Lake dispersed, leaving Jason, Juniper, and Tyler alone.

As Jason and Tyler sat atop the water, Juniper stood facing them. "Firstly, don't be afraid of my brother. This is just a game to him, so play his game."

Jason nodded, trying to keep a positive mindset despite knowing that if he lost, they would have to leave. *Why does Juniper never look concerned? I mean, she does know what happens if I lose. I guess she believes in me enough not to be worried,* he thought.

Juniper paced. "The competition is tomorrow, and knowing my brother, it will most likely consist of racing sea turtles, free diving, and a round of fighting. I will teach you how to race and swim fast, but for fighting, we will ask two of Arhat's best fighters to help you train."

Before they began, she handed him something. Jason studied it, curiously.

"Chew on this," she said. "We call it sek root. It's for memory, stamina, and focus."

Jason waited for Juniper's instructions. She asked Tyler to move several feet off to the side. She whistled loudly with her fingers, and the water beneath them gurgled until two giant sea turtles emerged beside him.

Juniper began to rub their shells. "I'd like to introduce you to Mamba and Zed. We're going to begin by learning how to race. First, I'll show you how to properly mount them."

Jason thought it looked easy, but when he tried, he lost his grip and slipped off Mamba.

Tyler cupped his hands around his mouth. "Come on, Jason, you got this."

Jason stood up. "It looks a lot easier than it is."

Eventually, he securely mounted Mamba, and Juniper walked him through how to direct her. "If you want Mamba to move at a moderate speed, say 'zell.' If you want her to increase speed, say 'nebraka,' and if you want her to stop, say 'menai.'"

Juniper led the first ride with Jason following closely behind her. He appreciated the slow pace, allowing him to adjust to Mamba.

Juniper looked back and yelled, "Okay, are you ready to go fast?"

Jason's eyes widened in worry. "Um, this pace is fine."

Juniper shouted "Nabraka," and both sea turtles jetted off at full speed. Jason held on for dear life, struggling to remember the command to slow down. Juniper eventually circled back and shouted, "Menai," which slowed Mamba down, guiding Jason back to the starting point.

Juniper slid off Zed's shell and walked over to Jason and Mamba. "Okay, this time, I want you to sink your hands into Mamba's shell." She guided Jason's hands, positioning them. "Keep your body low."

He nodded. "Got it! Thanks for the tip. I'll try not to fly away this time."

They practiced for another hour, and during a short break, Tyler encouraged him. "You actually looked pretty good out there. Keep up the good work, man."

The next phase of training, Jason came to learn, was free diving and swimming. He always thought he was a strong swimmer because he surfed for many years, but he soon learned that he was mistaken after watching Juniper.

With a smirk on her face, she picked up a stone, and using the surface of the water like a tabletop, spun it on its edge at top speed. She then dove into the water, swimming to the village and back before the stone stopped. Tyler and Jason's mouths hung open—they had no words for how fast she was.

Jason crossed his arms. "Impressive, but I don't think I can do that."

Juniper walked up to him. "Lesson number one, my love: never say you can't do something. First, you must try, and if you fail, try again."

Jason followed as she demonstrated how to maintain stamina and conserve energy while swimming. She also evaluated how comfortable he was holding his breath underwater. Together, they dove down, but after only thirty seconds, Jason couldn't hold his breath any longer and swam back to the surface. He appreciated Juniper's patience as she took him down a few more times, helping him stay underwater a bit longer each dive.

When they resurfaced, Jason slammed his fist against his palm. "Damn, I'm having trouble breaking one minute."

Tyler cheered him on. "Come on, man, I believe in you."

Before descending again, Juniper walked him through a series of meditation and breathing exercises to strengthen his breath work. On the next descent, Jason followed her exact instructions. They sat at the bottom of the lake, legs crossed, holding hands, and stayed calm. He focused on Juniper's teachings. Without realizing it, one minute passed by, then two, then three. They rushed back to the surface.

Jason picked her up and swung her around, kissing her all over her face.

Tyler gave Jason a high-five. "Not even surprised. Knew you could do it."

"You're really going to surprise my brother tomorrow," Juniper said. "Okay, are you ready for the next part of your training?"

Jason rested his knuckles on his hips. "I'm ready. Lead the way."

Juniper took them into the jungle to a place where villagers practiced fighting. When they arrived, Jason saw two of Arhat's warriors training.

Juniper walked up to them. "This is Rusaki and Adnanla, Arhat's best fighters."

Rusaki shifted his weight toward Jason. "Ready to get your ass kicked? We'll make sure you win tomorrow."

Adnanla gave Jason a bow. "It's great to meet you, Jason. It would be our honor to help you. We'll teach you the art of Aiujo. It's a cross between judo and capoeira. Arhat is the only place in the world that practices it."

Jason hesitated, then nodded. "Great to meet you guys. I can't thank you enough."

Rusaki waved him over. "It's our pleasure. Let's get started."

Jason timidly shuffled over to the fighting pit. *Damn, it's been so long since I did judo and these guys are pros.*

He and Rusaki entered a soft, mossy pit, and they squared up. What surprised Jason most was that Rusaki didn't move. He stood still with his eyes closed, meditating until he heard Juniper banging on a set of drums. Rusaki opened his eyes and began swinging his arms around, moving to the music.

Jason tilted his head. "This is a joke, right?"

Just as Jason lunged to take him down, Rusaki dodged and swiped out Jason's feet, putting him into instant submission. Jason was shocked by how quickly the man had brought him down.

Tyler called out, "Get it together, Jason. He's dancing around like a clown."

Rusaki smiled at Tyler, asking him to join.

Jason and Tyler surrounded Rusaki while he quietly meditated. Once again, his eyes opened as the music began, and he swung his body around in harmony. Jason remembered that Tyler used to be a wrestler, so he let him take the first strike, but Rusaki leaped over him. Jason ran up, trying to take him down, but Rusaki spun away, then jumped onto Jason's back like a spider, pulling him to the ground and placing him in a chokehold that made him tap out.

By the time Jason lifted his head, he realized Rusaki was already facing off with Tyler, who came running at him. Rusaki stuck out his leg, grabbed Tyler's shoulder, and tripped him to the ground, making him tap out as well. Jason was impressed. He and Tyler shuffled off to the side, catching their breaths.

Jason applauded. "Okay, we get it. You're superhuman. Please show me how!"

Rusaki smirked and then called for Adnanla to demonstrate a few moves. Jason watched Adnanla's endless barrage of counterattacks until he finally kicked Rusaki's back heel, bringing him to his knees, then crawled onto his back, clinging until he had him in a chokehold. Jason knew it was over for Rusaki, but as he watched him, he noticed a confident grin.

Rusaki shifted his eyes to Jason. "Watch closely. When you're in this situation, do this." He shrugged his shoulders in a way that broke Adnanla's hold on his arms, then he stood, brushing himself off. "And that's how it's done."

Jason had no words, but he felt grateful that they were so willing to train him and teach him moves like that.

For the first hour, they taught him how to move harmoniously with the sounds of the music, which was the art of Aiujo.

The next hour was spent reviewing counterattacks, strikes, and chokeholds. During a sparring session with Adnanla, Jason tried implementing all that he'd learned so far. Just as Adnanla got him into submission, something overtook Jason. He felt himself falling into a dark hole, imagining all his setbacks and all those who'd underestimated him. He broke free, and his attacks became stronger and more precise. When he finally came back to consciousness, he saw himself standing over Adnanla, who looked shocked and was clapping for him.

Jason silently caught his breath as he looked around. "Why are you all staring at me like that?"

Tyler stood up. "Man, you were a damn animal. You're going to crush him tomorrow."

Jason looked at Juniper, who winked at him.

Rusaki patted him on the shoulder. "You have a fire burning on the inside—use that strength tomorrow."

When the sun started to set, they returned to the village, and all Jason could think about on the way back was how grateful he was to have Juniper's help and Tyler's encouragement.

As they walked through the village, Jason admired how the evening light made Arhat such a tranquil atmosphere filled with vibrant energy from its people. Villagers strolled peacefully, conversing, and some sat around sharing drinks and food. The three of them lounged at a small teahouse that reminded Jason of a Mongolian yurt.

Nela passed by, then came to sit with them. "How was the training, Jason? Are you ready for tomorrow?"

Jason placed his hands in his lap. "As ready as I'll ever be, thanks to Juniper."

A smile grew on Nela's face. "You'll do great tomorrow. There's a party down by the beach. Would anyone like to join?"

Tyler's hand bolted up, but Juniper and Jason decided to stay behind to relax and continue chatting. Nela grabbed Tyler, and off they went, leaving Jason alone with Juniper just as they wanted. They became so lost in conversation, he barely noticed that the owner of the yurt had filled their cups three times already.

A few young kids played a game just in front of the yurt. Despite trying to keep his attention on their conversation, Jason couldn't help but ask Juniper about the game. "Sorry to interrupt you, but that game over there, I've seen it before. It's called mahjong, right?"

Juniper glanced over and responded enthusiastically. "Yes, that's a famous game in Arhat."

"Yeah, I recognize it, but isn't it traditionally a Chinese game?"

Juniper gripped her cup with two hands and brought it to her mouth for a sip. "Traditionally, yes, but we play it here too. Legend has it that many years ago, a man from the outside world like you also came to Arhat. He was the first ever, and an extraordinary world traveler. He'd lived in and visited almost every country, and one of the games he brought here was mahjong, from his travels around China. He stayed for many months, settling into Arhatian culture until he became one of us, and then one day, he was gone."

Jason crossed his arms and leaned in. "What do you mean, 'gone'?"

"Supposedly they searched for him all over the island, but they never found him. No one ever saw or heard from him again."

Jason tilted his head, thinking how strange that was. He sipped his tea and looked out, noticing that it was now golden hour, and how beautiful the lighting was over Arhat.

Juniper watched him closely. "Do you have a large family back home?"

Jason turned his focus back on her. "I was raised by my grandparents. My mother and father passed away when I was young."

The corners of her mouth drooped down and her gaze lowered. She rested her hand on his, then looked into his eyes. "I'm very sorry, Jason."

He gave a partial smile. "Thanks. I remember how much they loved each other, and me. Your parents kind of remind me of them, how playful they are with each other. When I was little, my mom would tell me things like 'I love you more than all the stars in the sky.'"

Juniper kept her focus on him. "I can tell they were wonderful people. And your grandparents?"

He jerked his head to the side and smiled. "My grandparents are lovely people. My grandmother has been ill for a while now. She'd want me to stop worrying about her so much though. I can hear her telling me I should be having fun and enjoying the moment."

She moved closer to him and held his hand. "I want to help you find a cure. We'll continue to pray for her."

Jason looked in her eyes, appreciating her. "I haven't told many people this before, but back home, I always felt stuck, with no direction or purpose."

"But that's okay, my love. You're okay, just as you are. It will come to you. I already believe in you so much and your potential. I'm confident that you will find your unique purpose in life."

He continued to hold her gaze. "I've never met a girl who makes me feel the way you do. It's like you understand me without me having to explain myself."

"And I feel that way with you. We've only known each other for a short time, but my heart already tells me how special you are."

He wrapped his arm around her shoulders. For a moment, they kissed, losing sight of everything around them.

"Can I ask you something, Juniper? In Arhat, it seems like everyone has found their unique gift. How did they do that?"

She shifted back. "My father told me growing up to follow these three words: 'Be-Do-Have!' *Be* your true self regardless of what others think. *Do* what is required of you in life, despite the obstacles, and one day you can *have* all that you strived for. Our people do what brings them joy; what their hearts call them to do."

Jason thought, *Be-Do-Have! Is that the magic formula I've been searching for?*

Juniper looked away. "And back home, do you have a wife or children of your own?"

His eyes widened in surprise. "I don't! Most people my age aren't married. And you? Any secret husbands I don't know about?"

Juniper laughed. "Of course not, my love. Have you ever been in love?"

"Not before coming here." Jason sighed. "Back home, I always dated people who never made me feel safe enough to get emotionally invested. With you though, it's a feeling I can't describe."

Juniper teared up and placed her hand on his face. "I've been waiting a long time to meet someone like you."

As happy as Jason was, the biggest issue that dwelled in the back of his mind was whether it was such a good idea to get involved. If he lost the bet, he'd have to leave, and regardless, he'd have to go home sooner or later. His whole life was in San Diego, including his grandparents.

Before it got too late, Jason and Juniper walked back to her place, both aware that he needed rest before his big day tomorrow. Despite his attempts to sleep, Jason tossed and turned throughout the night, too nervous about tomorrow to sleep, so he went for a walk. Along the way, he ran into Eshin, who was quietly sitting next to a lantern, smoking his pipe.

Jason stopped. *Why do I always run into him at the most obscure times?*

Eshin puffed his pipe. "Hello, young Jason. Shouldn't you be resting? Big day tomorrow."

Jason placed a hand on his hip, running the other through his hair. "Tell me about it. I can't sleep at all. And you? Are you always wandering around at this time?"

"Was never much of a sleeper." Eshin blew out smoke. "And why so worried? It's just a few games after all."

Jason took a seat in the sand, resting his head on his knuckles. "I'm just worried that if I lose, I'll have to leave Arhat and Juniper. I'm not ready to go yet."

"Giving up on yourself so soon?"

"Trying not to, but Titi's one of Arhat's greatest athletes."

Eshin chuckled. "The jungle is pretty vast. Plenty of places to hide."

"Thanks, Eshin." Jason smirked. "But I think I'll need more than a good hiding place. You think I can beat him?"

Eshin crossed his arms. "The question isn't if I believe in you, but if you believe in yourself. You must believe in your heart and your mind that you are more than enough."

Jason shook his head. "Easier said than done, but I'm trying, and I appreciate that."

Eshin smiled and then rose, arching over Jason. "Farewell for tonight, young Jason. I will be rooting for you tomorrow."

Jason walked back to Juniper's home to get some sleep, thinking about what Eshin said. It reminded him of something his grandmother once told him: "The most successful people have failed trying, but they succeeded because they never doubted themselves."

CHAPTER 22

OVERCOMING THE ODDS

When Jason woke the next morning, he lay still, letting his eyes adjust to the morning light. Eshin's words still pervaded his thoughts, and as he continued to meditate on them, he felt a surge of energy rise throughout this body, giving him the enthusiasm to take action. He reflected on how far he'd come just to reach Arhat. *Most would have turned back or given up, but not me,* he thought. *Doubt has always been my worst enemy, mostly because I've always been too scared to look fear in the face and tell it to take a hike. Eshin's right—our mindset is everything.* He clenched his fists and breathed harshly through his nostrils. He felt ready to face Titi today. He certainly wasn't about to back down as he had always done in the past—that version of himself would no longer stand in his way. *I'm not going to lose, but if I do, at least I'll know that I gave it my all,* he said to himself.

As he wiped his eyes and washed his face, he heard roaring cheers from outside Juniper's home, "Jason! Jason! Jason!"

He walked out to be greeted by not only Juniper and her family, but several villagers who wanted to walk with him down to Humtay Lake for the games.

Juniper personally escorted Jason, holding his hand as the crowd followed. Jason managed to spot Tyler, who pushed through to catch up with them.

"You didn't think I'd let you have all the fun without me, did you? We're in this together! Look at all these people—you're famous."

Once they reached Humtay Lake, Jason was led out into the center by a spirit guide and they waited for Titi to arrive.

Jason scanned the crowd. He didn't see Titi and secretly hoped he wouldn't come, but then he heard a voice from behind, "Guys, do you see this? Jason actually showed up."

Jason felt slightly sick to his stomach and tried to block out the negative gossip he heard in the crowd, "He doesn't stand a chance. Titi is too good!"

They looked at the guide, awaiting his instructions. Jason's legs and hands shook, and he was sure that Titi sensed his anxiety, but keeping eye contact with Juniper and Tyler gave him the motivation he needed.

The spirit guide announced, "The first challenge will be an underwater race. Each player must collect as many cactus shells as possible. The cactus shells will glow neon green. This particular challenge will test your breath work and agility."

Jason closed his eyes and began taking short breaths, preparing as Juniper taught him. He and Titi were each given a net for collecting the shells.

When the spirit guide's arm swung down, Jason and Titi dove underwater, swimming as fast as they could to the bottom. Although Jason could see the cactus shells glowing brightly, he found them in the most obscure places, under rocks and buried in the sand. He saw that Titi collected them with ease, and after gathering a few himself, Jason felt he had a chance—until everything went wrong. His net got caught on a rock, tearing it open and spilling all the cactus shells he'd collected.

Jason saw Titi laughing and he knew he'd lost this match since he could no longer hold his breath. He swam back to the surface. When Titi got to the top, he threw his fists up in the air, showing everyone that he was the winner. Jason shook his hand. Even though he felt anger and disappointment, he said to himself, "I'm not leaving Arhat! I got this!"

As they rested for a few minutes, Tyler came over to give Jason a pep talk. "Good try, man. I know you're mad right now, but this is only the first game. You got two more to go. Just remember what you learned yesterday. I told you, we're in this together, so no matter what happens today, I got your back, and we'll be okay. I believe in you, and so does Juniper. But for real, I'm not ready to go home yet, so kick his ass."

Jason smiled and gave Tyler a fist bump, feeling grateful for his support. He then looked over at Juniper and thought, *How does she do it? How does she remain so calm, appearing so assured even when things aren't going well?*

Hearing the spirit guide calling them back, Jason walked over to stand next to Titi, awaiting instructions for the next game. Suddenly, two massive shells emerged from the water. The spirit guide explained, "The next challenge will be a race across Humtay Lake through various obstacles."

Jason felt good about this one, especially after being assigned to Mamba, who he had practiced with yesterday. He rubbed her shell and whispered, "We got this girl, right?"

Titi peered over at Jason. "Hope you can at least get on her back."

Jason scoffed and easily mounted, sliding his hands into Mamba's shell.

Titi gasped sarcastically. "Well look at that! Good job, new guy. Now, let's see if you can race. It just happens to be my specialty. Hope you miss home, because after these games, you can say bye to Arhat forever."

Ignoring Titi, Jason remained focused, ready to ride. He listened as the spirit guide told them, "Whoever misses or bypasses any of the obstacles will be disqualified."

The guide extended his arm in the air, and when it came thundering down, they both yelled, "Zell!" and took off at lightning speed.

Jason struggled to see Titi through the mist, but he soon found himself soaring right next to him at an equal pace. Titi smirked before pulling ahead. Jason put his head down, shouting "Nebraka" to go faster. Titi tried to throw him off by zigzagging, but Jason stayed poised.

Just ahead, he saw the first obstacle, a giant water ring in the sky. Titi shot right through it, but Jason had no idea how to make Mamba jump into the air. Scrambling, he tried several things—pulling up, shouting, lifting his body—and just when he thought they were going to miss it, Mamba elevated and made it through. Jason let out a whoop, not knowing how they'd done it.

Refocused, he tried to gain on Titi. When they were side by side, Titi rammed into him, trying to knock him off course, but Jason made it through the next three hoops. He felt relieved, but up ahead, he caught sight of a swirling vortex.

Jason instructed, "Nebraka!" and was baffled when, after Titi went through, he could no longer see him. Nervously, he called "Nebraka," again, until a force of gravity pulled him through the vortex, and he found himself soaring through the sky, eventually landing on the water.

He was still on Mamba's back, drifting in the water, trying to gain back his sense of direction. When he heard the cheering of the crowd, he headed in that direction.

As he raced toward them, he continued, saying to himself, "I'm not losing this race." The only thing that worried him was he didn't see Titi anywhere—until he came flying through the sky, landing close to Jason.

Jason put his head down and kept going with the finish line now in sight. The two rocket-fueled warriors battled it out toward the last obstacle: a bend forming in the water. Titi drifted around it. With a "Nebraka," Mamba picked up speed, and Jason shouted, "This ain't over," kicking in his left foot into Mamba's side to shift weight and drift around the curve, shooting past Titi for the win.

Jason hopped off and looked at the crowd in disbelief. They all chorused, "Jason! Jason! Jason!"

When he went to shake Titi's hand, he was taken back by his comment. "Not bad, new guy! I was kind of impressed, but I let you have that one."

They followed the spirit guide into the jungle for the next challenge. Jason searched for Juniper in the dense crowd of villagers, but couldn't see her. Finally, he spotted her standing behind a couple people just a few feet away. He shot her a wink, feeling more confident as she smiled back at him.

With only one game left to determine the winner, Jason knew he had to really focus. Thankfully, the spirit guide allotted them more time to rest before beginning. Jason sat against a tree and Juniper and Tyler came over to talk to him.

Tyler jumped up and down. "That race was unreal! Okay, one more to go. You can do this."

Juniper grabbed his hands. "Jason, you were amazing out there. My brother is not an easy competitor, but I can tell you shook him up a bit, and rarely does anyone do that to him. This last challenge won't be easy, but just remember what Adnanla and Rusaki taught you. We all believe in you, Jason, no matter what."

He felt uplifted after hearing their enthusiasm, leaping up with a look of determination.

Titi strutted into the mossy green pit where Jason had trained yesterday. To show he wasn't afraid, Jason matched his body language, swinging his arms with his chest lifted.

He carefully watched Titi as he warmed up. *If there's one thing I learned about Titi so far, it's that he's very talented but overly confident.*

As he continued to focus on Titi, he heard Tyler from the sidelines, in his best Michael Buffer voice, "Let's get ready to rumble!"

CHAPTER 23

THE STRENGTH WITHIN

The spirit guide explained, "To win this last challenge, you must pin the other person three times and hold them down for no less than twenty seconds."

Jason could hear the pounding of drums, creating rhythms for Aiujo. The crowd clapped and yelled so loud that it reminded him of the Roman Colosseum. He noticed that all eyes were on him, which made his heart pound even faster.

Titi swung his legs and arms perfectly in sync with the music. He approached with his arms lunging directly at Jason, who deflected his attack and reciprocated with the same attempt.

Jason could sense that Titi was also reading him, trying to predict his next move.

When Titi's leg caught him in the cheekbone, Jason grabbed his face. Titi kicked out his legs and put him in a chokehold. Jason knew he had no option but to tap out.

As they began round two, Jason waited, anticipating Titi would make the first move, but Titi never did, and neither did Jason. Eventually, Titi flew toward him. While trying his best to deflect, Jason found himself in the same position, tapping out again.

He took a few breaths. He knew he couldn't lose this next point or it was over. *Listen to the music,* he reminded himself, and as he did so, his eyes began to flutter and his vision blurred. Those same negative thoughts from training yesterday streamed into his mind. With all his rage, he deflected Titi's strike, threw him to the ground, and held tight until he earned his first point.

Jason couldn't understand why he was experiencing this intense amount of anger. He could tell Titi was caught off guard. When Titi went for the strike again, Jason swiped his feet and pinned him for another point.

Jason shook his head, grabbing his temples to coax his vision back because everything was moving in slow motion.

Jason didn't care about the score—he just wanted to prove to himself that he could beat Titi.

Strategically, Jason and Titi circled each other until Titi charged. Quickly, Jason turned to the side and tripped him, but they both ended up falling. Titi jumped on his back, and Jason was helpless against Titi's strong grip.

Titi whispered in Jason's ear, "You did good, new guy. Now just submit." The words made Jason feel weak and devalued, but instead of giving up, he channeled that harsh feeling inward to motivate himself. He wasn't buying into the belief that he wasn't good enough—not this time, not anymore.

Out of the corner of his teary eye, he saw Rusaki slowly nod at him. By the look in Rusaki's eyes, Jason knew he was trying to tell him it was time to initiate the special move they'd practiced during training.

Breathing heavily, Jason made one big attempt, yelling at the top of his lungs, shrugging his shoulders upward, and hitting Titi directly in an area that caused temporary paralysis. Feeling Titi's grip loosen, Jason watched him struggle to move his arms. He quickly pinned Titi to the ground and held him there for the win.

Jason looked around in shock as the crowd ran toward him. They bombarded him, and Tyler and Hoko hoisted him up in the air. Everyone tried to touch him.

Jason was in so much shock that he was still questioning if he had even won. He called out, "Where's Juniper?" He finally saw her and asked the guys to put him down. Tyler and Hoko lowered him, and Juniper ran full speed toward him and jumped into his arms. He hugged her tightly, knowing that neither one of them wanted to let go.

When Jason saw Titi, he didn't know how he would react, but to his surprise, Titi grabbed his arm and lifted it to the sky with a smile on his face. Relief rolled over Jason, knowing that he'd won the bet and that he and Tyler could stay in Arhat as long as they wanted.

Jason saw Adnanla and Rusaki off to the side and ran over to give them hugs. Rusaki placed his hand on Jason's shoulder. "That, Jason, was your fire; your spirit animal. You are a lion."

Jason was distracted by one of the children pulling on him. When he looked down, he realized it was the boy from the moon festival. "Hey, I remember you. You're little Osito."

Osito became bashful. "You did it, big bro. I knew you could win. I'm so proud of you. I want to be like you one day. You inspire me."

Jason knelt and hugged him. "Yes. I did, little bro. And nope, I want to be like *you*, always a kid at heart."

Tyler's voice cut through. "Yo, Jason, I know you're excited, but who the hell are you talking to."

Jason shot Tyler a strange look. "It's little Osito," he said. But when he tried to introduce him, Osito was gone. "Um, well, he was here just a minute ago."

Juniper grabbed Jason's hand. "Come with me. Let's get out of here."

Jason agreed and followed as they ran until the sounds of the villagers faded.

"Where are we going?" he said.

Juniper didn't look back and kept running. "Just follow me!"

She took him to a secluded beach where they spent the rest of the day swimming in the ocean, dancing, and singing. As the sun set, they made a small fire and sat by the edge of the beach, where the ocean touched the sand. Waves washed over their feet as they stared out at the water stretched between two giant cliffs, the gateway to a never-ending ocean lit up by the moon and stars.

Jason felt like they were the only people on Earth. "Hello, world! Can you hear me?" he yelled. He tucked his arms around his knees. *I'm in a world that most people will never discover. Why am I really here though? Am I like the man who brought the game of mahjong, just passing through?*

Juniper rested her head on his shoulder. "So, you really like it here, huh?"

Jason lifted his arm to place it around her. "That's an understatement—I love it here."

He watched her remove a small rope bracelet from her wrist, decorated with little Arhatian charms, and tie it around his. She pointed out the charms one by one. "This one means love, this one is strength, and the other is friendship."

"And what about this?" Jason pointed to the letters *J & J* engraved into the heart charm.

She smiled up at him. "That's our initials—I was hoping you'd notice."

He smirked, and from his pocket, he pulled a white string bracelet and slipped it around her wrist.

He told her, "This one means love, this one means strength, and the other means friendship. Your sister, Lotusa, helped me make it."

Their emotions stirred, and Jason knew they both felt a wild energy for each other. As they spent the rest of the night on the beach, he watched the sky shift like a time-lapse and listened to the waves crashing against the rocks. He smiled with his gaze fixed on the endless ocean and Juniper curled up under his arm.

Walking through the village the next day, Tyler and Jason ran into Juniper's father, Tiko, who was lugging a giant pink snapper on his back. "Hello, boys, how are you today? You see this fish? I caught it with my bare hands. I can show you how if you want. Hope you boys are ready for another Arhatian celebration soon. Arhat's Lunar Som festival is next week."

"Really?" Jason said excitedly. "What's special about this one?"

Tiko adjusted the fish on his back. "The day is important because it marks the energy of Arhat at its strongest throughout the entire year. The collective prayers of the villagers deeply penetrate the subconscious minds of humanity, bringing peace and love to all for one whole day. Look up at the sky—you can already see the shade of the moon slowly transforming."

Jason observed a faint blue moon with hints of purple and felt excitement for yet another amazing festival to enjoy. But even so, thoughts of his grandmother brought him back to reality. His main priority was to find her a cure, and although he loved Arhat, he knew that soon he'd need to return home.

CHAPTER 24

THE FESTIVAL OF LUNAR SOM

As Jason really began to settle into Arhat, he grew accustomed to the ways of the village. Tiko took Jason and Tyler hunting and fishing. They also helped the artists prepare costumes and decorations, raced sea turtles with Titi, and explored the vast jungle with Juniper, Nela, Lala, and Hoko. Jason even decided to get into the habit of writing each morning, trying his best to record everything that had happened so far on his journey.

The day of the Lunar Som festival, Jason strolled the vibrant streets flooded with villagers adorned in jewelry and paint. Small fireworks exploded, musicians played, and people danced. Some were already praying while children chased local dogs.

Suddenly, Jason was pulled into a passing throng of dancers, surprised to find Tyler beside him. They broke away and went off to the side. Jason spotted Juniper running off with a group of girls, but she didn't hear him when he called. He was pleasantly surprised when Nela, Lala, and Hoko popped out of the crowd, bedazzling him and Tyler with colorful blue stone necklaces.

Nela marked Jason's face with paint. "Are you boys ready to celebrate?"

Jason pulled back. "Of course we are, but what about Juniper? Will she be joining us?"

Nela placed another necklace around his neck. "Later. It's a surprise. Let's go, boys."

Jason shrugged and followed Nela through the crowd, trying to keep up with her. He occasionally looked back to ensure Tyler and the others were also keeping up. They squeezed past people dressed in marvelous feathered headdresses. He noticed that all the women were wearing glittery blue-and-white outfits with a million gold bracelets on their wrists and forearms. Their hands were laden with turquoise rings, and some had glistening silver chains running from their nose to their ears. White and red flowers rained down from the windows of homes, and the smell of grilled meats and local veggies blended with the sweetness of fresh fruits, making Jason's mouth water. Finally, they entered a giant yurt, which served as a dressing room where villagers decked themselves out in traditional costumes, preparing for different dances throughout the day.

Amused, Jason watched as Nela grabbed various garments, holding them up to him and Tyler, imagining how they would look. Lala enjoyed painting them with symbols of peace while they dressed in vibrant lime-green and orange vests and white silk pants.

Hoko brought over two fancy headdresses and placed one on Jason. "For you, Jason. This one is closest to your spirit animal. You are a lion—brave, trustworthy, and strong."

Jason admired the reddish-yellow fur and feathers of his headdress. Next, Hoko placed one on Tyler. It was adorned with long orange, black, and yellow feathers that draped down his back. "And for you, Tyler. You are the tiger—cunning and bold."

Dressed in their festival gear, Jason felt ready to party. He noticed Tyler tapping a rhythm out on his legs in excitement. They followed Nela and the others through the village, pushing past people. Occasionally, they stopped to feast on small bites of food and to take gulps of refreshing tazwack.

As the group strolled the congested village paths, Jason and Tyler partook in games and were pulled into various dances. Jason marveled at the chaos and joy of it all. Children were making paper sky lanterns and lining them up in the street to be taken to the festival grounds later that night. He saw Tyler smash a few Arhatian piñatas that exploded with colorful yellow butterflies. Jason balanced himself on two coconuts while Lala, Nela, and Hoko created giant bubbles filled with their prayers, which were carried off into the world to reach people in need.

Nearby, Jason was unsurprised to see Tyler was enamored by all the jeweled necklaces and bracelets scattered on the ground after being indiscriminately tossed into the crowd. Jason rolled his eyes as his friend began to stuff his pockets. Tyler always got distracted by anything with monetary value.

Jason watched Nela kneel beside Tyler, gently grabbing his hand. "You know, my dear, this doesn't hold any value here. It's just for decoration."

Tyler looked confused. "You're telling me this ruby necklace is worthless? This is probably worth at least a million dollars."

Nela giggled. "Maybe where you're from, but not here. Our currency is love. Our wealth is measured by how much love we contribute to the world."

Tyler dropped the items, staring at them, then back at Nela. "Yeah, I guess you're right. If anything, those poor people I witnessed during the group meditation are the ones who truly need it. If I could use it to help them all, I would."

Nela kissed him on the cheek. "Now that's one way to make it valuable."

Is that the same Tyler? Jason thought. Passing up ruby necklaces. Was he finally having a change of heart? Had his perspective on wealth shifted?

As the sky grew dark, the sun moving like a ticking clock, everyone transitioned from celebrating in the village to the jungle.

Jason followed the others, awed by the mystical transformation of the jungle path into a grand stage, reminiscent of Narnia or Pandora.

Along a well-lit trail, he recognized Chanthira standing with a few people. Waving, he noticed something off about Chanthira's eyes. From afar, they were greenish blue, but as he passed her, they turned pure black and stared at him like a possessed porcelain doll. He looked away and then back to her. Her skin was a pale yellowish green with deep cuts and slashes all over her face oozing white pus. She gave him a crooked smile with her sharp teeth biting into her bottom lip, which caused blood to drip down her chin as her eyes shifted to red and fixated on him.

Jason blinked. Chanthira was normal again, laughing with the others. He shuddered, feeling a horrid drop in his stomach as goosebumps crawled up his skin. *Did nobody else see that?*

Tyler bumped his arm. "What's wrong with you, man? Everything okay?"

Jason rubbed his face. "Yeah, I thought I saw something back there. It's nothing, though."

Reaching the festival grounds, Jason found it to be even more magnificent. The landscape resembled the vast plains of Wyoming's Grand Teton National Park, with a dark, rich blood orange moon like a yolk slipping behind the mountains. The greenish grass was soft against his bare feet, unlike the jungle's moss and thick vines.

As night fell, the festival grounds were full of life. A giant fire burned in the center—the focal point for a proper Arhatian gathering, Jason thought.

He observed villagers who rang tambourines and played hand drums while others in colorful feathered dresses and creative animal masks juggled fire batons.

Jason and Tyler continued to lose themselves in the enchantment of the festivities. With magic in the air, the Arhatians exhibited a childish joy and zest for life. Young lovers basked in each other's presence, chasing their desires. Villagers of all ages twirled each other around, and a nearby spring was filled with people swimming.

Sitting by the fire, Jason surveyed the eclectic crowd. A man walked by in a panic, talking to himself, "Where's my Advocate? Have you seen my Advocate?"

Jason just watched the man in curiosity, raising his arms and shaking his head since he had no idea what he meant.

The old man stumbled on, continuing to murmur to himself.

"Hey, Jason, I need your help with something."

Jason turned to see Titi juggling a bunch of limes.

"I'm working on my spin kicks. Can you throw this lime at me? I'm going to kick it as fast and hard as I possibly can." Titi began stretching his legs.

Jason wound up like a pitcher and hurled the limes toward Titi. In a 360-degree motion, Titi's foot connected, launching the limes like a golf ball, which landed in someone's cup, splashing them. Jason and Titi fell to the ground in laughter.

Off to the side, Jason noticed poets creating stanzas, painters working on whatever came to their imagination, and sculptors carving things out of tree trunks. Musicians played alongside the poets, and the paper lanterns Jason saw earlier in the village were being launched.

He then felt vibrations in the ground as drums began to beat steadily. Mongurt and Katalan appeared, likely to give their usual speech. The rumbling grew, accompanied by the sounds of giant footsteps. Jason was shocked when two enormous white elephants emerged. Their tusks were long and rounded. Encased in woven pastel blankets and crowned with colorful jeweled headdresses, they stood on their hind legs and blew their trunks loudly.

The drums picked up speed, the flames of the fire changed colors, and spirit animals soared through the sky. The focal fire released elephants, falcons, eagles, and bears, but then all became calm. A soft flute and guitar followed the drum's pace, and everyone settled. The fire and all the surrounding torches throughout the grounds were put out.

A delicate female foot covered in Sak Yant body art appeared out of the darkness. She rotated her ankle to the music, revealing herself slowly. Her coin jewelry rattled as she twirled her hands and moved her hips. Her face was still hidden in the shadows, and her body was partially covered by a red shawl with her belly and legs exposed. She moved gracefully. An angelic smile greeted the crowd, which Jason immediately recognized. The woman was

Juniper, leading a group of dancers behind her.

Their hips shook like belly dancers', and their long wavy black hair fell down their backs. Their light blue crop tops clung to their bodies. Spirit animals reappeared, flying around and through them. Jason sat entranced, never taking his eyes off Juniper, mesmerized by the speed of her feet.

Millions of sky lanterns were released, carrying prayers. Then, like a light switch, everything went dark except for the glowing lanterns. Jason stood, clapping with the others for the incredible performance.

When the flames relit, the women bowed. Jason wasted no time navigating through the villagers to find Juniper. He could see that she was searching for him too. Reaching her, he hugged her from behind. She turned into him and he hugged her again. "You look so beautiful. Your performance was wonderful."

Afterward, Jason and Juniper followed everyone over to a long table for a grand feast. The table was filled with various fruits, desserts, meats, vegetables, and drinks. Jason sat with Juniper, taking in his surroundings. She was acting more flirtatious than usual, constantly gazing at him and keeping her hands on his. Feeling inseparable, they soon ventured away from the feast. Jason saw that their friends, including Tyler, were tossing a pomegranate around near the fire, but instead of joining the group, Juniper took Jason's hand and led him into the jungle.

"Hey, come with me. I want to show you another one of my secret places."

Jason followed without hesitation, as she pulled him through the dark forest. They reached a bed of glowing purple lilies. He felt the soft petals brush against his legs. Juniper turned toward him, wrapping her arms around his neck and caressing his face, pulling him down to lie in the flowerbed. Their cheeks pressed together, and Jason felt the warmth of her skin. He pulled her in, pinning her arms down as he kissed her neck and body.

Their kisses became more profound and their hearts beat faster. Juniper's hands ran through his hair, holding it tight. Their passion intensified, and simultaneously lightning burst in the sky, followed by thunder. Jason felt the moist heat clinging to their skin as they rolled in the lilies. Soon, they were like two volcanoes, ready to erupt, until a euphoric release overtook them. They lay there for a moment after, unmoving, staring at each other. Juniper brushed her fingers through Jason's hair and they laughed a little. He felt the rain but noticed that they were mostly protected under a large canopy of leaves.

Jason stroked her face. "Are you okay?"

She pulled him closer, holding onto him. They listened to the rain trickling off the plants. Jason knew, as did Juniper, that there had been much anticipation leading to this moment.

Despite his desire to start a new chapter with Juniper, Jason felt a lingering uncertainty. *Is it selfish if I leave now? Is it even more selfish if I try to take her back to San Diego?*

Juniper wrapped her body around him like a koala bear and placed her small hand on his chest. "Your heart is beating fast."

They lingered for a while, wishing that they could freeze time. Eventually, they stood and walked through the fluorescent petals, washing in a nearby spring. They tittered at the thought of rejoining the celebration but decided against it, preferring to be alone.

Suddenly, Jason felt the earth shaking. "Did you just feel that?"

"Yes, that was strange." Juniper stopped to listen.

"Interesting, do earthquakes happen often?"

She shook her head. "Never!"

When Juniper stood to stretch, Jason covered his mouth in shock. "Juniper, what happened to your back? There are bruises and cuts all along it. Those weren't there before."

Juniper caught the reflection of her back in the spring. She covered her mouth, buckling at the knees. She held a hand up to him and said, "It's not you. It's not even these cuts. Something is wrong, Jason. I know it. I can feel it. We need to find the others now."

CHAPTER 25

A DEMON IN THE GARDEN

When they reached the celebration grounds, Jason saw the disbelief on Juniper's face. Nobody was sleeping in the fields as usual. The place looked deserted, which made Jason shiver.

Juniper paced back and forth. "We need to go to the village at once. We're in danger."

Confused and worried, Jason ran after her. They arrived just in time for an announcement from Mongurt, "My brothers and sisters. Last night, a terrible sign was inflicted upon Arhat and our people. Our dear friend Eshin is no longer himself—evil has invaded his soul. Do not be afraid, for together, we are strong. To ensure our safety and the interest of humanity, please look after one another, so we can stop whatever evil is out there. Please do not be afraid."

Jason couldn't believe his ears. He trembled, placing his hands behind his neck. "Eshin! Did he just say Eshin? There's no way. Eshin wouldn't hurt a fly," he muttered to himself. Tyler, Nela, Lala, and Hoko ran over to them. Juniper hugged her friends, making sure they were okay.

"Jason, we may have seen some crazy stuff on this journey, but nothing like last night. Eshin transformed into the devil," Tyler said.

Nela recounted the details, "Juni, it was awful, absolutely awful. Never in my life have I witnessed such terrible things. We were all just having fun when a few young hunters came to the festival, dragging Eshin behind them. Nobody could believe it. They said they found him chanting in the jungle, dancing around a fire, and casting spells, and his skin appeared to be melting off his face. They said his body shape shifted between human and creature, and he would drop to the ground, holding his stomach in pain, and then try to stand back up. The most frightening part was when they said Eshin's head slowly spun until he locked eyes with them. They could even hear his bones cracking. At that moment, they said they knew they had to put an end to this, so they charged him, dragged him down, and tied him up. When they brought him to the festival before everyone, Mongurt was outraged and demanded that he be released. That's when they explained to Mongurt what they saw. When they were done, Mongurt turned to Eshin and said, 'Dear friend, tell me this is not true,' but Eshin never replied. Instead, he released a cackle and vanished in a puff of smoke."

Jason tried to piece it together, but nothing Nela said made sense. He reached out to console Juniper, but she pushed past him. "Jason, stay with Tyler. I need to find my family now. I promise I'll be back."

The rest of the afternoon, everyone dispersed and stayed in their homes. For once, the village was quiet and deserted. As Jason and Tyler walked the sandy trails of Arhat, they got a whiff of something familiar and delectable. It was Auntie Zaza's umberry bread.

Tyler peered at Jason. "After last night, I could definitely do with some umberry bread."

As they walked up to her hut, Tyler got distracted by Manana, and knelt to pet her.

Jason stopped before entering. “Are you coming in?”

Tyler kept petting Manana. “I’ll be there in a minute, you go ahead.”

Jason walked in. “Knock, knock, it’s one of your favorite people, Jason!”

He was relieved to see Auntie Zaza baking, likely to take her mind off last night’s incident.

She looked over at him. “What a lovely surprise. Come on in. And Juniper?”

“Thanks, Auntie. I couldn’t resist the smell of your bread. Juniper is with her parents and sisters. She’s concerned about what happened last night, as we all are. It’s crazy that this happened.”

“She needs you, Jason. We all need you. Hehehe.” Her high-pitched laugh and the way she phrased her comment seemed peculiar to Jason.

She asked for Jason’s assistance to take the bread from the oven, and when he went to help her, she wrapped her hand around his bicep. “I need your strong arms.”

She continued to make him feel uncomfortable, especially when she rubbed his arms again. Jason decided it was time to leave, but when he tried, Auntie Zaza stopped him, barring his way. “Oh no, I wouldn’t want you to leave now. I need you. We all need you,” she said, laughing hysterically.

Jason jumped back, pushing her arm away. Her eyes lost all color, and then turned red. They were the same red eyes that had been following him.

He couldn’t move, he couldn’t speak, and her devilish cackle continued until she asked, “Do I startle you?”

Jason trembled and stuttered.

She shut the door to the hut. "I don't expect you to say much. You're pathetic. You're worthless. How can Juniper consider you a man, especially once you leave her? And your grandmother, she will die too, hehehehe."

Jason mustered up the courage. "That's enough. What did you do to Auntie Zaza?"

"Hehehe." She mocked him further. "Somebody is getting upset, I see."

Jason tried to run, but she stopped him, swiftly crawling past him on all fours like a spider. She grabbed him by the throat with her skinny, veiny hands.

He looked with horror at her pale, blistered skin and dry, brittle hair. Her tongue slithered from her mouth like a snake's, covering him in saliva. She made little slashes over his face with her long, sharp nails, causing him to cry in pain, and he watched as she enjoyed the taste of his blood.

He heard a dog barking and was relieved to see that it was Manana. The dog ran up and bit Auntie Zaza on the leg, causing her to release Jason, but she smacked Manana aside, making her whimper and run out of the hut.

As Jason tried to regain his breath, Tyler rushed in, yelling for help.

Jason's vision became blurry, but he saw a few hunters enter the hut. Auntie Zaza hissed at them and escaped. At that moment, he passed out.

Jason woke a few moments later, slightly incoherent. He felt like he was being carried somewhere. Everything and everyone was so blurry, and he could faintly hear concerned voices.

"We can't let anyone know about this."

"We'll take him to a discreet location, by the cove."

"We must get a doctor."

As he lay there, delirious, he overheard Tyler, "Jun, it's hard for me to tell you this, but it was Auntie Zaza who attacked Jason. She was possessed."

"Not Auntie," she cried. "Not my Auntie Zaza. Please don't tell me that." She ran to Jason's side. "Oh, my love, you'll be okay. I'm not leaving you."

Jason then heard another woman's voice, "You must blot his head and lips with sisu root. It will help his lungs and respiratory system."

As Jason gained full consciousness, he looked around and saw everyone in a panic. He saw Juniper and Tyler speaking with Mongurt and Katalan.

Jason called out, "Guys, I'm okay. Everything is fine." He waved his hands around. "Can you hear me?"

Strangely, nobody responded, except for a small voice, "Don't worry, big bro, you're going to be okay. You're strong like a lion."

Jason looked beside him, and to his pleasant surprise, it was little Osito. "Hey, little bro. Of course I'm okay. Why does everyone look so concerned?"

"You'll be okay, big bro. I know you will. Can we go surfing soon?"

Jason high-fived him. "Of course, but Osito, are you the only one who can hear me?"

Osito looked up at him. "Love you, big bro. I have to go now," he said, and as he walked out of the medical hut, Jason passed out again.

He woke to Mongurt's deep voice. "He's waking up." Everyone rushed to his side.

Tyler stood over him. "Rise and shine, bud. We thought you were a goner."

Jason rose, bringing a hand to his aching head. "What? What do you mean? Tyler, man, we're going to be late. We got to get to the pizza shop. Art's going to kill us."

Tyler laughed. "Don't worry about Art—we're a long way from the pizza shop."

Jason shook his head. "Sorry, I'm fine. Where's Juniper? Is Auntie Zaza on the loose? You have to find her so she doesn't harm anyone else. Some evil took over her body."

Juniper hugged him. "I'm here, my love. Just rest, you don't have to speak now."

Katalan and Mongurt came to sit next to Jason and made sure he was okay before leaving him with Juniper to get some more rest.

When Jason fell back asleep, flashes of evil Auntie Zaza entered his mind. "Lucky boy, such a lucky boy. Your grandmother will die, this village will die, and so will your love with Juniper."

He woke in a cold sweat, realizing it was just a nightmare. Beside him, Juniper was sleeping peacefully. He stepped outside to get some fresh air. Still overly concerned, he wondered why his grandmother of all people had anything to do with this. Jason racked his mind for possibilities. *It's all so bizarre. Nothing makes sense—first, Eshin, and now, Auntie Zaza. And my grandmother?*

Could whatever had possessed Auntie Zaza have been watching him all along with those red eyes? If only he could speak to Eshin right now. He needed to find Jesepa first.

Quietly, Jason made his way to Jesepa's home, and when he entered, he saw him curled up in a dark corner, looking depressed.

Jason sat down next to him. At first they didn't speak. Finally, Jesepa broke the silence, "She's out there somewhere, ya know. My sweetheart. And here I am sitting on my ass. I'm happy you're safe though, Jason. I was notified that *it* escaped, not my wife."

Jason hung his head low, legs extended out on the floor. "Of course it wasn't Auntie Zaza."

Jesepa covered his face with his hands. "Why her though? Why my beautiful wife?"

Jason turned toward him and placed a hand on his shoulder. "We're going to find her and get to the bottom of what's happening around here, I promise."

Jason tried to give him hope but deep down, he was petrified, wishing he could leave Arhat immediately. But how could he abandon these people who had been so kind to him, and especially his love, Juniper?

CHAPTER 26

BARGAINING WITH BRAVERY

The next day, as Jason and Juniper walked through one of Arhat's local markets, a woman began screaming as she pointed at her baskets of fruit.

Jason rushed over. "Is everything okay?" The woman's face went pale. She let out another shriek before covering her mouth, her hand trembling as she pointed down at the ground. A giant maggot crawled out of from a plump mangosteen. Jason's eyes widened in a panic. He turned his gaze back toward the basket, knocking it to the ground. He crushed the scattered fruit with his foot. They were all infested with white sticky maggots.

Almost simultaneously, he heard Hoko yell in the distance, "She's sick! We need to help her."

Jason followed Juniper down to Humtay Lake, where Mamba was sprawled out, lifeless. Her once prominent shell was dull and faded like brown-skinned potatoes covered in spores. Her eyes were heavy and purple spots covered her skin. Jason saw a villager look at the sky, and when he looked up too, the day was slowly turning into night. The moon passed before the sun like a solar eclipse. The air became cold and images appeared depicting the demise of humanity: widespread war, famine, and catastrophic natural disasters.

Jason saw flashing images of his grandmother. He heard the sound of a teacup shattering as she fell to the ground in pain. He saw his grandfather help her inside so she could rest, and all he could hear her say was, "It's Jason. Something's not right. I'm worried about him."

The moon passed, bringing light back to the day, but the Arhatians were frightened. He was even more concerned now.

He didn't explain himself to Juniper, but he ran from Humtay Lake, leaving her and the others behind, and went to the secluded beach where he and Juniper had spent several nights. He needed to clear his mind as he became overwhelmed.

As Jason paced back and forth, he knew if anyone had the answers, it was Eshin. He had to find him, but what if he was still possessed?

He began to speak aloud, "Should I go alone? Should I bring Juniper, Tyler, or the others? No, I can't. I don't want anything to happen to them."

He paused his inner wrestling and made a plan to start by checking Eshin's usual spots, and if he wasn't there, then Jason would come back to the village before sundown.

With enough daylight left, he headed toward the jungle, undetected until a voice stopped him.

"You're not going alone." Juniper appeared.

Jason stopped in his tracks. "Juniper, what are you doing here?"

She walked up to him. "I know you're going to find Eshin, and I'm coming with you."

He placed his hands on her shoulders and leaned into her face. "I don't want anything to happen to you though. I think you should stay here."

"I love your confidence right now." She smiled, a hint of sarcasm in her tone. "But you should be more worried about yourself than me. I know this jungle."

Jason shook his head, grinning. "You win—let's go. I was going to check Eagle's Cliff first. He sometimes sits there smoking his pipe."

Juniper placed her finger to her chin. "He might also be at the Monkey Steps."

When they arrived at Eagle's Cliff, Jason was disappointed to find Eshin wasn't there. At the Monkey Steps, they climbed to the top and searched for him, but again, he was nowhere to be seen.

They stopped to rest for a few minutes and lay on their backs. Jason turned his head to her. "It's not looking so good. Should we go back to the village?"

Juniper sat up in a hurry. "The celebration grounds—we have to check there before we go back."

When they arrived, Jason called for Eshin and they searched everywhere, but he wasn't there. A sense of defeat rolled over him. He was frustrated and yelled, "Whatever is out there, if you want me, come and get me. Leave Arhat alone. Leave my grandmother alone."

At that moment, Jason looked down, realizing he had just stepped into a giant footprint. They followed the trail of footprints right to the edge of a cliff.

The smell of old cedar and licorice reminded Jason of Eshin. *He has to be here.* He called for him, "Eshin, it's Jason and Juniper. We need to talk. We know it wasn't you."

They heard nothing at first, and then a voice responded close by, "And they expect me to do something about it. After all, I'm just old Eshin. One day we're friends for hundreds of years, and the next, I'm reduced to their hunted prey."

Juniper found him. He was just beyond the cliff, floating in the KaRas dust. "Eshin, I don't blame you for anything. I know my brother and the rest of the village are after you, but I refuse to believe any of it."

Eshin chuckled. "Don't worry, you two, your doubts about me are understandable, and you don't have to justify yourselves. You're here now, aren't you?"

Jason rushed to Juniper's side. "Of course, Eshin, but how do we stop this evil?"

Eshin calmly smoked his pipe. "Arhat is trying to stop the evil that I came so close to defeating." He went into detail. "I was fighting with this evil the night of the Lunar Som festival and had almost banished it for good, but when the hunters dragged me down, it escaped, and now it's among us. It seeks destruction as a debt for the pain it endured in its earthly body."

Juniper looked at Jason, confused, then back at Eshin. "What are we dealing with here? What will become of our home if we don't stop it?"

Smoke from Eshin's pipe rose into the sky. "Unfortunately, my dear, we are dealing with a force so dark that even I struggled to overcome it. If we do not stop it, Arhat will be no more."

Juniper sank to the ground with a look of despair.

Jason turned to Eshin. "And my grandmother, is it true? Is her life also at risk?"

Eshin remained silent for a moment. "Unfortunately, it is. This evil is out to destroy all forms of love. It's not easy to tell you this, but it holds the power to accelerate your grandmother's cancer. If we defeat this evil, she will be cured."

Jason had difficulty processing his words. His mouth hung open, and his eyes were wide as he pushed against his forehead. "That can't be! We need to stop this evil together, right, Eshin?"

Again, Eshin paused. "I'm afraid this is not my fight, young Jason, nor is it Juniper's or any others'. Only you."

Jason laughed a bit hysterically. "Me? What do you mean, only me?"

Eshin chuckled. "After all you've been through, you still doubt yourself?"

Jason was frustrated. "Ha! Good one, Eshin! Just to remind you, you're basically telling me only I can stop the Devil himself. So, yes, I do doubt myself—you're one hundred percent correct."

Eshin took a deep breath. "Do you remember the story about the foreign man who came to Arhat? He learned our ways and even found a woman to love. They were an inseparable force, and their love was envied by all. They would spend countless hours at their favorite cove, discussing life and their future together. One evening, she sat alone, peering out into the ocean, and just beside her, she noticed a small paper scroll pinned under a stone. When she removed the stone, the message read, *'My love, you have given me more happiness than one could find in a lifetime of travels. You gave me purpose, a home, and a family. I'm sorry, but I can no longer stay here with you for reasons I cannot explain. The world has called me to continue my journey. I feel that if I do stay, I will only cause you pain. My days grow shorter for reasons I rather not reveal, and I would never want to put you through that pain. I want you to know that I will always love you.'*

"She almost fainted at what she read and didn't want to believe it, so she placed the letter back under the stone and pretended that she never saw it. To her, life wasn't worth living without him. Over time, she grew distant from everyone and slept each night at the cove in case he returned.

"Days turned into months, and she no longer felt any purpose for hanging on. She believed that the only way to free herself from this pain was to give her spirit up to the sky. She went down to the cove overlooking the ocean, a normal escape for her, but this time, she wasn't leaving. As the sun rose, she turned to the ocean, cast a spell, and fell backward, instantly transforming into a dove, her spirit animal. She flew out into the distance, but instead of peacefully crossing over, she burned up, and her ashes scattered across the ocean. This place became known as Katrice's Cove. She had rested peacefully for many years, or so we thought. When I spoke with Katrice that night, during the Lunar Som festival, she said she wanted to prevent anyone from ever loving again. This is where you come in, Jason. You and Juniper, your love has awoken her. She wants to destroy the bond you two have and everything that you love."

Juniper inched closer. "How is this possible? I never heard this part of the story before."

Jason stayed silent, staring at the ground. He looked up. "How do I stop her?"

"All the answers live within you, young Jason."

Jason wasn't convinced by his cryptic answer. "Come on, Eshin, I need real solutions right now. I need your help."

Eshin blew another puff of smoke. "I must go now. I feel myself still too weak after fighting with this evil. You shall prevail, if you choose to believe in yourself."

He disappeared into the sky as Jason tried to reach out for him. "Eshin, wait—I still have questions. Please, you can't leave us like this."

All went silent. He was gone.

Jason fell to his knees. "Why me? I can't do this."

Juniper placed her arms around him. Both were afraid but confident in themselves to do all they possibly could to save Arhat and his grandmother.

Jason insisted they needed to return to the village to get the others before the sun set. As they ran through the jungle, he looked around in worry as it became dark, and the trees grew increasingly withered and depleted.

"This isn't real," Juniper cried out. "This cannot be happening to my home; my beloved Arhat. I need to find my family, Jason."

As they ran, the sounds of dying animals and crying babies tormented them. Some even mocked Jason.

"Why me?"

"Why me?"

"I can't!"

"Hehe."

He tried to block it out as he saw Juniper shake her head and shout, "Stop it! Stop it! It's not real!"

Jason grabbed her hand. "What's wrong?"

"It's my little sister Lotusa. I can hear her." Tears were streaming down Juniper's face.

Jason could also hear Lotusa's voice. "Help, Juniper, help me. We need you, hehe," but that devilish laugh was proof to Jason that they were only being teased by the evil spirit.

The sky lit up with the largest shock of lighting Jason had ever seen. Everything around them became clear, including each other, and then dark again. Jason rubbed his eyes. "What was that?" But he heard no answer from Juniper. He called for her, "Jun, this isn't a time to be playing games." Nothing. He screamed out her name, "Juniper! Juniper!" but the only voices he heard were the creepy children mocking him. "I'm not leaving until I find you, Jun. Just like you didn't leave my side until I woke."

But his search became hopeless. Sitting there in the darkness, feeling defeated, he talked to her, "I should have never brought you along. I'm sorry. I'm going to find you. I promise I won't let anything happen to you."

He got up and ran back to the village, and what he saw when he arrived left him in complete and utter shock. He dropped to his knees for a moment, thinking, *How could this have happened?*

CHAPTER 27

POINT OF NO RETURN

The village was a barren wasteland, making it seem like a fallout town. All the homes were abandoned and dilapidated. People's possessions were broken, torn, and scattered in the streets. Some of the villagers ran around with goblin faces, hiding in the shadows. The golden sandy streets were no longer warm and soft; instead, they resembled black volcanic ash.

Jason spotted Hoko on his knees, covering his stomach with his hands. When Jason asked where the others were, Hoko looked at him with sad eyes and vomited massive amounts of blood beside Jason's feet.

Jason ran away from Hoko, searching for the others, and found Lala next. She was madly stomping on something and shouting, "I hate you! I hate you!" She had gathered all the little gifts that Jason and Juniper had given to each other and was breaking them to bits, laughing. She spat at Jason. "I hate you and Juniper. I hate you both, hehe."

Jesepa had also fallen victim. When Jason found him, his face was blue, and his stomach was bloated and as big as a beach ball. There were tons of food platters around him. It looked like someone had force-fed him until he choked to death.

Arhat's warriors, including Titi, were no longer hunting animals but their own people. They were throwing spears through them, slashing their necks, and slinging rocks at their heads.

Jason grabbed his chest, taking several deep breaths. His legs felt like they were made of lead, but he knew he had to keep moving or else they would spot him.

He managed to sneak by them unnoticed and was only steps away from Mongurt and Katalan's home. It seemed to be the only yurt in the village that was vibrant—the smell of delicious food lingered and music played. He crept over, and when he peeked inside, it looked like they were having a great time.

He shook his head in disbelief. "This is despicable."

When he walked in, he saw Katalan lounging on her side, naked, smoking a hookah, and being fed grapes by some of the hunters from the village.

Mongurt was sitting on a throne, grasping a cup of tazwack.

Jason was distraught. *How can they lie around like sloths while their people die?*

Katalan waved him over. "Ahhh, Jason, make yourself at home. Join us."

"Come, Jason, this is one of Arhat's most glorious moments. We're purging. We're going through a cleansing process to produce everything new. Isn't it splendid?"

Mongurt extended his arm, pointing to a slithering serpent next to him. Jason noticed the shape of a small animal outlined in the snake's stomach.

Mongurt tilted his head back laughing hysterically. "It looks like your little friend Manana was a nice treat."

Jason reared back, his heart pounding. Manana, the little village dog that saved him from Auntie Zaza, was in the stomach of this slithering beast.

Katalan's eyes bore into Jason's. Images flashed in his mind of Juniper being raped, and her family being executed, but he broke away from the hypnosis and ran out of the yurt.

He searched desperately for Tyler and finally heard his feeble voice, "Look at me, man. Look what she did to me."

Jason hurried over to his friend. "Ty, is that you? What's wrong?"

In agony, he cried out, "Look what she did to me, man."

Jason pulled Tyler's hands away from his face to reveal that his eyes had been replaced with two shiny green emeralds, blood dripping around them. Jason fell back in fear, stumbling in the sand, and shielded his eyes. He stood hastily and moved backward but tripped over a stone.

"It was Auntie Zaza!" Tyler screamed. "She offered me the treasure from the temple, but Nela called me away. I chose Nela. I chose this place, not the treasure, so Auntie Zaza took my eyes."

Jason dodged as Tyler tried to lunge out and grab him. "Ty, man, I'm so sorry I left you. I'm sorry I convinced you to come here in the first place. I promise I'm going to get you out of here. You have to believe me. I'll be back, I promise."

As he walked away, he heard Tyler cry out to him, "Don't leave me like this. Look what she did to me."

Jason carefully made his way through the village, hiding behind homes in his path. He felt hopeless and had no luck finding Juniper. As he hyperventilated, he leaned his back against one of the village huts. Tears flushed his eyes, and knots formed in his stomach, and he tried his best to keep his hands from shaking, but it was useless.

He recited to himself, "This has to be a nightmare. This has to be fake. Wake up, Jason, wake up." He sank into a hidden corner, tucking his head into his knees, wishing it would all disappear.

A gust of wind blew over him—the same familiar warm current that once blew throughout Arhat. Images of his journey passed through his mind as well as all the wonderful people he'd met along the way. More than ever though, flashing visuals of his grandmother came into his mind—moments of her smiling, and when she'd supported him, believed in him, and helped him grow.

He stood up and wiped away his tears. "I need to try for her, for Juniper, for Tyler, and everyone who helped me on this journey even if that means giving up my own life."

Suddenly, Jason noticed the necklace that Preeda had given him lying in the sand right beside him. He'd been carrying it in his pocket, and it must have fallen out. He looked intently at it as he slowly picked it up. "When Preeda gave me this on the flight, she said that it would keep me safe on my journey."

He placed it around his neck, and it pulsated intensely. He diligently thought up a new plan, and when he was ready to go, he felt the presence of someone nearby. Turning, he was shocked to find Auntie Zaza staring at him with a look of sorrow.

They stood only a few feet apart, like a standoff between a sheriff and an outlaw. Auntie Zaza, looking feeble and frail, remained silent for a minute before finally speaking, "I can help you, Jason. Listen to me."

He was skeptical, knowing she was probably trying to trick him.

She tried to inch forward, and he stepped back.

"You must seek him—only he can put her to rest. Listen to me, Jason."

She pointed toward the dark jungle, signaling to where he should go next. Then Jason heard another voice calling for him. It was Juniper.

He jumped. "I'm coming for you, Juniper. Stay strong, my love!"

Auntie Zaza reached her frail arm up to him. "No, Jason! You must not go. Please listen to me."

Jason ignored her and moved toward Juniper's voice, but Auntie Zaza cried out again, "No! No! You mustn't. Go and seek him—only he can put her to rest. Trust me, Jason."

He found himself in a tug-of-war, unsure of who to listen to. He exhaled deeply and looked into her eyes. He focused on them, wrestling with his emotions. "Why should I listen to you? You're not Auntie Zaza."

She stood silent, and Jason noticed that the hauntingly red, evil eyes that he remembered from when she attacked him were now soft and gentle. They were the same oceanic eyes from when he first met her. As he studied her closely, everything about her physical appearance convinced him that she was evil. Her skin was like leather, with bones protruding and inflicted with wounds. Maybe this was the evil trying to trick him, he thought.

Jason was distracted again by Juniper's voice calling for him, "Jason, help me. It hurts."

He puffed out his chest, blowing air from his nostrils, and made his decision.

He ran in the direction Auntie Zaza had told him. He had no rational explanation other than his heart was telling him to listen, and her eyes were the only source of truth.

The jungle he once knew had fallen victim to deforestation. Trees were limp and cut down. Snakes, rats, and roaches were the primary inhabitants, and all the trails were now unfamiliar. His only way to navigate was by the light of bioluminescent insects. Often, he contemplated turning back out of fear, but where else could he go?

Jason sorted through his thoughts aloud. "Auntie Zaza could be walking me right into a trap, but I don't know what to believe anymore."

Evil continued to deter him at every step. Tormented souls screamed through the darkness. The trees oozed blood, and even his grandmother's voice called to him, "Jason, why did you leave me? How could you leave me for all these months?"

Jason's body locked up, but then he clenched his necklace. He ignored the fake outcries that antagonized him. He yelled out positive affirmations as the bioluminescent lights guided him.

Soon, the lights burned out, and in the darkness, he tripped, tumbling down a small hill, collecting debris and bruises.

Jason stayed put for a minute as his body ached. Rising, he found a glowing tree. He noticed symbols deeply carved into its trunk. Jason traced the glowing symbols, and read that a young person would one day come to Arhat to save the village, and in turn, save humanity through love.

The luminosity of the tree grew faint, and Jason heard the sounds of leaves crunching. He quickly became defensive, ready to fight, but the steps paused, and the mysterious figure retreated. Jason pushed past the brush, only to find another bioluminescent trail that led him to a small bridge with a stream beneath it. This place felt different, resembling the Arhat he once knew before evil took over.

A person stood on the bridge. The man was tall and old, with a white beard and wavy white hair around the sides of his bald crown.

The man shifted his weight. "Isn't Arhat beautiful? It's everything you could have imagined and more." When the man turned, Jason stared, finding him familiar.

Jason sighed. "It used to be, but have you seen what's happened here?"

The man leaned against the bridge. "We only see what our minds tell us to see. The Arhat I know has always been beautiful, even without its physical existence."

Jason moved closer to get a better look at him. "But who are you? Have we met before?"

The man nodded. "Of course we've met—how could you forget? I led you to Arhat after all."

Jason had no recollection of meeting him until the man reminded him, "Don't you recall? You were so fascinated by my game of mahjong that day in the Bangkok market."

The man walked into the light, revealing his face, and Jason shook his head in disbelief. "It's you? Can it really be you? But why are you here now?"

CHAPTER 28

A PERFECTED SOUL

The old man remained quiet for a few moments, allowing Jason to process everything, before he finally spoke, "I came here once, long ago. You were my only way to return and see her again. Unfortunately, it was the love you and Juniper shared that woke her. No one could have foreseen such wrath. Your love for each other is more important than you know. It precedes the prosperity of Arhat and your grandmother. Humanity depends on it."

Jason recalled Eshin's story about the foreign man who came to Arhat and left. "So you're him? What about my grandmother? Juniper and my friend Tyler, will they be okay? Will Arhat be okay? What do you mean by 'humanity depends on it'?"

The man rushed past him. "Jason, there's not much time. Take me to the village."

Jason ran ahead, leading the way, and despite the man's silence, he assumed he was following until he stopped to check. The man was gone.

Bone-chilling yellow eyes appeared in the darkness, glowing. A pack of panthers emerged from the underbrush. They slunk closer. Jason watched, terrified, as they stretched their mouths open, revealing their fangs. They surrounded him, and all he had was a sharp rock near his foot to defend himself.

He recalled Titi's hunting advice: "*Always be one step ahead of your prey.*"

One of the panthers lunged at him, but simultaneously, he heard the roar of a mighty lion. The panthers shrieked in fright as the lion's prowess made them back away. A blinding flash cut through the darkness, and Jason had to shield his eyes. A lion spirit moved fiercely through the bodies of the panthers, causing them to claw at it. The spirit then passed through Jason's body, making him roar, which scared the panthers away.

Jason sat on the ground, shaking, watching as a person came into focus. It was a child.

"Hey, big bro. You did it. You found your courage. That was your spirit animal. I knew you could do it."

Jason jumped up, baffled to see Osito.

Osito kept his distance. "I've always been with you, but now I have to go. Mother is calling me. I will always love you, big bro. Thank you for everything."

Jason tried to go after him, but he vanished into the darkness.

He stared for a moment, trying to process it all. He ran back to the village, hoping to find the man there, but as he got closer, the ground became damp, and his feet sank.

When he reached the village, it was apparent that the island was sinking. The ocean had flooded all of Arhat's sandy streets. He recalled from the temple that Arhat came from the ocean, and it appeared as if the witch was taking it back.

He noticed a singular stream and followed it, finding himself at Katrice's Cove. Nobody was around except for a young woman sitting on the beach.

"Juniper!" he cried out. He ran over, and when she turned, he was relieved to see that it was definitely her. "I thought I lost you forever." Jason hugged her tight. He scanned her appearance to ensure she was okay. "Where are the others?" He looked into her eyes.

Juniper was broken down. "They're gone. Everyone is gone, Jason. My entire family."

Out in the mist, Jason witnessed something moving at the edge of the ocean. The cold wet wind blew harshly against them, and as the mist subsided, he saw a woman with a black ripped shawl draped over her hunched body.

He grabbed Juniper's hand and moved her behind him, acting as her shield. It wasn't Auntie Zaza, but a terrifying creature. Veins bulged throughout her pale undead body, and her long rotting nails were as sharp as blades. Her presence was so strong that it caused Jason's knees to shake and buckle. She floated toward them until she was only a few feet away. She stared at him and Juniper in envy. Jason could see the pain, rage, and hatred in her red eyes. As she moved closer, he stayed put, keeping Juniper behind him until the witch was face to face with him. She slowly grabbed Jason's neck and squeezed tighter and tighter. Juniper made an effort to pull her away but was swatted back.

"Take me! Take me instead," Juniper screamed.

Jason had hoped the witch wouldn't listen to her, but she could see the concern in Jason's eyes, so she dropped him. He tried to stop the witch from moving toward Juniper but didn't have the strength.

The witch circled Juniper's petrified body and placed both hands on her head. She whispered into Juniper's ear, "He will only leave you. He doesn't love you." The witch then grinned at Jason. "Ah, yes! First I will take Juniper, and then I will take your grandmother. That's what will cause you the most pain."

Jason dragged his body toward them, his hand reaching for Juniper. "No! I'm who you want, not her. Just let her go."

He watched as she clawed through Juniper's hair and dug her nails into her wrist, bringing Juniper to her knees, crying in pain as blood streamed everywhere.

Jason continued to try to move toward them but felt like he was held back by some force.

Juniper was shaking, but then she became calm. She looked Jason in the eyes, tears falling from her face. She stopped trying to escape and accepted her fate. "I promised to protect you, Jason, remember? If that means giving my life to save you, then so be it. I'm sorry it has to be this way, my love. I will always love you."

The witch whispered into Juniper's ear, and she fell lifelessly to the ground.

Jason screamed out for her, feeling that his heart had been ripped from his body. An indescribable agony overtook him. He had let the love of his life slip from his fingers. He felt helpless, knowing that Juniper and all he'd come to love about Arhat had been taken from him before his eyes, and soon his grandmother would follow.

As Jason collapsed in defeat, pounding his fists, he listened to the witch cackle at him until he felt he no longer had anything else to lose. He stood and faced her. "If you've taken her, you'll have to take me too."

The witch floated over to him and threw her fist into his chest, launching him backward. He tried with all his might to hold up his necklace, knowing it would protect him.

"No, please, no, it hurts. Stop, it hurts," the witch teased him and then smacked the necklace out of his hand.

As she loomed over him, he screamed furiously, "You're not an evil person—you're just in pain." This only made her angrier. She began pressing her nails into his chest, going straight for his heart. Jason was in so much pain that he couldn't speak, but then he managed to whisper, "Leave... my grandmother... alone. She... doesn't deserve to die. You can try to take away everything... that I love, but you'll never... destroy Arhat. It's more than a place."

Jason was barely coherent when he heard another voice.

"Katrice, stop and let him go."

It was the old white-bearded man.

He calmly walked up to her with his hands in prayer position. "My dear, I loved you more than life itself, but I caused you the pain I tried to avoid by leaving." He reached out with one hand while his other rested on his heart. "My rare disease had spread, and my time was limited, and if I stayed, I might have put you and the others in danger. When I left, I realized this world would be cold and lonely without you. When I tried to return to Arhat, it was too late. My health had dwindled and I could no longer go on. I suffered more knowing that I would die alone rather than in your arms. I never forgave myself for leaving you and our child. I'm sorry, my love."

The witch pulled her nail from Jason's chest, causing him to almost pass out, but he hung in there, watching as the interaction with the man unfolded. She extended her pale arms, floating toward the man, and screeching, "You left me! You left us!"

The old man walked toward her with his arms open as well. It seemed like the witch was going to destroy him, but then she stopped at the sound of a little voice.

"Mom, can we go home now?"

The witch shuddered in astonishment as the little voice held her back.

"Mom, can we go home now—you, me, and Dad? Can we, please?"

Jason recognized the voice—he had heard it many times before.

When he looked over, it was little Osito. Jason called out to him, "Osito, what are you doing? Stay away from her!"

Osito waved to Jason with a smile. "It's okay, big brother. You were the best brother I ever had. I learned so much from you. I'll love you forever, big bro, but it's time to go home."

Jason watched as Osito walked over to the witch and grabbed her cold, bony hand. Before his eyes, the most miraculous transformation happened. The witch's skin became warm and regained its brown tone. Her jet-black hair flowed down her back, and her cheeks filled with a red blush. She was nothing short of an angel, bending down to pick up her son.

It all made sense now, Jason realized. Osito was a guiding spirit, the unborn child of Katrice.

The white-bearded man transformed into a younger version of himself. He stood tall with thick brown hair combed to the side. He wrapped his arms around his family.

As Katrice and Osito waited by the ocean, the man walked over to Jason, helping him up, and instantly, Jason felt himself heal.

The man looked into his face. "Thank you, Jason. Because of you, I am reunited with my family, bringing peace to them and myself. Bravery and courage, my friend—that is what you stand for now. You stayed strong in the face of darkness. You believed in yourself and persevered when all hope was lost. By no means did you accomplish this alone, for it was the love of many people who helped you along your journey. As you've come to realize, even

Arhat has its imperfections, so I leave you with one question: is happiness found in a place or within? Your path in life has been in front of you all along. Arhat as we know it will be restored, and as for your grandmother, she will be healthy once again."

Jason saw a vision out in the ocean, and realized it was his grandmother. A ray of light penetrated her body, and her pain subsided as she filled with vitality. He knew that by defeating the witch, the Ancestors must have offered him a gift as a thank you for saving Arhat.

Before the man departed, he laid a hand on Jason's shoulder. "Please don't make the same mistake I once made, many years ago. She's waiting for you. Be well, Jason."

Jason watched as the man and his family walked out into the ocean. Their bodies became spirits, heading toward the sunrise and becoming brighter until he could no longer see them. A sudden feeling of fulfillment flowed through him. He thought about what the man had said. Never in a lifetime would he have described himself as brave and courageous.

CHAPTER 29

A DANCE WITH DESTINY

The sky brightened and the rain ceased. Before his eyes, the village returned to normal, and the jungles gained back their vitality. He could hear several birds, monkeys, and animals singing in harmony. The black sand beneath him glistened pink, and he felt a touch on his shoulder. Turning, he saw it was Auntie Zaza, radiant and full of energy. A burst of joy overcame them as they hugged.

Back in the village, Jason saw that homes were restored, the sandy streets were warm, and the dogs greeted them with licks.

"Jason, man!" Tyler emerged from the crowd of villagers coming toward them. "I had the worst nightmare ever. The island went evil and Auntie Zaza gouged out my eyes."

Jason smiled and pulled him in for a hug, barely able to contain how happy he was.

Like bears coming out of hibernation, everyone left their homes, including his friends, looking around as if they were experiencing life for the first time.

Hoko was strong and virile and there was Nela, Lala, Adnanla, Rusaki, Titi, Jahira, Jasmina, Lotusa, Tiko, Mongurt, Katalan, and every single person who Jason had thought perished. Everyone was hugging and embracing one another. Jason pushed through the crowd, getting smothered in kisses. They hoisted him into the air and covered him in yellow paint, celebrating their victory as a people and Jason's great contribution to Arhat's salvation. All the while, he searched for Juniper. She seemed to be the only person missing.

Mongurt and Katalan expressed their gratitude, and Jason was also greeted by his old friend, Eshin.

"Eshin, we did it. We saved Arhat!" Jason exclaimed.

Eshin's beard swayed as he shook his head. "No, Jason, you saved Arhat. I am proud of you."

"Thank you for believing in me, Eshin. Where's Juniper?"

"I think only you would know that, young Jason." Eshin winked at him.

Jason stared back for a moment, thinking, and then a smile formed on his face. He had a good idea of where she'd be.

He managed to escape the crowd, running off to find her. He went to the spot where she'd helped him overcome his fear of heights, shuffling along the cliff's edge until he made it into the cave. On the other side, he saw her sitting there, admiring her village and people.

Jason stayed silent because he didn't want to disturb her, but she heard him and turned immediately. Her face lit up with shock, hesitating for a moment, and then they ran toward each other, hugging as if the world were ending.

"Juniper! I thought I lost you forever." Jason swung her around. "Back there on the beach, you gave your life for me. Why did you do that?"

She pulled back to look at his face, kissed him, and then looked again. "Because I love you, Jason! It's that simple. I truly love you."

He couldn't get his next words out and just kissed her lips, neck, everywhere. He looked at her again. "I love you so much! Despite all that happened, coming here was the best decision of my life. Everything just makes sense when I'm with you."

They stood silently for a moment, glancing at each other with smiles of gratitude. With their hands intertwined, they slowly made their way back down the winding path to the village. Their steps were slow as if they had all the time in the world to embrace the rejuvenation of the lush green jungle surrounding them. The sound of distant laughter and music greeted them the closer they got to the village, and they clenched each other's hands tightly in excitement because they knew their family and friends were waiting to welcome them home.

As the day passed, the sky transitioned into hues of indigo and pink. Jason and Tyler sat on a wooden dock as the sun dipped over Humtay Lake with their fishing lines cast out into the golden water that reflected off the sun. They talked, first of their adventures, then of how far they had come not just on this journey, but as people.

Tyler cast his line again. "I don't know about you, Jason, but I feel different, in a good way. This place has been transformative. I feel very humbled. Wealth, for instance, I define that in a very different way now. Wealth is not just about how much money you have, but how much love you have and give to others. I've been thinking, when I go back home, I want to help people in a big way. Maybe start a foundation. And Nela, man, I love her, but in all honesty, I'm ready to go home. I was planning to tell Mongurt tomorrow that I'm leaving. Are you coming with me?"

Jason thought for a moment as he reeled his line, marveling at how his best friend had grown in ways he never thought possible. "I'm really happy for you, Tyler. I love this new goal of yours. So, you're no longer worried about the gambling debt?"

Tyler looked out into the ocean with a smile. "You know something? Not as much as I was before coming to Arhat. I mean, my parents will kill me, and I may lose a leg, but it's my responsibility. I need to own up to it. I'll find a way."

"I know you will."

"And you? I know you were hoping to find a cure for your grandmother."

Jason let out a deep breath and cast out his line. "And as for my grandmother," he said, voice wavering, "something tells me she's going to be alright as well. But I guess I should go home too."

Tyler glanced over. "Are you actually coming back?"

Jason looked at him with a confused expression. "Of course, that's my life."

"True, but what about Juniper?"

"Well, just like you said, I'll always love her, but how can I not go home? How can I never see my grandparents again?"

Tyler shrugged. "You crack me up, Jason. Even after all you've been through, you're still taking the safe route, huh? I'll support you no matter what you decide. All I'm saying is, if you love her, why leave?"

Jason nodded. "I get what you're saying, but it's a tough call, and honestly, it makes me sad thinking about it." All his moments with Juniper passed through his mind in a slideshow. He reeled in his line and stood up. "I forgot I have to help Juniper's parents with something. Let's tell Mongurt tomorrow that we're leaving."

When he met up with Juniper, they went back to the spot on the beach where they often camped out. They danced together by the fire.

"How was fishing with Tyler?" she said.

Jason twirled her. "It was pretty good. He's thinking about going home."

Juniper followed his lead. "And you... Will you go as well?"

Jason paused. "Well, I don't know yet. That's what I wanted to talk to you about. What if you came with me back to San Diego?"

He could see that she struggled to find the words to reply. "I would love to, but my family is here, Jason. I need to look after my sisters. My family needs me. Of course I want you to stay, but I also understand you have your family as well."

All went silent between them. Jason could sense that she was upset and her words didn't match her feelings.

"I don't know about you, Jason, but I'm convinced I love you, and I was sure of that the day I met you. I know you feel the same way. Promise me we'll always have that love for each other even if you decide to leave Arhat."

Jason turned away and then back toward her. "Ah, Juniper, I loved you from the moment I met you, and I want to stay here with you, but my whole life is back home."

A tear fell from her face. "I don't get it. Why would you leave if this is where you want to be? I just want you to be happy, whether you stay or if that means letting you go."

He had no response.

Juniper stood on her tiptoes and kissed his forehead before walking away. "I need some time alone, my love."

As Jason sat, he pounded his fists into the sand. *This is the hardest decision of my life! I want to stay here with Juniper. I love her so much, but my life and my home is back in San Diego, and my grandmother needs me. What am I supposed to do?*

As he contemplated his decision, Eshin paid him a visit. "So, are you ready to go home, young Jason?"

Jason kicked some sand. "I'll never be ready to leave Juniper and this place, but I'm not going to leave my grandmother behind. I just wish I could speak to her."

"Then why don't you?" Eshin twisted his beard.

Jason looked up at him. "What do you mean? How would that even be possible?"

Eshin took small steps along the beach. "More things are possible than you think—you should know that more than anyone by now. Come with me, Jason. I need to show you something."

Together they walked off the beach and rather than heading into the village, they strolled along the outskirts to an area that had several small temples and hanging lanterns. Jason immediately recognized some spiritual presence about the place, which made him feel calm and tranquil. He couldn't take his eyes off an illuminated willow tree up ahead.

Jason walked alongside Eshin's mighty presence. "What is this place?"

"One most never get to visit," Eshin confirmed. "It's very sacred to Arhat as well as that willow tree. Only a few of Arhat's people have ever walked through its branches. It is a direct link to our Ancestors."

Jason tried to touch the willow, but then pulled his hand back. "Then why me? Why did you take me here?"

Eshin parted the willow's branches. "For your sacrifice for Arhat, the Ancestors have granted you this opportunity. Within that willow tree, your grandmother waits for you. Go now if you wish to speak with her."

Feeling confused, Jason looked at Eshin, then at the willow. He hesitated, then slowly walked inside, shielding his eyes from its luminosity. To his surprise, it was empty, but a voice guided him. "Close your eyes, Jason. Be calm now." He followed the voice along, feeling his body become weightless. A blinding white light flashed before him like a camera, and when he opened his eyes, he found himself in another world—a white desert below a blue sky.

He thought he was the only one there until a voice called out, "Jason, is that you?" When he turned, he saw his grandmother standing a few feet away.

At first he wiped his eyes, unsure if she was real or not, but then ran to hug her. "Grandma, what are you doing here? Are you okay? I'm sorry I never checked in with you. I didn't mean to leave you both behind. It's just... I ended up on this island."

Jason tried to explain, but his grandmother stopped him. "It's okay, Jason. It's okay. I'm fine, and so is your grandfather. I think I'm dreaming right now because last I remember, I was reading my book before bed. It doesn't matter though. I'm just happy to see you. Tell me, are you coming home soon?"

He walked with her. "I don't know. Maybe it is all a dream, but seeing you now means more than anything to me. How are you feeling? What about the cancer?"

His grandmother stopped and turned toward him with a serene expression. "Oh, Jason, my dear boy. Let's just say miracles do exist because the doctor said I'm free of cancer. They don't know exactly how, but I'm healthy. Are you okay, wherever you are?"

Jason felt his eyes tear up and he hugged her again. He proceeded to tell her about his journey, how he and Tyler ended up in Arhat, and all that they faced and overcame. He also told her everything about Juniper and how they fell in love. By the look in his grandmother's eyes, she was blissfully happy for him, but at the same time, she could tell something important was on his mind.

"Why do you appear so conflicted?" she asked in a soft voice.

"Conflicted? What do you mean, Grandma?" Jason bit his bottom lip, puzzled.

She placed her hands on her hips. "I know that look when I see it, Jason. Are you thinking of coming home? What about that lovely girl? Your grandfather and I will be just fine. Do what is in your heart, my dear."

Jason exhaled and shifted his weight. "I had a feeling you were going to say that, but how can I just leave you both like that? I love Juniper, but you're my family."

"And we always will be your family, my dear," she said. "We're not going anywhere, Jason. I want you to know that you have brought me and your grandfather more joy than you could ever imagine. We will always love you."

"Grandma, are you sure about this?" His eyes fixed on her, waiting for her response.

"Yes, we're sure. You already know the answer." She hugged him.

Jason had no words and just hugged her back, but like a fleeting dream, she vanished. A flashing burst of bright white light hit his eyes. When he opened them, he saw that he was back where he started, standing under the willow tree. He stayed still, reflecting on their conversation, grateful at the thought of how deeply his grandparents loved and accepted him. The reassurance of her health brought him comfort, and her support for his decision to stay eased the weight of his uncertainty.

CHAPTER 30

A LIFE UNTETHERED

On the day of their departure, the village became a giant party. Music played from the moment the sun rose and the smell of Jesepa and Auntie Zaza's food was once again in the air. The local craft makers weighed Jason and Tyler down with necklaces, bracelets, and fine clothing. Jason tried to keep his smile and attention on everyone, but his eyes constantly drifted around, searching for Juniper.

Mongurt and Katalan gave a speech in the village center. "Arhat was blessed favorably the day these two young travelers found themselves here," Katalan announced. "They came to us as two lost people, and in little time, became our friends and family. They are Arhatians." She gently kissed them both on their foreheads and hugged them.

Mongurt turned toward them. "You will always have a home here in Arhat and be considered family. We are forever grateful. Now, before you go, I have something for you both. Tyler, on your journey, you have realized that money and possessions do not make a person any more fulfilled than a fancy title, nor do thousands of women amount to one great woman. I grant you access to the treasures you first encountered in our temple. You will take with you an abundance of wealth, but that comes with great responsibility. I wish you to live a purposeful life, one that makes you happy, but by no means squander your fortune, or else it will be taken from you. I wish you to bring peace and change to this world by helping others, and to find a good woman who makes you happy. Sometimes when we stop chasing the things we want, they naturally come to us when we're ready to receive them. Jason, now to you, my fine friend. Although it saddens us to have you leave, we will always be with you. We will always be looking after you and your family. People of Arhat, we owe a great deal of gratitude to our friend Jason, who exhibited bravery and courage, contributing his life to save Arhat and humanity."

Mongurt wrapped his arms around them both, then asked the crowd, "Now, who will see our two friends off to ensure they have a safe journey home?"

Jason could hear everyone cheering and yelling, offering to take them. He stayed quiet, still searching for Juniper, hoping she'd be the one.

Tyler whispered in Mongurt's ear, and as he nodded, he said, "You three over there, dear friends to Tyler and Jason, will you see them off?"

Hoko, Nela, and Lala stepped forward.

Jason followed Tyler and their friends down a trail of praise. The flowers flowed like champagne all the way to Humtay Lake.

Jason called out for Juniper, but the roaring crowd overpowered him.

Then he heard her soft voice shouting back, "I'm here. I'm here, my love."

His eyes frantically shifted as he scanned the crowd, searching until he spotted her. He inhaled deeply, and his heart raced faster than ever. As she moved closer, he reached out his trembling hand, desperate to grab hers. With every ounce of strength, he pulled her through the sea of people into his arms.

She said, "I'm sorry, my love, that I avoided you."

"There's nothing to be sorry about. I love you so much," he replied as he hugged her tight. He shut his eyes, embracing the warmth of her cheek against his, feeling her arms wrapped around his body. All went silent for a moment, he noticed, as if they were the only people in Arhat, and he never wanted to let go.

The six of them reached the edge of the lake. The crowd stayed a short distance behind, waving and shouting.

The friends paused, and as they grinned at one another, Jason knew they were all thinking the same thing.

"On three," Hoko said, and then, counting on his fingers, "One... two... three."

The six friends ran across the lake, gliding on their stomachs and feet. Their laughter echoed for miles. They splashed each other. Hoko fell through the water, and so did Tyler and Nela. Lala and Juniper were still dancing along the surface until they both fell through as well. Jason plunged in and purposely snuck up on Juniper and grabbed her legs, pulling her under. She splashed him a few times, laughing, and Jason moved closer, drawing her in. For a moment, they hesitated, floating in the water, silently paddling their legs. He gazed at her and a sense of lightness washed over him. Her eyes always had a way of telling him that everything would be okay, no matter what. It was a feeling he could never quite put into words, something he'd only ever felt with her.

"Hey, love birds, get over here," Hoko yelled, breaking them from their spell.

The group gathered, placing their arms around one another and forming a circle. As they put their heads together, Hoko told them, "You're my family and our friendship will never die, no matter how many years go by after today."

A smile formed on Jason's face. He shook his head, feeling so blessed for the special friends he'd made as he knew they were rare to come by.

Jason felt the water gurgle beneath him and it came as no surprise when Mamba surfaced to take him across the lake toward the jungle. He hopped on her back, and Tyler climbed onto the other sea turtle that rose next to him. Juniper got on with Jason to escort them.

Tyler waved the others over. "Hey, aren't you guys coming with us?"

Nela placed her hands on her heart. "We love you, Tyler and Jason, forever and ever. Juniper will bring you the rest of the way."

"Ahhh, guys, I'm gonna miss you so much, and this place. Never saw me cry before, huh?" Tyler wiped a tear from his face.

Jason embraced the kisses that Nela and Lala blew at them, and the way Hoko pounded his fist against his chest and up to the sky. And for one last time, Jason said goodbye.

The three of them soared off across the lake, leaving their friends and Arhat in the distance. When they reached the beach, they jumped off, and Jason rubbed Mamba's shell. "We made the best team, didn't we?"

Through the jungle, they soon reached the cave, a swirling sky-blue vortex that pulled them through. The well-lit tunnel was warm and bright. There was soft moss below their feet, and they walked until they arrived at the area where Jason and Juniper had seen each other for the first time. As they stood staring at each other, embracing their last moments, Tyler gave Juniper a big hug and said, "Jun, I'll never forget this place—or you. Thank you for everything. You're like the sister I never had." He laughed, rubbing the back of his neck. "Seriously though, how do we even get home from here?

Juniper smirked, giving him a playful punch on the arm. "And you're like the brother I never had. I'll miss you too, Ty. Just follow that trail up there. When you reach the top and step out of the tunnel, you'll be home."

Tyler shook his head. "If only it had been that simple getting here. Jason, I'll wait for you up top. Take all the time you need."

Alone together, Jason and Juniper stood facing each other. He took her hand, his fingers brushing over hers. Her gaze stayed on the ground.

"Jun," he said softly, tilting her chin up until her eyes met his. "This isn't goodbye."

As she gazed back, she let out a laugh, brushing a tear off her cheek. "I was just thinking about the silly things we used to talk about by the waterfall of colors. Do you remember?"

Jason smiled. "Of course—every one of them." He paused. "You know, I used to make fun of people who believed in soulmates, but I know now they exist."

She stepped closer, wrapping her arms tightly around him. "They are real," she whispered. "We're a good example. I'll love you forever, Jason."

He closed his eyes, resting his head against hers. Her warmth, the citrus scent of her hair, he savored it all. A tear slipped down his cheek as he held her tighter, wanting to freeze this moment. Finally, he pulled back and kissed her soft lips one last time.

"Thank you, Jun," he said. "For always seeing the best in me, even when I couldn't see it myself. You never doubted me. You always believed in us and our love for each other."

Jason took a step back. As he turned toward the trail, he felt a knot in his stomach and a lump in his throat. Every step felt like he was making the biggest mistake of his life. He didn't look back because it was so difficult leaving her behind.

Once Jason was at the top of the hill, Tyler sighed. "Jason, man, I didn't think it would be this hard. I'm really going to miss Arhat, but I'm ready to go back home. And you?"

Jason said nothing for a moment, and then looked up at Tyler. "Yeah, I'm ready. Let's go."

He tried to walk ahead, but Tyler put out his arm to stop him. "Hold up," he said as he watched Jason drag his feet with his shoulders and head slumped. "You're not going anywhere like this. Look at you, man."

Jason pushed his arm away. "Ty, I've already made my decision. It's hard enough just thinking about it. Everything will be okay."

"Will it though? Will it be okay, or will you just wake up one day realizing that you made the biggest mistake of your life?" Tyler pressed.

Jason had no words, so Tyler continued, "But hey, if you want to go home, that's cool too, man. We got our whole lives ahead of us."

He began moving toward the rock blocking the entrance, and the bright light pierced through.

Jason grabbed Tyler. "Wait."

"What?"

"I'm not going with you," Jason blurted. "I'm staying here, man. I'm staying with Juniper."

Knowing that his grandmother was healthy and that she had encouraged him to stay made his decision easier, allowing him to do what he had wanted all along.

"Are you sure about this?" Tyler asked.

"You know, man, I've always been sure, but just too scared to admit it. I spent years questioning my purpose, always feeling lost and comparing myself to others who seemed to have it all figured out. I can't say I ever had the strongest self-worth. I relied so much on external validation, believing that if everything was perfect in my life, then I'd be happy. I desperately searched for love and acceptance, but the truth is, love surrounded me all along, and I've realized we can't grow alone because people often bring out parts of us we'd never find ourselves. You helped me. Juniper helped me. My grandparents and so many others helped me discover that self-confidence and happiness is something to find within ourselves. We have to learn to love ourselves enough not to give up on pursuing consistent personal growth. Ty, man, all I can say is thank you for always pushing me to grow and being the friend I needed."

Tyler smiled proudly. "Way to go, man. I knew from the start you two were madly in love with each other. And you know something, you helped me as well more than you realize, buddy. For most of my life, I've been obsessed with money, women, and status, but as you said, so many people along our trip and in Arhat showed me a different way, one that gains satisfaction by how much we give rather than how much we gain. So, now what? Guess this is goodbye, huh?"

Jason shook his head. "Naaaa, man, it's not. I'll be back again one day. This is just the beginning of a new chapter. If you need anything, you know where to find me."

Tyler placed a hand on his shoulder. "Proud to be your friend. You inspire me, Jason. Now I'm not going to get all sentimental, but I will miss you. I might have a lot of friends back home, but there was always only one friend I look up to, and that's you."

Jason removed his necklace, the one that had protected them, and placed it around Tyler's neck.

"Jason, you can't give this away," Tyler protested.

He smiled. "Of course I can. I want you to have it. This is yours now, and no matter where you go, it will keep you safe. Nothing in this life really belongs to us anyway, right? We're just borrowing stuff until it's time to pass it on to the next person."

"What about your grandparents? What should I tell them?" Tyler fretted.

"Tell them that I love them very much. Let them know that I'm happy and that I followed my heart."

"You got it, man. They will always be taken care of, I promise."

"Thank you, Ty. Wait!" Jason leaned against the rock wall and grinned. "One more thing: Be-Do-Have."

"What?" Tyler's brows furrowed.

"*Be* your true self regardless of what others think. *Do* what is required of you in life, despite the obstacles, and one day you can *have* all that you strived for."

"A poet and a philosopher! Get over here, buddy." Tyler hugged Jason. "You got yourself a little lady waiting for you down there. Go and get her, tiger."

Jason nodded with a smile. "Love you, man. We'll meet again someday."

"I love you too, bro. I don't doubt it. Be cool, homie." Tyler moved past the boulder, disappearing into the light.

Jason rushed back down the tunnel, hoping that Juniper hadn't left. He slowed when he heard her weeping, and then saw her wiping away her tears. He stayed out of sight for a moment, watching her, admiring her beauty. When her eyes opened, and she saw him, Jason smiled and rushed over, and once again she was in his arms.

"What are you doing here? I thought I lost you!" Juniper exclaimed.

"You'll never lose me." He leaned back, looking into her eyes. "I'm tired of ignoring what I've wanted all along. I love you so much."

They stayed in the moment for what seemed like an eternity.

EPILOGUE

SUBLIMITY

Jason's grandparents were taken care of as Tyler promised, and their dreams were filled with magnificent images of Arhat. Their happiness became intertwined with Jason's, even if it meant only connecting with him through their dreams.

Tyler went on to fulfill his destiny and pay back his debts. Using the Arhatian wealth granted to him by Mongurt, he founded the largest global nonprofit dedicated to serving impoverished communities and became one of the most influential people in the world. He often stayed out of the spotlight, having discovered a simpler, more humble way of life since Arhat.

He reunited with his soulmate, Jessica, who had never forgotten about him. Together, they had two beautiful children named Jason and Juniper.

Ten years passed since his journey to Arhat, and not a day went by without Tyler thinking about his friend. One afternoon, he sat outside his usual café, sipping a cortado and daydreaming about Arhat, when he heard a father tell his son, "Be-Do-Have." Tyler's hands trembled, thinking for a moment that it was Jason, but it wasn't.

A book had fallen from the boy's backpack. Tyler went to call after him, but the boy and his father were gone. As Tyler picked the book up and flipped through its pages, he realized it told the story of Arhat and his and Jason's journey. It spoke of their time in prison, the many celebrations of Arhat, overcoming the evil witch—everything.

Tyler looked for the name of the author, but the title page read, "by Anonymous." Then he read the epigraph: "When one knows a true friend, they know their greatest gift." In that instant, the necklace Jason had given him glowed bright and warm against Tyler's chest.

THE END

ACKNOWLEDGEMENTS

Thank you to my family, friends, and all those who helped me grow over these past few years. Your support, inspiration, and encouragement were catalysts in bringing this book to life. To all the talented professionals who helped make this book a reality—I'm forever grateful.

ABOUT THE AUTHOR

Michael Bucci is a novelist and lifelong traveler. His writing is inspired by his journeys through 17 countries and the unforgettable people he's met along the way. A proud New Jersey native, he lives in Hoboken. When he's not jet-setting, you'll find him dancing salsa, discovering new restaurants, or catching live electronic music around NYC.

Connect with Michael:

MICHAELBUCCI.COM

INSTAGRAM: @WHATSBUCCII

www.ingramcontent.com/pod-product-compliance
Lightning Source LLC
Chambersburg PA
CBHW021240020826
48980CB00026B/692/J
* 9 7 9 8 9 9 9 7 5 5 5 1 3 *